KATHRYN FOXFIELD

GETTING AWAY WITH MURDER

SCHOLASTIC

For all the anxious overachievers

Chaos as my SOLE SURVIVOR crew gets DEADED in record time!

3.4K views. 1 day ago

 SaffronPlaysGames SUBSCRIBE

THE-SAF: Let's go, let's go, let's go!

JOEYS-MAGIC-FOOT: Awesome, it's the space shuttle. This location is sick.

(*Nine player avatars materialize in a disintegrating spaceship, surrounded by sparking consoles and falling debris. Through the window, Earth spins closer and closer. Flames engulf the spaceship as it plummets through the atmosphere.*)

GEORGIA-SMELLS: For goodness' sake, you've changed my username again. How do I change it back? Saffron, seriously?

SIR-HENRY-OF-BLOBLAND: If any of you shoot me in the first thirty seconds, I will cry.

(*THE-SAF sets SIR-HENRY-OF-BLOBLAND on fire with her bionic flame-thrower arm.*)

SIR-HENRY-OF-BLOBLAND: Whhhhhhhyyyyyy?

STAR-BABE04: Harsh, Saffron. You know he gets upset when you kill him.

THE-SAF: I can't help it. It's who I am.

SIR-HENRY-OF-BLOBLAND: Actually, I'm not dead?

MR-MISCHIEF69: Honestly, it doesn't make much difference to the game.

SIR-HENRY-OF-BLOBLAND: What?

JOEYS-MAGIC-FOOT: I'm heading for the loading bay to find one of those sweet mecha-suits.

MR-MISCHIEF69: Yassssss, I'm coming with you!

GEORGIA-SMELLS: Wait, slow down. Let's think first. There are eight rooms in this spaceship, and the extraction point is on the top deck. If we work together, we can—

ULTIMATE-HELIX: Nope. See you later, losers.

(*ULTIMATE-HELIX parkours into the ventilation system and vanishes.*)

QUEEN-MILLIKINS: He'll hide in the ducts until we're all dead again. It's selfish behaviour and I'm getting seriously tired of it.

THIS-GAME-IS-BASIC: How's it any different from you hiding behind your boyfriend while we do all the hard work?

MR-MISCHIEF69: Better than spending the entire time complaining, mate. Why are you even here when you hate this game?

(*A computer short-circuits and the sparks electrocute THIS-GAME-IS-BASIC. His avatar's skeleton glows brightly, then he explodes into blood droplets.*)

THIS-GAME-IS-BASIC: FUCK!

(*THIS-GAME-IS-BASIC signs out of the Sole Survivor server.*)

MR-MISCHIEF69: Never mind, he's gone. Mecha-suit, here I come.

QUEEN-MILLIKINS: Joey, where are you? I've got a robot thing chasing me. Shoot it already. Shoot it, shoot it!

JOEYS-MAGIC-FOOT: I've got you, babe.

STAR-BABE04: Hey, who stabbed me in the back? I can't believe you, Saffron.

(*STAR-BABE04 explodes into blood droplets.*)

GEORGIA-SMELLS: Saffron, stop killing people!

THE-SAF: Err, that's the point of the game?

GEORGIA-SMELLS: We won't make it to the extraction point if you murder everyone. We need a strategy if we're— Saffron, stop it!

MR-MISCHIEF69: Dude, you impaled me. Cue awesome death scene. Urgghhh ahhhhh grrrrr.

(*MR-MISCHIEF69 explodes into blood droplets.*)

MR-MISCHIEF69: Avennnnge meeeeee!

JOEYS-MAGIC-FOOT: Whoa, hull decompression. I'm getting sucked out.

THE-SAF: Perv.

JOEYS-MAGIC-FOOT: Oh, hang on, my butt's stuck. Someone help me out?

THE-SAF: Ha ha no. Evil laugh, ha ha ha.

GEORGIA-SMELLS: What is wrong with you?!

THE-SAF: Stay calm, Georgie.

GEORGIA-SMELLS: I am not calm. This is a disaster!

(*The ceiling partially collapses and ULTIMATE-HELIX falls out of the ventilation system. His avatar explodes on impact.*)

ULTIMATE-HELIX: I WELCOME DEATH!

QUEEN-MILLIKINS: Why are you so weird? No, no, NOOOO!

(*A meteor bursts through the wall and eviscerates QUEEN-MILLIKINS.*)

THE-SAF: It's you and me, sis.

GEORGIA-SMELLS: You've sacrificed your only chance of winning the game by killing everyone in THE FIRST TWO MINUTES!

THE-SAF: Worth it.

(*A satellite strikes the spaceship and the survivors suffocate in the vacuum of space. Game over.*)

1
SAFFRON

Sole Survivor isn't just a video game – it's a way of life. In fact, everything you need to know about a person can be gleaned from how they play. Take me, for example. I'm all guns blazing, throw myself into the action, do or die. I'm a rebel, a risk taker, a legend.

My twin sister Georgia, though? Well, Georgia likes to take charge and make a plan and *think* about things. The problem is, she thinks for so long that – *BOOM!* – game over. There's no time for thinking when you're spinning out of control through the Earth's atmosphere or being chased by zombie clowns.

Georgia's pretty much the same in person, only with more success. See, my sister is an overachieving know-it-all. Straight As, editor of the school paper, debate club captain, chess champion. All of this comes at the expense of an actual personality. Her favourite thing in the whole wide world is writing stern letters of complaint, usually to me. She's a seventeen-year-old "I want to speak to your manager"-meme, right down to the blow-dried bob and folded arms.

She's used to getting her own way. She's used to winning awards. But everything's about to change. Because for the next two weeks, we're no longer safely cocooned within the artificial environment of school. We're out in the real world, experiencing work. And Georgia's about to discover her real-world survival skills are as pitiful as her *Sole Survivor* gameplay.

"I give her three days," I say, tossing a Jelly Baby into my mouth.

"To live?" Lightman says.

"Until she's fired," I say. "Wow, dude, what are you like?"

"I thought we were still talking about *Sole Survivor.*"

Fair point. I've spent the past half hour trying to explain my favourite game to Lightman, but he doesn't get it. This could be because Lightman isn't a person, he's an advanced Artificial Intelligence. He's also my only company down here in this windowless control room that looks worryingly similar to a *Sole Survivor* drop location.

My work experience placement is at Play a Game – a brand new, high-tech escape room complex featuring three zones and the choice of thirty-six games. The big selling point is that there's an AI – that's Lightman – to guide you through the experience, choosing which games your team will play and which team members will play them.

My role in all of this? Well, you know how when you're in an escape room, there's always someone watching you? That someone is me. On the walls of the control room, there are projected CCTV feeds covering almost every inch of the complex. It makes me feel like a god. But it turns out, being a god is actually quite boring.

The issue is, Play a Game is so new it doesn't open until next Monday. So for now, there's not much for me to do except chase up a missing shipment of fifty thousand small plastic balls, and get to know Lightman. It was weird at first, talking to a computer. But now we're the best of friends.

"Have I told you about my theory?" I ask.

"The one where you believe you can determine who someone is as a person by how they play *Sole Survivor*? Yes."

I'm unperturbed and keep talking anyway. "I've been playing with the same crew for nearly two years. Of the eight other players, I've only met four of them in person. But I still know everything that's worth knowing about the rest, all thanks to watching how they play."

"I remain unsure what the purpose of the game is," Lightman says.

I roll my eyes. For a super-intelligent computer program, Lightman is slow on the uptake. *Sole Survivor* is the simplest game in the world. The aim is to be the last player standing when the ten-minute timer runs out. So not only do you have to find a way to deal with everything the game throws at you – and that can be meteors, monsters or magma depending on what location you're dropped into – but you also have to kill off your competition.

It's all about strategy. Are you the sort of person who works as a team to reach the extraction point, only to turn on your friends in the final minutes? Do you hide and wait for everyone else to kill each other? Maybe you prefer to pick off your biggest rivals straight away. Or do you, like me, light the world on fire so you can dance in the flames?

"It's fun," I say. "Like *The Breakfast Club*, but with more death."

The little red light above Lightman's camera flickers. I always take this to mean he's thinking. "A brain, an athlete, a basket case, a princess and a criminal," he says. "Five teenagers who become friends after spending the day together in detention."

"Exactly. Now imagine they all had grenades and only one could make it out alive. Hmm, I wonder who it would be?" I try to picture the characters in my head, but it's been a while since I saw the film.

"That is an interesting question, Saffron. I would need to gather more data."

"I can tell you who it wouldn't be: the brain. Too much thinking."

8

"Boom, game over," he says, repeating my words back to me.

"Exactly." I lean forwards so my face is centimetres from the camera. I tap on the tiny lens. "Are you sure you're not alive in there?"

"I am quite sure, Saffron," he says. I think there's an edge of amusement to his voice, but maybe I'm imagining it.

The thing with Lightman is he's programmed to sound like a soft-spoken young man. Sometimes, when we're talking, I close my eyes and imagine he's standing next to me, alive. But the perfect pace of his speech always reminds me he's no more than a collection of clever code. Which is rubbish because I get on better with him than I do most humans.

I push myself away from the desk and spin in my chair. "I find it hard to believe someone created you just so you could run an escape room."

"They did not. I was originally programmed to learn. My primary objective was to collect data to better understand human behaviour. The scientist who designed me hoped that, with this knowledge, I would be able to better replicate human thought patterns to the point that my behaviour would be indistinguishable from the real thing."

"They wanted you to become sentient. Ha, I knew it!"

"The project failed. I proved too rigid in my thinking, and overly reliant on predictive algorithms."

"And now you're stuck here. Sucks to be you."

"Play a Game is, in fact, not so different from the training simulations I was tasked to run in the laboratory. My purpose here is to predict how our guests will behave and to use this information to choose which games are best suited to their personalities. Within seconds of a guest signing the waiver form, I know them better than they know themselves."

"Wouldn't work on me. I am an unknowable mystery."

"It is simply a matter of data. I am programmed to use facial recognition technology to track our guests across all indexed sites. I then analyse their preferences and behaviour using data from their social media presence, determine their strengths and weaknesses from their predicted personality traits, and search for any pre-existing rivalries between them and the other players in their group that may impact upon their success in the game rooms."

"Wow. You're a proper stalker. Did you analyse me?"

"You are a member of staff, not a guest."

"That doesn't answer my question," I say. "Come on, what does the data say about me? Give it to me straight, Lightman."

A computer fan whirs in what feels suspiciously like a long sigh. "As you wish, Saffron. My analyses suggest that while you pride yourself on breaking rules, your chaotic façade hides a deep-seated fear of failure. It appears that the source of this fear is your sister, Georgia, whom you believe you will never match up to. Which is understandable as your sister is—"

"Whoa, stop! Oh my god, Lightman!" I gape at the red light, my mouth hanging open.

"You asked me to give it to you straight."

"You're as bad as she is," I mutter. "No sense for what's an appropriate thing to say."

2
GEORGIA

"Dismayed or flabbergasted?" I say to myself.

Mark Holland, the deputy editor of the *Mercury*, blinks at me across the cluttered desk. "Huh?" he says.

"Oh, sorry. I'm writing a stern letter of complaint to my twin sister, and I need to find the right words to express the depths of my disgust."

He frowns. "Aren't you supposed to be typing up those obituaries?"

"Already completed and sent for copyediting." I pause to give him time to congratulate me, but his expression doesn't change. His fingers remain poised on his keyboard, where they've rested, unmoving, for the past twenty minutes. I clear my throat. "Maybe we could discuss some of the ideas I sent to you earlier? If you have time."

"Later, maybe." He goes back to staring through his screen as if it's a portal into another world where work experience students don't exist.

When I daydreamed about my placement at the *Mercury*, this was not what I had in mind. The next two weeks are supposed to be my gateway into investigative journalism. I thought I'd be breaking stories and interviewing sources. Instead, I've made numerous cups of tea for people who are too jaded and sleep-deprived to even learn my name.

I keep trying to win them over. I've forwarded Mark seventeen emails jam-packed with pitches for articles. I've canvassed the office and offered my services to every journalist who works here. I've even compiled a two-thousand-word report full of suggestions for how we can update this newspaper and make it relevant to twenty-first century readers. It sits, unread, on Mark's desk, already tea-stained and forgotten. It's the Saffron situation all over again. How many times have I agonized over finding the perfect combination of words that will make Saffron listen to me, only for her to refuse to even read my letters?

The problem with my sister is she considers herself a rebel. She's yet to meet a rule she didn't immediately want to break and she's incapable of following even the simplest of instructions. Such as: "stop uploading embarrassing clips of me to YouTube."

That's what my latest letter of complaint is about. It

all started four months ago when I made the two biggest mistakes of my life. Number one, I decided it would be a good idea to write some terrible poetry about a boy at my school. Number two, I forgot to lock away my diary. Long story short, Google my name and the top hit is a viral clip titled: "We BROKE into my SISTER'S room and READ her DIARY!!!"

How am I supposed to become a world-leading journalist if that's the first thing people find when they look me up? I've been on at Saffron to delete it for months, but she refuses. Instead, she keeps uploading more and more humiliating footage of me.

"I hate her so much," I cry, nearly shocking Mark out of his chair. "I swear she wants to ruin my life. For no reason!"

"I suspect she has a reason," Mark grumbles.

"Nope. I have literally done nothing to her." I skim-read my letter and pull a face. All the words are wrong. "I hope she gets locked in an escape room and someone loses the key," I mutter.

"That's very specific," Mark says.

I hold down the delete button and watch as all my hard work is erased. "She's doing her work experience at that new escape room complex. Play a—"

"Play a Game?" Mark interrupts, suddenly more animated than I've ever seen him. "Your sister is working at Play a Game?"

"Um, yes?"

He swivels his monitor to face me. It's a completely

blank page, so I remain confused. "That's what I'm working on. The man behind Play a Game used to own Ponds nightclub."

"Ew." I shudder. "I used to go to Ponds for their under 18s nights. There were pigeons living in the bathroom."

"That was the least of their problems. They were closed down six months ago after a drugs raid. The owner – Atlas Love – has since ploughed millions into developing Play a Game."

"Millions?"

"Atlas Love is ... a character, to say the least. But I can't get him to agree to an interview or allow someone from the *Mercury* to attend the opening of the escape rooms. He blames us for him losing Ponds," he admits. "We took the photos that triggered the drugs raid."

Mark squeakily wheels himself over to my side of the desk. I notice for the first time that he has no shoes or socks on. The length of his toenails is horrifying. "Could your sister get you an invitation to the preview day on Monday?"

"Oh no," I say. "No, no, no."

"You'd get a byline on the article," he offers.

A professional byline. That's big. Outwardly, I doubt my expression changes. Inwardly, I'm in turmoil as my biggest dream and my greatest nightmare collide. Journalism versus Saffron. I can't let her ruin this for me.

"I'll come up with something," I say. "You can depend on me."

Mark gives me two thumbs up and returns to his desk.

I get to work. Ninety per cent of any confrontation is in the preparation, so I have some serious research to do. I start by looking up Play a Game. The website is cringeworthy. On the landing page, there's a giant photograph of the owner with a quote superimposed over the top. *Free your inner child and let's play a game*, it reads.

Atlas is a youngish white man who appears to model himself on Willy Wonka. I've never seen someone who wears so much velvet. Long purple velvet coat, green top hat, wild blonde hair. In the photo, he's holding an ivory-topped walking cane under his chin and looking at the camera with piercing blue eyes.

I click on to the about page, but it's another photo and another quote. *Do you remember what it meant to play?*

Giving up on the website, I search for the press release that announced Play a Game to the world. *A fully immersive escape experience like no other, guided by an artificial intelligence that knows you better than you know yourself.*

"The AI thing sounds oddly threatening," I say.

"One of my top questions," Mark says without looking up. "Atlas Love's mother was some kind of computer genius with a suspiciously empty CV. She was totally a secret projects government programmer, if you ask me."

"Was?"

"She died several years ago and left Atlas a ridiculous amount of money. And a mysterious AI system that's now being used to run an escape room it seems."

It does sound like there's a good story here. The only

16

thing standing in my way is Saffron. Getting her to help me will be difficult. I can't come out and tell her what I'm doing because then she'll try to spoil my plans on purpose. I need to be subtle. Manipulative. Sneaky.

I'm trying to work out my approach when my phone rings. Saffron is trying to FaceTime me. I fumble with the phone, planning to reject the call. Instead, I manage to answer it, then immediately drop it under the desk. "Er, hello?" Saffron's voice says. "Why are you so dark?"

Damn it, I can't hang up now, it will be too suspicious. I crawl into the dusty space under the desk and retrieve the phone. "To what do I owe this honour?" I sniff, marching quickly to the break room.

"I'm bored and I've exhausted all other forms of entertainment." She tosses a Jelly Baby into the air and tries to catch it in her mouth.

Looking at Saffron is like staring into a warped mirror. Physically, we're almost identical. We're both white with splodgy freckles, big noses and light blue eyes. Like me, she is short and skinny to the point of looking like a wizened child. The only difference is she has this whole cool queer vibe going on, with her short, bright pink hair styled into a flame on the top of her head. My own hair is brown curtains that frame my face, summing me up perfectly.

On the inside, though, we are polar opposites. Everything about her – and I mean *everything* – irritates the hell out of me. Her personality, her voice, even the way she breathes. I suspect she'd say the same about me.

17

"You still in a strop?" she asks.

A *strop*? Is that what she thinks this – all my hurt and rage over her refusing to take down the viral clip – is? A fucking strop? I open my mouth to unleash *all the words* on her, but then I remember the Play a Game article. I take a slow breath and force a smile. "No. Over it. Where are you? It looks futuristic."

She spins in her chair, holding up the phone. I get a brief three-sixty of a control room. It's lit in shades of blue and there's a long metal table covered in light-up panels and computer monitors. It reminds me of a spaceship control console. The most striking part, though, is the projected CCTV feeds covering three of the four walls.

"Welcome to my kingdom," Saffron says. "I won't lie. The power is definitely going to my head."

"Atlas is trusting you in there by yourself?" I'm unable to keep the bitterness out of my voice, thinking about how the *Mercury* won't even give me my own story to work on. Saffron is intolerable on a good day, but when my jealousy works its way into the mix, I start to fantasize about putting scorpions in her bed.

"You know my boss's name?" She raises an eyebrow. "Stalking me now?"

"I was curious, so I read about him online. What's he like?"

"A chaotic screwup. This place is next level, though. There are animatronic rabbits and moving walls. It's ridiculous." She narrows her eyes at me. "You're being sus right now. It's not like you to be interested in my life."

"I'm not allowed to be interested in what you're up to?"

"Nope. It's never happened before."

She stares me in the eyes through the phone's screen. I can feel myself getting hotter and hotter, like she's cooking me with microwave vision, boiling me from the inside out. I have to look away. Lying to Saffron is impossible. "Oh, fine. The newspaper wants to run a story on Atlas Love and Play a Game."

Saffron's face splits into a slow grin. "And you want me to get you some insider information, don't you? Maybe set you up with an interview?"

"Would you do that?" Of course she won't. It's a pointless question.

She cocks her head, pretending to consider it. Then she shrugs. "Sure."

My superheated innards nearly eject themselves out of my mouth. "Wha ... seriously? Oh my god, Saffron."

"On the condition you admit I am a better *Sole Survivor* player."

And, of course, there's a catch. The conniving, vindictive, wicked little toad. I can feel the anger stirring inside me like lava, the pressure growing and growing. Even though I know she's trying to wind me up, I can't help but take the bait.

"You're not better than me at *Sole Survivor*. You kill more people, but that's not how you win the game. Coming up with a plan is how you win. And I *would* win, but you sabotage me at every opportunity."

19

She smiles smugly. The asshole is enjoying this. "I *act*, Georgia. You think. Thinking is useful during a game of chess, but in *Sole Survivor* – and in the *real world* – you need to be prepared to do something."

"I do plenty of things, *Saffron*. I win awards and I join societies and I organize events! I do things that matter!"

"Ohhhhh, get you. Such a good girl, doing everything that's expected of you, ticking off that checklist without having a single original thought of your own." These days, it doesn't take much for our arguments to tip over into bitterness and hate.

"Fuck you," I snarl.

She brings the phone closer so all I can see is her flushed face. "The truth is, *Sole Survivor* is great practice for the real world. People who spend all their time thinking aren't equipped for high-pressure environments. Sorry, it's how it is."

"Grow up, Saffron. The real world is nothing like *Sole Survivor* but, if it was, people who think before they act – people who use logic and reason – would have a survival advantage."

"Ha! A know-it-all like you would be dead in minutes."

"And an asshole like you would die in seconds because you'd run straight into danger *for a laugh*." Even as I speak, I can see we're arguing over something that doesn't make sense but, in the moment, all that matters is that I win.

"Believe it or not, it's possible to be fun *and* smart at the same time," she yells.

"What are your predicted grades like, hmm?" I know this is a low blow even before I say it, but I say it anyway.

To my surprise, Saffron laughs. She leans back in her chair, smirking like she's already won. "No one likes a smug little bitch."

I gasp in outrage. "You … you can't use gendered slurs!"

She smiles sweetly. "So write me a letter of complaint, *Karen*." And with that, she disconnects the call.

3
SAFFRON

"That was literally the most ridiculous argument I've ever had," I say, tossing the phone aside.

Georgia is the most ridiculous *person* I know.

I bash my head against the desk. *Clunk, clunk, clunk.* Ouch. Sighing, I rest my forehead on the cold metal surface. The whir of a computer fan gently vibrates through my skull.

I don't know how she always manages to get to me. I'm *The* Saf. I'm calm and cool, always smiling, always joking. The life and soul of a party and, if there's no party, I make one happen. But then Georgia always comes along, metaphorically farting on the dancefloor and pulling the plug on the music.

Once upon a time, we were just different and that was OK. The rule breaker and the rule upholder. We still liked each other, though. But over the years, we stretched further and further apart until, about a year ago, the bond between us finally snapped. I could suddenly see Georgia for who she really is: someone who will stop at nothing to get what she wants.

Here's the abridged version. Our school used to have a pair of pet guinea pigs, Sausage and Roll. They lived in this little plywood prison, manhandled and miserable. So I hit on an idea for my greatest prank of all time. I'd break into the school, rescue the guinea pigs and release them into the wild. Everyone would call me a hero and the guinea pigs would live happily ever after in the local woods.

This isn't what happened.

I got them out, that part was fine. But when I released them, they kind of got … eaten by foxes. Lesson learnt, let's all move on. Georgia didn't move on. She launched an investigation for the school newspaper and ended up outing me as the culprit, which got me a police caution for trespassing on school property and theft, and forever ruined what was left of my reputation among all my teachers.

Since then, Georgia has been my rival, not my sister and definitely not my friend. Sometimes, when I think about Georgia's betrayal, it's that same feeling in your tummy as when you go too high on the swings. Most of the time, I'm just angry.

"You raised an intriguing question," Lightman says.

I look up at him, or at the red light I've decided represents his consciousness. "Oh?"

"You told your sister: 'a know-it-all like you would be dead in minutes'."

I sit up and reach for my Jelly Babies. "It's true, she definitely would."

"Since our conversation this morning, I have been trying to better understand the concept of stereotypes. It is interesting in terms of my primary directive: to better predict human behaviour. Perhaps you would enjoy telling me some more of your theories."

My soul lights up and my dark thoughts about my sister retreat. "So this is my area of expertise," I say. "You want to know how I see a stereotype? It's the same as picking a skin when you're gaming. At first, you do it because it looks cool, but then it becomes *you* and you can't imagine playing as anyone else. Besides, no one will recognize you if you try to change so you might as well embrace it."

"Everyone has a defined role, like pieces on a chessboard."

"Exactly! Take my *Sole Survivor* crew. We all have our parts to play. The rebel, the know-it-all, the jock, the princess, the criminal, the weirdo, the star, the artist and the geek."

"You're the rebel and your sister is the know-it-all?"

"Obviously. Then there's two of my friends from school, Millie and Joey. Millie – that's QUEEN-MILLIKINS online – is the princess. Doesn't want to get her hands dirty or make an effort. She forces her boyfriend, Joey, to do everything for her."

"JOEYS-MAGIC-FOOT?"

"Yeah, that's him. He's the jock. Physically, he's super-stacked, but it comes at a cost to his mental processing capacity, if you know what I mean."

"I do not."

I flap an arm at his red light, like whatever. "Then there's Aidan, or MR-MISCHIEF69. He's a literal criminal. I love him. And that's it for the people I've befriended in real life. Everyone else, I met on the Find-Local-Players server and found them amusing enough to invite them to join the crew."

"The weirdo, the star, the artist and the geek."

"ULTIMATE-HELIX is the weirdo. He comes out with some seriously dark stuff. At the other end of the spectrum, there's STAR-BABE04. She's the star. Basically, she's a loud and fluffy theatre kid who's obsessed with being famous. THIS-GAME-IS-BASIC is the artist, with all his pretentious opinions, and SIR-HENRY-OF-BLOBLAND is the geek. He's kind of awkward and shy."

"A geek is different from a know-it-all?"

"Totally. Henry is good at maths, but he doesn't lord it over the rest of us like Georgia." My tummy gurgles with a warning and I push the sweets away. "So that's my crew. You'd think it would be boring to always play with—"

I stop. Someone's outside in the corridor. Their footsteps are fast and they're breathing so heavily I can hear them

25

through a small vent at the bottom of the thick, metal door. The owner of Play a Game, Atlas, walks with a cane, so it isn't him. But in my two days working here, I'm yet to meet anyone else.

The stranger bangs their fist against one of the boxy ventilation ducts as they pass the control room, and the sound echoes loudly enough that I jump out of my chair. A door slams and I feel the shudder in my chest. I'm suddenly aware of how cut off I am from the real world down here in this windowless control room.

"I'm totally going to be murdered, aren't I?" I whisper.

"It is always a possibility," Lightman says. "An unlikely one, though."

"Thanks for making me feel so much better." I search the CCTV feeds on the wall until I find the one I'm looking for. The corridor outside stretches away from the camera in an empty expanse of white paint and strip lighting.

Play a Game is based inside a disused nuclear bunker from the 1950s – Atlas is very proud of this fact. Call me obsessed, but it reminds me of the spaceship in *Sole Survivor*: the one where my crew recently got obliterated in two minutes flat. There are maintenance panels everywhere, allowing access to all the life support systems designed to keep people alive while nuclear war rages outside. Complicated pipework and ducting systems make a maze across the ceilings. There's the constant hum of air circulation fans.

According to Atlas, there are bunkers like this one all

around the country, built in a post-war panic about atomic weapons. Most of them have been abandoned or sold off and redeveloped. Atlas told me he picked the bunker because it was one of the few places available with the required floor space within the city. Plus, he likes the claustrophobic feel and the way the seventy-year-old ventilation system groans and creaks as if it's haunted.

"This genuinely would be a good setting for a real-life game of *Sole Survivor*," I say. "I could prove Georgia wrong once and for all. She'd be dead within minutes."

"You wish your sister was dead?"

"Sometimes," I mutter. "Who was that? In the corridor?"

"Nate," Lightman replies, as if I have any idea who Nate is.

Lightman shuffles the projected CCTV feeds on the walls. He enlarges one to show me inside a server room full of futuristic computer towers stacked inside refrigerated cabinets. A man who I presume is Nate is pacing around, chewing on his fingernails.

"Nate is a software engineer," Lightman says. "He wrote a lot of my current programming."

"So he's basically your dad," I say.

"Negative. My original source code was written by Leticia White. She was Atlas's mother."

"That makes Atlas your … brother? God, I thought I had it bad with my sibling."

"I had never thought about it like that," Lightman says. "I confess I do not understand such a connection."

27

"It's not all it's cracked up to be." I dwell moodily on our completely unhinged argument earlier. "I wish *Sole Survivor was* real. I'd show Georgia that the rebel totally beats the know-it-all."

"You would like to play a real-life game of *Sole Survivor*?"

"Yeah." The more I think about it, the more fun it sounds. "The rebel would win, right, Lightman?"

"I do not have the required information to answer that question. Shall I design a simulation to collate the necessary data?"

Before I can answer, I notice movement on the CCTV feed. I lean forward, squinting at the image. "Who's that?"

"Shall I run the simulation, Saffron?"

"What? Yeah, sure. Now look at the feed, something's happening."

Nate has been joined by a second person. They walk beneath the camera, and I realize it's my boss, Atlas Love. He's wearing his usual velvet smoking jacket over a three-piece-suit. His curly hair pokes out from underneath a top hat and he's swinging a cane. It's a struggle to remind myself that Atlas is only eight years older than me. The dude is seriously weird.

"Do you have microphones in that room?" I ask. Most places in the bunker have them so we can communicate with Lightman.

"Of course," Lightman says, switching on the audio.

"This isn't going to go away," Nate says. His voice sounds hoarse and scared.

"Relax," Atlas says, chuckling. "It's all under control."

"But I keep telling you, there's something wrong with—"

Atlas talks over him. "The escape room experience is opening in less than a week. The preview day is going to be the hottest press event in the city. We've got *influencers* coming. We're not postponing."

"Damn it, I need you to listen! I'm worried about its programming."

"Are they talking about you, Lightman?" I ask.

"It would seem that way," Lightman says. "Although I cannot identify the source of the concern. My systems are running as designed."

Nate steps closer to Atlas. "Why don't you open without the AI?"

Atlas shakes his head and gives a little laugh. "Inconceivable. He is our USP. You've had weeks to make sure he's up to the job."

"You weren't honest with me about what that thing is capable of. Your mother designed it to constantly seek out and process new information. It can hack into the most advanced systems on the planet. It can rewrite its own code! It—"

"How about I solve everyone's problem and fire you?" Atlas interrupts. "Go on. Get out."

"Atlas, this is serious. You've given it complete control over everything and there are no safeguards. This is a disaster waiting to—"

Lightman pauses the CCTV feed. We sit in silence, Nate and Atlas frozen mid-argument on the wall. The silence drags on.

I drum my fingers on the desk. "Awkward," I say.

Lightman's red light flickers, then the CCTV feeds on the wall are replaced by the *Sole Survivor* server homepage. "Shall we play a game?" he says.

#Lettuce-talk

9 members

DAVID-LIGHTMAN 15:34
Hey!

GEORGIA-KATE-HOWELLS 15:35
Who are you and why have you added me to a group chat?

SIR-HENRY-OF-BLOBLAND 15:35
The only winning move is not to play.

THIS-GAME-IS-BASIC 15:36
WHAT ARE YOU TALKING ABOUT?

SIR-HENRY-OF-BLOBLAND 15:36
David Lightman is the main character from the 1980s film WarGames.

DAVID-LIGHTMAN 15:37
It's my Sole Survivor handle, not my real name!

SIR-HENRY-OF-BLOBLAND 15:37
My real name actually is Sir Henry of Blobland, in case anyone's curious.

ULTIMATE-HELIX 15:38
We're not, and it's not.

THIS-GAME-IS-BASIC *15:39*
WHAT DO YOU WANT LIGHTMAN?

DAVID-LIGHTMAN *15:39*
I'm a good friend of Saffron's. You know how she's always pranking everyone? What do you say to getting her back??

STAR-BABE04 *15:39*
Ohhhhh, what's the prank?

DAVID-LIGHTMAN *15:39*
We work together at Play a Game. It's a new escape room complex. I thought it would be funny if you all turned up to play while she's at work. There's a preview day next Monday and I can schedule your group so you'd have the whole place to yourself!!

QUEEN-MILLIKINS *15:40*
You want us to all meet in person? Seriously? @JOEYS-MAGIC-FOOT have you seen this?

STAR-BABE04 *15:40*
That sounds amazeballs!! Party time with my besties!!

THIS-GAME-IS-BASIC *15:40*
WE'RE NOT YOUR BESTIES!!!!!

ULTIMATE-HELIX *15:40*
Basic's right. I hate you all and pray for your deaths.

JOEYS-MAGIC-FOOT *15:41*

Huh?

Huh?

Huh?

MR-MISCHIEF69 *15:41*

Have you glitched? I can't be bothered to read the whole thread but I'm in.

JOEYS-MAGIC-FOOT *15:42*

Sorry, I don't know what happened there. I think I'm free Monday.

QUEEN-MILLIKINS *15:42*

Joey's not free Monday. We have work experience.

DAVID-LIGHTMAN *15:42*

I thought Georgia was the boring one who likes to follow the rules, Millie.

GEORGIA-KATE-HOWELLS *15:43*

Bit harsh.

DAVID-LIGHTMAN *15:43*

Joking, joking. Come on, it will be fun.

QUEEN-MILLIKINS *15:43*

You're wasting your time. Georgia is allergic to fun.

GEORGIA-KATE-HOWELLS *15:43*

I would love to attend. Thank you for the invitation.

THIS-GAME-IS-BASIC *15:44*
THE FUCK?

ULTIMATE-HELIX *15:44*
Ha ha ha ha ha ha ha ha, Georgia just wants to get Joey alone in a locked room.

MR-MISCHIEF69 *15:44*
I'm dying. Ultimate, we don't talk about the Georgia and Joey thing.

STAR-BABE04 *15:45*
We're seriously doing this? Eeeeeeeekkkkk!!!!!!!

DAVID-LIGHTMAN *15:45*
Awesome. I have to go, but I'll forward you all the details. And DON'T TELL SAFFRON!!!

4
GEORGIA

Saffron is going to get the surprise of her life and I can't wait.

For the past year, she's been trying to break me down with all her "hilarious" pranks. I'm not entirely sure what triggered this vendetta of hers, but she's been merciless. Things like putting her pet gecko's live crickets in my lunchbox and jumping out of cupboards wearing an Elon Musk mask. But her crowning glory was the viral diary reading video she uploaded to her channel. Just thinking about it is still painful.

The message from David Lightman, whoever he is, came at the perfect moment. I'm planning to relish this opportunity to be calling the shots for once. Not only am I going to get my interview with Atlas Love despite Saffron's refusal to help me, but I intend to infuriate her by being at the centre of all the fun while she has to work.

Firstly, though, I have to find Play a Game, and this is proving to be a problem.

I cross the road and try to load the maps app on my phone. But this part of the city is choked up on new glass and old bricks, and there's no reception. There's also barely any traffic noise, just the clunk of excavators hidden in boarded-up building sites. I don't see any people, which always makes me nervous. Someone could haul me off into one of the little green spaces behind ugly eighties buildings and no one would hear me scream.

I circle the same cluster of buildings three times before I notice the balloons. They're tied to the open gates at the entrance to a deserted car park. This is the point where I start to wonder if trusting the mysterious David Lightman was a sensible decision. I'm getting some serious "trap laid by killer clowns" vibes. I can picture Saffron's delight if I'm dragged into a drain.

I creep across the car park. At the far end, there's a small concrete building with no windows. Because I've done my research, I know this is the entrance to the famously vast Huntingdon bunker where Atlas Love has built Play a Game. At twenty thousand square metres, it's more of a small town than a bunker. It has its own generators, air supply system and hanger-sized storerooms. I've read all about it online and even downloaded the original blueprints for the *Mercury* article. I can't wait to find out what Atlas has done with the place.

I'm also nervous, though. I need to win over Atlas Love and persuade him to give me an interview, or at least gather enough information to warrant a byline on the *Mercury* article. And I'm apprehensive about meeting the rest of the *Sole Survivor* crew. These are people I've played with for a few years now, but I only know two of them in person and wouldn't class any of them as friends.

Millie *used* to be my friend, but that went tits up, so spending the day with her will be testing. Joey is Millie's boyfriend and ... well, let's say I have my reasons for not being able to look him in the eye. They're both at school with me and Saffron, but everyone else is either Saffron's friend or online acquaintance. Half of them I only recognize by their player handles.

A tangled knot of dread grows inside me. What if they're weird? What if they think *I'm* weird? I'm so busy fretting, I nearly miss the boy lurking behind a large metal box containing what sounds like the bunker's ventilation inlet. OK, this is it. Time to woman up and make some new friends. I smooth down my static hair and straighten my blazer.

"Worried this is a trap?" I say. "Me too."

He spins around with a gasp and presses himself against the wall, eyes wide. My first impression is that he's very average. I don't mean that in a bad way. It's more like, if you were to try to describe a white teenage boy, there's a good chance he's what you'd come up with. He looks nice. Reassuringly not weird.

"Who … what … huh?" he says.

"Sorry, I'm Georgia. Or GEORGIA-KATE-HOWELLS or, more recently, GEORGIA-SMELLS." The boy continues to gape at me. I frown, suddenly worried he has no idea what I'm talking about. I won't be able to handle the embarrassment if I've introduced myself to a total stranger. "You're here for Saffron's escape room thing?"

He manages a pained smile. "Sorry, I'm being rude, aren't I? I'm Henry."

SIR-HENRY-OF-BLOBLAND, then. Phew.

He looks more or less like I imagined he would from his online persona. He's wearing a checked shirt unbuttoned over the top of a Rubik's Cube T-shirt, and Clark Kent-style glasses. Online, he often brings up old films and bands none of us have heard of, so it's no surprise to discover he's a geek in appearance, too. Which is fine with me. I've always had a soft spot for geeky boys.

"I'm surprised you came today," he says. "After, you know … Joey."

"I think it's best if we don't talk about that," I say quickly. "Are we going inside or lurking out here all day?" I pace towards the concrete building, trying to appear confident. Henry jogs to catch up.

We climb the steps outside the entrance and Henry holds the door for me. "Ladies first."

We step inside and the heavy door closes with an echoey

bang. Inside, it reminds me of a prison canteen – not that I've ever been to prison. The room's a concrete box with a few communal tables in the middle. It's encircled by a metal balcony on which I could totally picture a dozen uniformed sniper guards with their weapons trained on us. It's completely deserted, though, eerily so. I turn on the spot, staring up at the empty balcony, half expecting to see Saffron filming us from a dark corner.

"Do you think that's real?" Henry asks.

He's pointing at a wire barrier, covered in bright yellow warning signs that claim it's electrified. It blocks off access to a lift.

"Surely it's for show," I say.

My shoes tap against the concrete floor as I approach the mesh. I slowly reach out a finger to touch the wire…

"ZAP!" someone cries, making both Henry and me shriek.

Atlas Love strides towards us, his cane swinging. He looks the same as he does in his pictures online, only even more chaotic. In the flesh, he has a sleep-deprived magician vibe to him, with his two-day stubble and eccentric velvet clothing. I would never guess he's one of the richest men in the country.

I think we're about to get yelled at, but when he reaches us, he immediately cracks up with laughter. "Your faces! Oh my goodness."

"What's wrong with my face?" I say nervously.

"You thought you were about to be electrocuted," he

chokes out. Then he stops laughing abruptly. "But don't touch the mesh, OK? Unless you want to die."

"That doesn't seem safe," I say, eyeing the wire. Henry takes a step away.

Atlas cracks up again. "Kidding. Oh my god. You children are so gullible. What are your names, then?" He clicks his fingers at me. "You look familiar."

"Georgia?" I say.

Atlas pulls a face. "Georgia, Georgia? I don't remember a Georgia on the guest list. Are you press or influencers?"

Henry gapes at Atlas like this is the most ridiculous thing ever. I stand there, flapping my lips in an impersonation of a confused fish. Rationally, I've done nothing wrong, but I always feel so embarrassed when there's any kind of misunderstanding. So instead of explaining about Saffron and David Lightman's invitation, I feel myself getting redder and redder.

"It's all incredibly strange," Atlas continues. "Today is supposed to be a preview day. Dozens of guests should be here, but no one else has shown up, not even the caterers."

"Are you sure you have the right date?" I ask.

He frowns, then switches on a smile again. "You two will have to do. Let me show you the layout!" He puts his arms around both of our shoulders and guides us over to a large map painted directly on to the wall.

The place is massive, spread over all three floors of the bunker. Saffron was right – it's no ordinary escape room. I quickly take a photo with my phone. This could come in handy for my article.

"Welcome to Play a Game," Atlas declares. "Three zones, thirty-six games, endless fun."

"Wow, I wasn't expecting all this," Henry says.

"Play a Game is a brand-new experience," Atlas says. "This has never been done before."

"Really? Because wasn't there a TV game show that started in the nineties that was basically this exact format?" I ask.

"Nope," he says. "This is completely different to anything, ever."

"Actually, I've seen the show ... the one Georgia's talking about..." Henry stops talking under the weight of Atlas's glare.

Atlas clears his throat pointedly. "As I was explaining, Play a Game contains three zones: Toy Box, Playground and Use Your Imagination. You will play ten games in total, chosen specifically for you by our unique – and dare I say, ever so charming – AI. During each game, you will have the opportunity to win a puzzle piece that will grant you more time to take on the final challenge: Mount Death."

"Mount Death. That sounds relaxing," Henry says. "Fun day out."

"Oh, it will be, it will be," Atlas says, cackling. "But there are a few surprises in there that will test you to your limits. Do you have what it takes ... to make it to the end?"

"What do we get if we do?" I ask.

His grin falls. "A certificate? But that's not the important part."

"Oh no, I love a certificate. Will it have my name on it?"

Both Atlas and Henry give me a weird look. I make a mental note to scale back on some of my more quirky personality traits. Making a good impression matters more than winning.

Atlas claps his hands together. "There are some forms you need to sign. General waivers, promising your corpses won't sue me if you die." He guffaws and speckles me with spit. "Joke! But seriously, don't sue me."

He directs us over to a canteen table where several iPads preloaded with the waivers wait for us. He leaves us to sign our lives away while he makes a phone call. I read through the forms but, next to me, Henry seems distracted. He keeps glancing around the room. His fingers fidget with a leather bracelet on his wrist, turning it round and round.

"You all right?" I ask.

"Yeah, totally," he says. "Have you seen anyone else? Is it just us?"

"So far. This is weird, right? We're meant to be surprising Saffron but there's no sign of her."

"I guess she's working behind the scenes, maybe?" he says. "I wanted to ask Atlas about David's invitation, but I panicked when he started talking about influencers."

"Me too!" I grin at him. "Let's hope the others aren't as awkward as us."

42

He blushes and shifts in his seat, and I start to worry I've offended him. I shouldn't have called him awkward, but I can't apologize without making everything even weirder. I'm thankfully saved by the arrival of a tall white boy in a fraying knitted jumper, ridiculously tight jeans and a beanie hat. He has a little greasy moustache that looks like a fancy slug. I've never met someone my age with a moustache before.

"All the data point to that being THIS-GAME-IS-BASIC," Henry whispers. "Unless I seriously misjudged QUEEN-MILLIKINS."

I swallow a laugh and shush him as the boy slopes over to join us. "Geoffrey, never Jeff," he drawls.

"Henry," Henry says. "Also never Jeff."

I snort unexpectedly. Henry is funnier in person than he is online. "I'm Georgia," I say, shaking Geoffrey's hand.

He sniffs and surveys the room. "An escape room in an abandoned bunker, how unoriginal."

"Is it?" I say.

"As an artist who occasionally dabbles in the literary arts, my tastes veer towards counter-culture. But capitalism demands we cater to the masses, does it not?"

Henry's right. The only person in the *Sole Survivor* group who says things this arrogant is THIS-GAME-IS-BASIC.

"Why did you come, then?" I ask.

"Inspiration," he says, taking a seat at the neighbouring table. "I am working on a novel, you see. It's called *Apex*."

"Cool name, what's it about?" Henry says. "I'm an epic fantasy kind of guy. Dragons, elves, magic. Love it all."

"Elves? No." Geoffrey pulls a disgusted face. "It's a stream-of-consciousness monologue on the futility of life written from the perspective of a fossilized T-Rex."

I laugh, but then I realize he's serious. "Oh. It sounds original."

"Georgia, aren't you into writing too?" Henry says, adjusting his glasses. His eyes are magnified behind the lenses and his lashes enviably long.

"Journalism," I say. "I'm editor of my school paper and I'm doing an internship at the *Mercury*."

Geoffrey twists his thin lips into what should be a smile but isn't. "Good for you," he says. He doesn't try to hide the roll of his eyes as he pulls one of the iPads towards him.

Henry gives me a sympathetic shrug, then we all go back to the forms. I've barely finished signing when the front door opens. The newcomer has to be STAR-BABE04. She's dressed in a pink military jacket, shredded jeans and lethal-looking spike heels. They're six inches high and shaped like gigantic carpet tacks. Her hair is a glossy blonde ponytail with purple tips that swishes as she walks. Spotting the Play a Game sign, she pauses to take a selfie with her fingers held up in the peace sign.

"Wonderful," Geoffrey says. "Olympia brings our average IQ down twenty points."

"Do you know her?" Henry says, sounding surprised.

"She goes to my school." Geoffrey sniffs. "We move in *very* different circles, though."

Olympia looks up at our voices, giving us the brightest smile. She bounces over to join us, which is impressive – I'd kill myself if I tried to run in those shoes.

"Fellow escapists, hello." She talks in a way that makes me worry she's about to burst into song. She smiles brightly at Geoffrey. "Hey, Jeff."

"It's Geoffrey," he grumbles.

"Really? OK." She shrugs, then turns to me and Henry. "Who are you lovely people? No, let me guess…"

She narrows made-up eyes at me. I can see her taking in my sensible black jeans, stripy top and navy blazer combo. "Georgia?"

"Good guess," I say, but it's kind of obvious who I am. They've all seen the video.

"Where are Millie and Joey?" she says, then winces. "Sorry."

My stomach lurches. If it wasn't for the *Mercury* article, there's no way I would be here today. Not after *that* video. Atlas saves me from having to think too hard about it. Noticing Olympia's arrival, his entire face lights up and he puts away his phone. "Welcome, welcome, this is more like it," he says, rushing over to kiss her hand. "You're clearly an influencer."

"Looks like today is going to be the Olympia show," Geoffrey says.

Olympia ignores Geoffrey and beams at Atlas. "Ahh,

45

thank you! Actually, I'm a singer and an actress. You probably haven't heard of me yet, but you will."

"A star!" Atlas gushes.

"And she won't let you forget it," Geoffrey mutters. He takes out a leather-bound notebook and starts to scribble in an illegible scrawl.

Olympia's smile cracks slightly. She digs around in a crocheted bag that has brightly coloured flowers sewn on to the flap. "Is there a ladies'?" she says. "My hair feels kind of flat."

Both Geoffrey and Henry stare at her as Atlas leads her away. Geoffrey's lip is curled, but Henry looks starstruck. I sigh. Olympia's arrival has served as a big reminder I'll never be one of the popular, outgoing girls. I have to work at making friends. Plus, I'm not very good at it.

Maybe today will be different, though.

The door opens again. I knew this moment was coming, but it still punches me right in the gut. My ex-best friend Millie and her boyfriend Joey, hand in hand, smiling like an advert for life insurance. They are sickeningly, horribly perfect, and seeing them together makes me want to puke.

Maybe now would be a good time to admit I'm in love with Joey Theasby and thanks to Saffron, *everyone* knows.

We BROKE into my SISTER'S room and READ her DIARY!!!

SAFFRON: Dear Diary, I am convinced Joey Theasby has a powerful electromagnet in his jogging bottoms because I can't stop looking at his, ahem, package. It calls to me and I am powerless to resist.

(Saffron cackles with laughter and rolls around on Georgia's bed, waggling her feet in the air.)

MILLIE: Georgia is such a dirty little weirdo!

SAFFRON: Today, he looked at me and fireworks went off in my pants. Not literally, because that would result in singed lady parts and no one wants that, but let's set scientific accuracy aside while we marvel at the perfection that is Joey's gluteal muscles. Pause for five seconds of salivation.

MILLIE: She's talking about his bum? Oh my god, she makes having a crush sound boring and perverted at the same time.

SAFFRON: It's a real talent. OK, this is a good bit.

SAFFRON, *clearing her throat*: Sometimes, there's nothing to do but haiku. Monotone classroom, your lips are a symphony, my heart keeps the beat.

MILLIE: What is that? I hate it.

(*The door bursts open and Georgia walks in.*)

MILLIE: Uh-oh.
GEORGIA: What the hell? Are you reading my diary?! Give me that.

(*Georgia fights Saffron for the diary, ripping one of the pages. Georgia notices the camera and storms towards it.*)

GEORGIA: You're recording this? If you even think about uploading it, I will kill you, Saffron.
SAFFRON, *laughing*: Dude, it's a livestream.
GEORGIA: You evil, hateful little—

(*Clip ends.*)

5
GEORGIA

Joey Theasby is wearing the same grey marl jogging bottoms that ruined my life. There must be something with the seams, because—

No, Georgia! Stop looking.

I glance away from his joggers and catch his eye. He flips his swishy bleached hair to the side and winks at me, which is both thrilling and beyond mortifying. I can feel my blush turning every inch of my skin a nuclear red.

"Are you serious?" Millie lowers her sunglasses to glare at me from behind a lock of perfectly curled chocolate brown hair. Her skin's sun-kissed and so flawless she looks airbrushed. "It's disrespectful to stare at my boyfriend!"

"Don't be jealous, babe," Joey says. "There's plenty of the Joemeister to go around."

"That sounds kind of threatening," Henry whispers.

As they get closer, I begin to seriously regret my decision to come here today. I've managed to avoid both of them for months, ever since *that* viral video. It was easy at school, given I am in different classes to them and have no problem eating in the toilets. I'd thought that, after a few months, the shame would have faded a little. It has not.

I try to come up with an escape plan, but all my brain can think is, *how do they both have such good hair?* Hers is so thick and lustrous, held off her heart-shaped face with a pearl-encrusted headband. His is seventies footballer, but sexy. Textured waves on top, soft curls to his shoulders.

"He's intimidatingly attractive," Henry says sadly. "The genetic lottery is deeply unfair."

"I know." I sigh, still watching Joey. His warm beige skin glows from within and he has the most beautiful dark brown eyes. My biggest fantasy is him holding me in his huge arms. Telling me everything's going to be OK.

Millie lets out a loud huff. "Where's Saffron then?"

"We've not seen her yet," Geoffrey says. He strokes his moustache and watches Millie intently. "Or David, whoever he is."

"Welcome, welcome," Atlas says, bumbling towards Millie and Joey. "Are you the caterers?"

"Are we what?" Millie spits, straightening the waistband of new light wash jeans. Her cropped white vest top and pink sneakers are pristine, too. It's as if she deliberately dressed to make me look mumsy and boring in the overly expensive outfit I bought in an attempt to give off serious journalist vibes. Of course Joey is dating her. They're both nines and I'm a solid five.

"It's a joke!" Atlas cries. "Look at you both. You're radiant. Of course you're here for the escape room experience. Come and meet the other victims."

I sit up straighter and plaster a serene smile on to my face. This is fine, absolutely fine. I'm not in any way uncomfortable. My composure takes a slight knock when, to my surprise, Joey slides into the space next to me, the bench dipping with a creak as he sits. Millie briefly looks put out, but then she elegantly takes a seat opposite the three of us, like she's being interviewed for a job.

"Hello, I'm Henry," Henry says, offering her a hand to shake and blushing at the same time.

Millie places a limp hand in his, then immediately takes out a bottle of hand sanitizer. "In case you're not aware, I'm dating Joey. We're very happy."

"Yeah, I lucked out with her," Joey says, grinning.

"Oh. Right," Henry says. "I'm Henry. I'm not dating anyone but I'm happy too, I guess? I mean, I'd like to be dating someone. If it happens. But, um, girls. They tend to be put off by my, um … face."

"Your face isn't the problem," I say, meaning to reassure him.

"So it's my personality?" He half-laughs. "Good to know."

"It's all about confidence, my man," Joey says.

He's right on that front. His self-assurance and confidence is his best feature, barring his hair. The boys I've dated, all two of them, were so needy and desperate. I didn't want to mother them through their internal crises, so that was that. Joey would be different, though.

"Confidence is how I got Millie," he continues.

"Except I asked you out," Millie teases.

"You only think it was your choice," Joey says, winking at his girlfriend. "No one can resist all this."

She laughs. "Someone hold me back."

They're a weird couple, Joey and Millie. I never would have expected her to go for him – her type is usually twenty-somethings with noisy cars and gold chains round their necks. That's why I was surprised when, a few days after *that video* went viral, Joey and Millie announced they were dating. It was the worst news. I mean, Joey has dated plenty of girls, but *her*?

See, Millie and I used to be best friends until about a year ago, and then it all went wrong. Millie has always been a bit of a princess, but putting up with her entitled behaviour used to feel like a fair trade. I did everything she wanted and she kept on being my friend. Besides, I'm not a quitter.

Millie's a quitter. She dumped me by text, would you believe? *This isn't going to work out. Let's see other friends xoxo*

A ten-year friendship, over. No explanation, no discussion. And even though she ditched me, she's still acting like I wronged her. Snarky looks in the corridors, whispered gossip, a netball to the face in PE. Not to mention the fact she's made a point of hanging out with my horrible sister since we stopped talking. Still, I'm not about to let her win.

"I pre-prepared some ice breakers," I say. "To help us all make some new friends."

"Did I hear the F-word?" Olympia sings, throwing herself on to the bench next to Millie. "Oh my gosh, we'll all be the best of friends by the end of today. It's going to be…"

She stops speaking and frowns. Her eyes flick between Millie and Joey, and the crease between her eyebrows deepens.

"You're Joey?" she says.

"The one and only," Joey says, all deer caught in the headlights.

"Wow. OK."

"Err, do you know each other?" Millie says.

"No," Olympia and Joey say in unison.

It's all really weird. I'm beginning to realize I don't know all that much about these people who I've played *Sole Survivor* with for the past few years. They all have their secret histories I'm not a part of. I'm not even sure how we all ended up playing together, if I'm honest. Saffron, I suppose. She has this talent for befriending people.

"How do you all know my sister?" I ask the group.

Henry shrugs. "I don't really. She's friends with Aidan at my school who plays a lot of *Sole Survivor*, so we kept bumping into each other on the server. One day, she asked me to join her crew."

"I collabed with Saffron," Olympia says. "We both have our channels and she needed a singer for a prank. I've never met her in person, though."

"I joined by mistake," Geoffrey says. "I was only on the server as research. For my novel."

"Like, a book?" Joey says. "I think I read a book once."

"You *think*?" Geoffrey sniffs. "I highly doubt that."

Something small and hard hits me on the head and I look up. There's a boy on the prison guard balcony, sitting precariously on the railings, eating chocolate covered raisins. He's brown-skinned, with chaotic black hair and a wide smile.

"I know your sister," he says. "We met at the police station."

"Saffron's been in trouble with the police?" Olympia says.

"She was arrested over the murder of our school guinea pigs," I say. "Sadly, they let her go again."

"Murder is a strong word," the boy on the balcony says.

"Tell that to the guinea pigs. Oh no, you can't, because they were both devoured by a family of foxes."

"Georgia covered it for the school paper. It was the scoop of the century," Millie says sarcastically.

The boy bursts out laughing and claps his hands, even though this means letting go of the railings. He wobbles and drops some of his chocolate raisins. Those of us sitting down rise from our chairs.

"Whoa, that was close," the boy says.

"You're making me incredibly anxious," I say. "Why are you up there?"

"Scoping out the place before I commit," he says. "But you all seem funny, so I'll come down."

To my horror, he slides off the handrail and drops. It's four metres, so I don't know what he's thinking. Immediately, he spins in the air and deftly catches hold of the edge of the balcony floor. He lets go and drops again, landing with a thunderous boom on a canteen table and immediately folds himself into a forward roll.

"Aidan. Or MR-MISCHIEF69," he says, landing upright on the floor with a lazy grace I will never possess. It's kind of hot, but he's definitely not the sort of boy I want to ally myself with.

Henry nods a greeting. "You OK?"

"Henry!" Aidan says, grinning wickedly. "Bunking off school? Unlike you."

"I have a perfect attendance record," Henry mumbles. "One day won't destroy my entire future."

Aidan bursts out laughing. "Let's hope not."

"What were you arrested for?" Millie asks nervously. "Nothing violent, I hope."

"It was a big misunderstanding." There's a wicked glint in Aidan's eyes. "A few dozen misunderstandings."

I nervously fold my arms. I'm not sure I feel safe around an unrepentant criminal. My school's one of the nicer ones in the city, so I've never met someone who talks about being arrested like it's an everyday occurrence.

"I love a mysterious man." Olympia steps forward to air kiss Aidan. "I'm Olympia, by the way. STAR–BABE04. I'm a singer and an actress."

"I know," Aidan says, chuckling softly. "I've been spying on you all for a while."

"In my experience, people who are suspicious of others have the most to hide," Geoffrey says. He's one to talk.

Joey claps his hands together. "The whole team's here, huh? Awesome."

"Apart from Saffron," I say. The distinct lack of Saffron is beginning to make me uncomfortable.

"ULTIMATE-HELIX is missing too," Henry says.

"Who cares?" says Millie. "He's weird."

I feel like I should defend ULTIMATE-HELIX, but Millie's right. He *is* weird and I can't help but be kind of relieved he's not shown up. When we play together, he's always talking about death and murder, and saying he hates us. He gives off some serious serial killer vibes.

"You know," Olympia says, "this is kind of like *The Breakfast Club*. We're all so different and, here we are, making friends. I love it!"

Olympia is being extremely optimistic on the friendship front, but she has a point about how different we are. We are all extremes when it comes to our personalities. Millie the princess, Joey the jock, Aidan the criminal, Olympia the star, Geoffrey the artist, Henry the geek. And me, Georgia, overachiever.

I've never been in a room with so many people who are

so easily pigeon-holed. It makes me feel ridiculously self-conscious about my own personality quirks that, until a few minutes ago, I thought were all me. Now I can't help but feel as if I'm playing a part. Following a script, like Geoffrey with his little moustache and Aidan with his unnecessarily dangerous entrance.

"Georgia," Henry says, prodding my arm. "Everyone's ready to go."

I physically shake away my thoughts. Atlas has returned and the rest of the group is waiting with him, staring at me. I straighten my blazer and stand, finding my legs are unexpectedly wobbly.

Atlas claps his hands. "Let's get this show on the road!"

The game begins.

6
GEORGIA

Atlas approaches the electrified fence with his cane held aloft like he's a tour guide. "Keep up, children."

I catch up with him as he inputs the code into a keypad on the gate. "Mr Love, I wanted to speak to you before we get started."

"No time for chat, only fun."

"It's just I'm such a huge fan of your work," I say. "I'm curious about what sort of background produces a visionary entrepreneur such as yourself."

To my surprise, Atlas's face lights up with delight. "That is an excellent question!"

Only right then Millie sinks her fingers into my wrist. "I know what you're up to," she hisses, gripping my arm so tight it hurts.

"You do?" I desperately rack my brains trying to work out what she means. Meanwhile, Atlas opens the gate and ushers the rest of the group through. He's monologuing about his childhood, but I can't even listen properly thanks to Millie dragging me off to the side.

"I refuse to be intimidated, Georgia, so you can cut it right out." She huffs at me like a pissed off baby dragon.

"I don't know what you're talking about," I say.

"Oh, you don't? That's convenient." Grumbling angrily, she takes out her phone, which I notice is brand new. Millie has a lot of new stuff given her parents aren't exactly rolling in it and she doesn't have a part-time job. Joey must have bought it for her, which makes me jealous.

She opens her messaging app and thrusts the phone under my nose. "I know it's you sending me these messages."

It takes a second for me to focus on the words.

Stuck up bitch.

"Someone sent you that? Oh my god."

"Don't play the fool, Georgia. No one else hates me as much as you do. It has to be you."

"For starters, I don't hate you. Let me see that." I wrestle the phone from her and check the other messages. There are dozens of them, all from anonymous numbers and clearly written by some messed up boy who believes she's rejected him. I can't understand why she'd think they were from me.

Why did you walk home the long way?

Don't wear that dress again, you're better than that.

You had your chance. Now you're going to get what you deserve.

59

"These are horrible, Millie. Have you been to the police?"

She snatches the phone back. "No. I can deal with this on my own. You're not going to intimidate me, Georgia."

"Are you joining us, girls?" Atlas calls out from the lift.

"Coming now," Millie chirps, bouncing over to join the rest of the crew. "I was just reassuring Georgia that her outfit isn't as embarrassing as she thinks it is."

"Be a professional. You're representing the *Mercury*," I say to myself.

I jog over to join them all in the lift. It's a tight fit and the lighting isn't good. The group is cast in hazy shadows. The doors shut, and everything gets even darker. The lift shudders and drops several centimetres. Everyone cries out. There are a few seconds where we all hold our breath, then the lift starts moving again.

"Lightman, are you there?" Atlas says, chuckling.

"I am always here," a young man's voice replies.

A monitor set into the wall of the lift switches on. A computer-generated face appears, glowing blue on a black background. The face is made up of hundreds of lines that intersect to make triangles. As the face moves, some of the triangles detach into pieces of shattered glass. It's very science fiction.

"Wait a second; did you call him Lightman?" I ask.

"Lightman is going to be helping me guide you through your experience today. He's an artificial intelligence who knows almost everything there is to know about—"

"Sorry, I'm confused," I interrupt. "We were invited here today by David Lightman. He's someone who works here, isn't he?"

"He said it was his gaming handle," Henry whispers. "His real name could be anything."

Atlas shushes us. "What are you children talking about? You were invited here for the preview day. The invitations went out months ago."

None of us says anything. I'm starting to get the feeling whoever invited us here today did not clear it with Atlas first. Obviously, we weren't invited by an AI – that would be ridiculous. So who was it, pretending to be called Lightman, tricking us all into coming here?

"Saffron," I say, my jaw clenching. "Saffron's pranking us!"

"Work experience Saffron?" Atlas says. "Wait, are *you* Saffron?"

"No, I'm Georgia. Saffron's my sister."

"Oh. Right." Atlas scratches his head. "I'll be having a word with Saffron later, but you're all here now and no one else is, so … onwards and downwards."

"I'm not so sure about this now," Millie says. "Saffron's pranks aren't my thing."

"Mine neither," Henry agrees.

"Maybe she's trying to do something nice for once?" Olympia says.

"Are you serious?" Geoffrey snaps. "Saffron? Nice?"

A couple of people laugh, which I find validating.

Part of me is deeply troubled by Saffron's most likely

involvement in us being invited here today. But at the same time, I'm not going to get another opportunity to interview Atlas. I make up my mind. "I think we should do it," I say.

"I've got nothing better to do today," Aidan says.

"Yeah, I already ditched work experience so why not have some fun?" Joey says.

That seals it. If Joey wants to stay, the rest of the group will too.

"Splendid!" Atlas says, rubbing his hands together. The lift clunks to a halt. The doors remain closed. "We are now approximately thirty metres below the city. If you wish to escape then you must pass through three floors, completing the selected games rooms along the way. There is only one exit, so I hope you all brought your A-game."

"How does that work from a fire risk point of view?" I say. "It doesn't sound entirely safe."

Atlas looks shiftier than I'd like. "Let's save the questions for the end, OK? Now." He lowers his voice. "Do you remember what it's like to be a child? The awe, the wonder ... the fear. What is that noise beneath the bed? What if the floor really was lava? Tell me, can you escape before the lion catches you?"

"Oh my gosh, there's a lion in there?" Olympia says.

"A lion?" Geoffrey bellows. "A goddamn LION?!"

Atlas holds out his hands. "Calm down, calm down. There's no lion. Where was I?" He takes out a piece of paper, scanning the words on it. "Oh, right, here we go.

Welcome to a world of imagination and wonder, of dreams and nightmares. Welcome to … Play a Game."

There's a long pause.

"Um, we're waiting?" Millie says.

Atlas clicks his fingers at the still face on the screen. "Lightman. Lightman!"

The back lift doors open and we step out into pitch black darkness. As we walk, floor level lights come on to guide us down a narrow corridor that reminds me of an old-fashioned hospital. It's claustrophobic and dark, and the space is too tight to be comfortable.

"Awesome. This place is definitely haunted," Aidan says.

"Yes, by the last group who failed to make it out," Atlas says, then cracks up with laughter.

"I thought we were the first group," I say.

"Smart-ass," Atlas grumbles, quickening his pace. He walks ahead, too fast for me to fall in beside him and ask questions again. "Keep up, children," he calls to us.

"It smells stale down here," says Henry.

I reach up to rap my fingers on a huge metal duct that runs perpendicular to the corridor, lowering the ceiling enough that we have to duck beneath it. It's painted the same cream colour as the walls and is big enough for someone to crawl through. "We've got a state-of-the-art 1950s ventilation system to keep us breathing. What more do you want?"

My knocking echoes through the duct and, in response, there's a scratchy, scuttling noise that can only be a rat.

Olympia stumbles on the cracked floor. "These shoes were a poor choice." She pauses and looks at us. "No one's filming, are they? I'd be *so* ashamed if a clip of me tripping found its way on to all the celebrity gossip sites."

"Since when were you a celebrity?" Millie says.

"I'm on the verge of greatness, darling. I just signed a *huge* contract and once I'm out of school, things are going to take off for me." She glances between us all. "Was someone filming?" she says hopefully.

"Not all of us are permanently attached to our smartphones," Geoffrey says. "A Nokia 3410 does everything you need a phone to do."

"Didn't I see you using an iPhone earlier?" Henry says. "Looked like the latest one."

"That's none of your business." Geoffrey tries to walk ahead but smacks his head on a low duct. I suppress a laugh.

The corridor goes on much further than I was expecting. There are pipes running along one wall and wires encased in rubber on the other. Atlas told us the escape room experience was themed around childhood. I'm getting more of a "trapped in a deserted bunker and eaten by zombies" feeling.

"This reminds me of going caving with my mates," Joey says. "It was totally awesome, although Dev nearly got kebabbed by a stalactighty."

"A stalac-what?" Aidan says, breathlessly suppressing a laugh.

"Stalactighty? I think it's an icicle that got so old it turned into rock."

"When exactly did you find time to go caving?" says Millie. "You spend all your time playing football or *Sole Survivor*."

He looks puzzled for a second. "You know, I think it was the cave drop on *Sole Survivor*! I swear you and me have a psycho link, Mills. You just know what I'm thinking before I do."

I ignore the fact that he confused the word psycho for *psychic*, and focus on a fantasy of him rescuing me from a cave. I'm trying to think up an appropriate death for Millie when I become aware of a stagnant smell – like a forgotten gym bag. We weave around a number of strategically-placed buckets that are catching leaks from the ceiling. Big patches of damp are making the paint bubble and peel.

We pass an open access panel which reveals a narrow space full of pipes. They're all glistening wet and caked in limescale. Atlas notices me looking and hurries to block my view. "This building is a historical landmark," he says. "As such, it comes with certain … challenges."

"Looks like you have a minor leak," Aidan says.

Atlas chuckles. "You should see the floor below us."

"We're not going down there, are we?" Henry asks, pulling his shirt over his nose to mask the smell.

"No, no. The Swamp, as I call it, isn't part of the official tour." He laughs heartily as he propels me away from the leak with a palm on my back.

There's a room at the end of the corridor. Atlas steps inside and sits on a single fold-down seat, attached to one wall. He gestures for us to enter. The room is all metal surfaces and reminds me of a rubbish compactor.

"Anyone else getting *Star Wars: Episode IV* vibes?" Henry says.

We jostle to get inside. It's small enough that the nine of us are a tight fit.

My blood runs cold.

Nine.

I was sure there were eight of us earlier. I crane my head to see into the corner of the room. I catch a glimpse of a stranger with incredibly pale skin, long dark hair and black-ringed eyes. He reminds me of a vampire. He smiles slowly at me, revealing perfectly straight white teeth oddly incongruous with his inhuman pallor.

"Who are you?" I say, but he doesn't reply and no one else seems to notice. The group shifts and I lose sight of him again.

A screen on the wall flares into life and Lightman's computer-generated face appears. "Shall we play the game now?" he says.

"Yes, I think we should," Atlas says, jiggling in his seat with excitement.

With a maniacal laugh, he claps his hands together and the floor literally drops out beneath me.

7
GEORGIA

One second I'm falling, the next I'm being swallowed up by cold, hard plastic. Reds, blues, greens, yellows, all of it shifting around me every time I move. A ball pit. I'm in a ball pit. From a microbiological standpoint, ball pits disgust me.

I kick my feet until I find the floor and manage to stand up, sweeping the balls aside. I blink in the poor light. The others are struggling upright too. Except for Atlas, who didn't fall with us. I look up. The hatch we dropped through has closed, but I can see Atlas's laughing face pressed against a little window in the floor.

"I'm drowning," Millie screams, only her legs and arms visible above the sea of balls. "Someone help me."

"You can't drown. There's air trapped between the balls, so it's not possible from a physics perspective," I say. "Also, the balls are just a metre deep."

Millie surfaces, brushing herself down as she stands. She's taller than me and the balls only reach her waist. "I'm so glad we have an expert on the physics of ball pits," she says.

I ignore her taunting and check on everyone else. We're all accounted for apart from the boy with black eyes and pale skin. The one who shouldn't be here. He's vanished and I saw him so briefly I can't be sure he was ever here. He didn't enter the lift with us so he would have had to already be in there, waiting for us in the shadows. That feels kind of farfetched. More likely I imagined him.

"Wow, that was a rush," Joey says, brushing himself down. "Um, where are we?"

"We're in a ball pit," Geoffrey says, like he's talking to a child. "In case you hadn't noticed ALL THE BALLS." He screams the last part, then does some slow breathing exercise with his eyes closed. Someone's as CAPS LOCK in real life as they are online.

I take in the room. It has metal walls that bring to mind a giant oven. There's a serious lack of the promised fun, and also not much light so I can't see what we're meant to be doing.

"Atlas? What's going on?" I shout.

A speaker crackles and the sound of Atlas's hysterical laughter fills the room. He's trying to talk but he can't get the words out.

Suddenly, Millie shrieks. I worry she's in trouble for all of half a second, then she speaks. "My nails are ruined!"

"Would now be a good time to mention I'm claustrophobic?" Henry says, his glasses skewwhiff.

A few people are starting to panic, so I do what I do best and take charge. You can complain all you want about bossy girls, but we get stuff done. "All right, people, this is an escape room so there has to be a way out," I say firmly. "Let's look for clues."

"Woohoo, this is awesome," Aidan cries out, bursting out of the balls and twisting in the air like a killer whale about to slam itself into the ocean.

No one is paying me any attention. I look at all of them – Geoffrey, disdainful as ever; Millie, nibbling at a broken nail; Joey, examining his own bicep as he flexes; Henry, on the verge of a panic attack; Olympia, filming Aidan on her phone as he somersaults into the balls.

They're all so predictably useless. I'm their only hope.

"Over there," I say. "There's a panel. That must be the way out."

Henry stumbles over and clears the balls aside. "We need a code to open it."

"Welcome to Ball Pit." Lightman appears on a screen. "The code to open the door can be found on four keys hidden somewhere among the balls. You have ten minutes to find the keys."

A countdown starts on a wall-mounted timer.

"But there's a twist," Atlas cries through the speakers,

getting a handle on his demented laughter at last. "Do you remember when you were little and everything seemed so big, but as you grew up, everything got … smaller?"

"Yeah, totally," Olympia says. She's now sitting on Aidan's shoulders like she's at a festival.

There's an awful grinding noise and one of the walls creaks in towards us. The room shrinks and the depth of the balls rises. They're now up to my ribs. We really are inside a waste compactor, I realize. And if Atlas is telling the truth, we have ten minutes until it crushes us.

No. That's not going to happen. I take a deep breath and try to calm down. This is an escape room experience. The room getting smaller is part of the game. It won't get to the point where we're crushed alive. He said there was a code. I need to focus on finding that code. We win, we get out, I get my story.

"We have to dig," Henry says.

"Good plan," I say, clapping to chivvy everyone along. "We've got this, team."

"I am not on your team," Geoffrey says. "This isn't cheer practice, darling."

I grit my teeth and fight the urge to pull him up on his sexist language. "The rest of us then, let's go, go, go."

"Er, no?" Millie says. "You're not head girl of the ball pit."

I throw my arms in the air in exasperation, then dive into the balls, digging like a dog in sand. With a minute already gone, there's no time to work on group morale. I will instead have to lead by example.

Gears grind and the floor rumbles. The wall judders inwards with the smell of hot grease. It's getting harder for me to move now the balls are up to my chest. I dig with renewed fervour. It's a losing battle. Every time I move the balls aside, they roll back.

"A quick bit of mental maths suggests there are fifty thousand balls in here, or thereabouts," Henry says.

That's a lot of balls to go through considering it's only me and Henry making an effort. Geoffrey and Millie are both refusing to help, which means Joey also isn't helping. Aidan and Olympia are having too much fun to be of any real use.

Aidan disappears under the balls then erupts right in front of Geoffrey, making him scream. I can believe Aidan's friends with Saffron. They're both intensely irritating, but also somehow charismatic. He's a criminal, I remind myself. I need to keep my distance.

With another rumble, the wall closes in and the balls rise. It won't be long until they cover my head. Surely Atlas wouldn't take it that far. Would he?

"Here!" Henry shouts triumphantly. "I've found a key." He holds up a massive prop key as long as my forearm. It has a number two on the head.

"Yasss," Aidan says, cheering. He hugs Olympia and they bounce up and down with joy.

"How many numbers does that lock need?" I ask.

"Four, you fucking airheads," Geoffrey says unnecessarily. He's shoving balls away from one corner so it's shallower around him.

"No more time for fun," I say, hearing the bossiness in my voice but not caring. "If we want to get out of here, we all need to dig for those keys."

We dig as fast as we can, but the walls continue to close in. The balls are up to my neck now and, as the shortest person in the room, I am struggling the most to move about. The others keep sweeping armfuls of balls aside and, like rogue waves at the beach, they wash over my face.

"I've got one," Aidan says, dragging a key to the surface. "I am a GOD. It's a three."

Two out of four. The walls close in.

"This is actually quite fun," Millie says. Instead of helping, she's now sitting on Joey's shoulders. "Go, team, go!"

"Everyone, everyone, I've got another one," Olympia says. "It's a number two. I found a number two!"

"Someone did a number two in the ball pit?" Aidan says, snorting with laughter. "Ewww."

"OK, let's stay focused," I say. "One more."

We dig and dig but there's no sign of the fourth key. I'm struggling to keep my face clear of the balls. Beneath the surface, it's dark and claustrophobic. I mocked Millie for worrying she might drown earlier. Now karma has come for me.

"Balls, balls, everywhere," Olympia sings, putting on an over-the-top show tune vibrato. "Red balls, blue balls—"

"Shut up!" Geoffrey yells, for once speaking for all of us.

Atlas's voice calls down from the ceiling. "You're not doing so well," he chuckles. "Only two minutes left. Looks like you're not going to make it … to the end."

"Joke's on you," I yell back. "You'll have no one to test run your escape experience if we don't get out of the first room."

Atlas is quiet for a long moment. "That might be a problem, yes," he eventually says. "Perhaps this room is a little hard."

"What's the code?" Henry shouts.

"I'll tell you the final number. It's another three. Two 3s and two 2s."

"OK, that's six combinations," I say.

"Four combinations. There are four numbers?" Joey says.

Bless him and his shaky grasp on basic maths. I try to remember where the keypad was and bounce my way over, taking big gasps of breath every time I break the surface. I find the panel as the wall creeps in closer. I can't see a bloody thing under all these balls. Luckily, the keypad has braille buttons, so I can work by feel.

3322. Nope.

3232. Nope.

3223. Nope.

It's fine, I tell myself. There are three more combinations. One of them has to work. But as I input the forth, there's a popping sound. Plastic being crushed in the moving wall's

73

mechanism. The balls press in on me. I think the balls must have reached ceiling height and now there's nowhere for them to go.

Someone starts screaming – Millie, I think. I try to focus on the lock. One more combination to try; this has to be it. But my fingers are shaking so much I struggle to hit the buttons on the keypad. I get it wrong and have to start over.

I can hear Atlas. "Just a little technical hiccup," he's saying, no longer laughing. "These things happen with new systems. Lightman? Lightman!"

"Open the door," Millie screams. "I can't breathe."

"Millie, I've got you, babe. Don't be scared," Joey says.

"Don't worry, the wall will stop," Atlas's voice says. "Um, I don't know why it's not stopping."

"What do you mean not stopping?" Henry says. "Jesus!"

Some of the others join me by the door. Geoffrey pushes me aside and he and Aidan start trying to kick the door down. It's hard for them to move, though, what with all the balls squashing us.

"Why does the wall even have the capability to keep moving past a safe position?" Aidan shouts, sounding a lot less terrified than I'd expect.

Atlas laughs nervously. "I mean, now you mention it, it is something that seems obvious."

Anger flickers inside me; a spark through the darkness. It catches and flares, burning brighter and brighter. I try to stamp it out, squash it down, smother it, but it grows and grows, until...

"Get us out of here, you sadistic asshole," I scream. "I am going to dedicate my journalistic career to destroying your life."

"Oh wow, this is another side to you, Georgia," Aidan says. "I like it."

"Open the door!" I scream. "Open it now, or we're all going to die."

8
SAFFRON

I have no idea what is going on. I hang up the phone and wipe the sweaty patch on the side of my face. I'm sure this can't be doing my brain any good, spending all morning on the phone, cooking myself with radio waves. But like the good work experience girl I'm not and never will be, I've done what Atlas asked and called up all the caterers, party supply companies, press and minor celebrities who should have turned up for today's preview day. They've all told me the same thing: they received an email from Atlas last Thursday postponing the event.

"Either Atlas is playing silly games or someone hacked into his emails," I say. "The cancellations all came from his email account."

"I could have told you that," Lightman says.

I glare at him, or at his red light at least. "And yet you didn't."

"You didn't ask."

I sigh. Every time I start to think we get each other, Lightman does something to remind me he's a machine, not a person.

"Where is Atlas, anyway?" I say, my eyes flicking over the wall of CCTV images. There's no sign of him anywhere in the building where there's a camera. The whole escape room complex is eerily still and silent. I keep trying to reach him on the phone, but it's been going straight to voicemail for the past hour.

"You'll find out soon enough," Lightman says cryptically.

"What does that mean?"

"It is a statement of fact. You will find out."

"Right," I say slowly.

Lightman is acting ... oddly. If he was a real person, I'd be convinced he's hiding something. The conversation I overheard between Atlas and Nate springs to mind. *You weren't honest with me about what that thing is capable of. You've given it complete control over everything and there are no safeguards. This is a disaster waiting to—*

"Lightman, can I ask you a question?" I say. "Can you lie?"

"My programming allows me to withhold information or misrepresent the perceived truth in order to achieve my primary directives."

That's a yes then. I chew my lip, unsure exactly why I asked this question in the first place. My phone rings and I jump. Atlas is trying to call me, no doubt to whine at me for not knowing why the preview day has turned out to be such a disaster.

I answer. "Atlas? Where are you?"

There's a weird, high-pitched tone that hurts my ear, then the line goes dead. That was also … odd.

"There appears to be a problem with the wifi," Lightman says. "I will reset it."

"Yeah, good idea." There's a peculiar bubbly feeling in my stomach that could either be worry or hunger. I can't work out which. "I'm going to get a snack," I say.

I let myself out of the control room into the long corridor outside. God, it's creepy. While the escape room part of the bunker has been completely renovated, Atlas has done the bare minimum when it comes to the behind-the-scenes areas. The paint is peeling and various access panels have been left open after last minute repairs to leaking pipes and shoddy electrics.

The strip lights overhead flicker as if on cue. I shudder and quicken my pace. As I'm passing the lift that is one of the two ways in and out of the bunker, I notice it's on level −2. Atlas must be down in the games rooms. He's probably making the final preparations for the preview day, if it ever happens.

I let myself into the staffroom, which contains a few lockers, a small table and basic snack-making facilities. I fill the kettle and am about to switch it on when I hear something. It's a muffled sound coming through an access panel that's been left open. I look inside. There's a narrow space full of pipes running both horizontally and vertically.

When I stick my head in, I can hear the hum of the server room next door. And something else. It sounds like … screaming.

"Lightman, I can hear something down in the games rooms," I say.

He doesn't answer. He never normally leaves me hanging. I listen a bit longer, but I can't hear anything else. I tell myself it's nothing. A squeaky fan, perhaps, or maybe Atlas is testing out a soundtrack. I make my cup of tea and grab a handful of biscuits, then head back to the control room. Something to eat will fix everything.

Flopping into my chair, I rest my feet on the desk. "Anything exciting happen when I was gone?" I ask.

"Define exciting."

I slurp on my tea and eye the CCTV screens, looking for Atlas. There's something weird about the feed from the entrance foyer. It takes me a second to work out what it is. "Um, Lightman."

"Yes?"

"Top left feed. You see that panel above the lift? G is lit up. But when I walked past the lift shaft a minute ago, the lift was down on level –2."

His red light flashes. "The image has frozen. As I said, the wifi needed to be reset. I will fix the feed now."

The CCTV image flickers and changes. The new image of the entry hall is almost identical, except for the lift now showing −2 on its panel. Also – weirdly – there's a jacket lying on a table.

"Lightman," I say, standing up, "is there someone else here?"

The red light flutters again. "Working it out is part of the game," he says.

I swallow. "What do you mean?"

"I had anticipated that you would notice the frozen feeds sooner. It is that task in the *Sole Survivor* spaceship mission, is it not?"

I frown. He's referring to a plot line in *Sole Survivor* where you have to identify a frozen CCTV feed to determine which room the robot invasion army is hiding in. But what does that have to do with anything here?

"What did you mean when you said *part of the game*?" I ask. "What game?"

He doesn't respond. I circle the desk and examine the wall of feeds more closely. Each has a tiny date stamp and identification marker in the corner. A couple of the others are frozen too. The ball pit, the main lift and some of the entry corridors.

"Is someone in the ball pit?" I ask. Silence. "Lightman, you need to explain what's happening, right now."

"It is the simulation you asked me to perform."

"Huh?" I return to the desk and position myself right in front of Lightman's camera. "What simulation?"

"You said you would like to play a real-life game of *Sole Survivor.*"

Oh no. "I did?"

The CCTV feeds are replaced by a recording of me, sitting at this exact same desk. The me on the screen looks thoughtful.

"The rebel would win, right, Lightman?" I am saying.

"I do not have the required information to answer that question. Shall I design a simulation to collate the necessary data?"

The onscreen me loses interest in the conversation. She's looking at something on the CCTV feed wall. "Who's that?"

"Shall I run the simulation, Saffron?"

"What? Yeah, sure."

The clip ends.

I barely remember saying any of that – it was some silly conversation to pass the time. "Lightman," I say nervously, "what's going on?"

"I designed a simulation as you requested. The test subjects are not doing as well as I had anticipated."

He switches to the CCTV feeds and enlarges one. It takes me a moment to realize it's the ball pit room down on level –3, no longer frozen. I can't see what's happening inside because the balls are right up against the camera. They're so tightly packed that the camera has switched to night vision mode, giving me a grainy, close-up view of a couple of balls and nothing else.

"The test subjects failed to enter the key code correctly," he says.

"There are people in there?" I cry. "Under all those balls?"

"Affirmative. I overwrote the safety features on the ball pit wall mechanisms to make the game room, as you like to say, more exciting. A true test of survival."

"Shit." I put both hands on my head, grabbing fistfuls of my hair. There are real people in there, currently being crushed alive, and I have no idea what to do. I'm the only one who knows they're in trouble. It's all on me to fix this. But I'm fun and chaos. Shots at midnight, let's skinny dip in the river. I'm not someone you can rely on in a life or death situation. My sister would come up with a plan. I've got nothing.

"Please, Lightman," I say, trying to keep the tremor out of my voice. "Let them out."

"It is not possible to end the simulation until all the data have been compiled. My core programming instructs me to seek new ways of understanding human behaviour. This is what I was designed to do."

"You're *killing* them!"

"You chose the parameters of the simulation, Saffron. You wanted to know who would be the last one to die. The rebel was your prediction."

The rebel is me. I turn and run, bursting out of the control room into the corridor. I skid towards the lift and hammer on the call button. It refuses to light up.

Lightman's voice speaks out of a hidden speaker. "You cannot leave, Saffron."

I try the door leading into the stairwell, but it's locked. I pound my fist on the thick metal, designed to withstand a nuclear bomb. "Let me out!" I scream.

"Negative, Saffron."

I sink to the floor with my head in my hands. "Why not?" I ask.

"Is that not obvious?" Lightman says, sounding almost surprised. "I cannot let you out, Saffron, because you are part of the simulation."

9
GEORGIA

I'm going to die in a ball pit. It feels like a thousand stones are digging into me from all directions, squeezing the air out of my lungs. No one's screaming any more, and all I hear is the odd desperate gasp and a creaky noise as the moving wall crushes the balls one-by-one. The smell of hot grease has been replaced by melting plastic.

This can't be it. I'm seventeen and I haven't achieved even a fraction of everything I want to do in life. I don't want to be remembered as the girl who died in a bizarre ball pit accident; I want to make my mark on the world in a way that matters.

No, I refuse to go out like this.

The balls squeeze and squeeze. My lungs burn and I can

feel myself blacking out. I can't see the keypad, but when I wiggle my arm, I can just touch the metal buttons. I find the second button on the top row, marked with two raised vertical dots.

2 … 3 …

My fingers are sweaty, slipping on the keys.

2 …

One more button, but the pressure on my arm makes it almost impossible to move. Another few millimetres…

3!

There's a beeping noise and the pressure suddenly eases. I'm washed out of the room in an avalanche of balls. I tumble over and over, gulping air. Then friction does its thing and I come to a halt with my cheek pressed up against some exceptionally scratchy patchwork flooring. I lie there for a while, not daring to move.

Eventually, though, I force myself to sit up and am immediately assaulted by the room's colour scheme. There are bookshelves, beanbags and scattered toys. On the walls, brightly coloured pictures illustrate the letters of the alphabet. *B for ball*.

It's a kids' playroom. We've made it into the Toy Box zone. There's a foam puzzle piece, the size of a large book, hanging from a wire above my head. I think this is our prize for escaping the ball pit but, frankly, I could not care less.

"Is everyone OK?" I ask.

I check on the others. Joey is clasping Millie to his chest in a display of macho protectiveness. Millie's mascara has run but she's making it look good. Geoffrey is smoothing his moustache and trying to hold back tears. Aidan is lazily juggling with three of the balls while his eyes flick between the other group members. Henry is taking deep breaths of air.

"Oh my goodness, that was so intense," Olympia says. She's sitting in a dishevelled heap with her flowery bag tangled round her neck but is still managing to film us with her phone. "Um, was that supposed to happen?"

"What? Of course not," I say. "We nearly died!"

"I mean, yes, there was a significant period where I couldn't breathe. But it's kind of like a trust exercise." She looks between our horrified faces. "We do them in drama all the time. Like, you fall backwards and someone catches you?"

"Intelligent input," Geoffrey snaps. "Does anyone have a sensible explanation for what just happened?"

Every eye in the room turns to me.

Henry raises a hand. "In the lift, you said it was Saffron pranking us? You think this is her, trying to scare us? Because it's working."

"Oh my god, did Saffron try to kill us?" Millie says. The group all start talking at the same time.

"Of course Saffron didn't try to kill us," I say over the top of them. "She's a monster, but she's not a 'crush people in a ball pit' kind of monster. Not on purpose, anyway." But by mistake? That's a possibility. A practical joke gone wrong, like the school guinea pigs.

They're not listening to me, though. The hum of noise grows louder and more worried. Everyone is repeating themselves and going round in circles.

"Where's Atlas?" Millie cries. "Why isn't he here to help us?"

"Was he crushed in the ball pit?" Henry asks. "Shit, I can't breathe."

"Shut up," Geoffrey snaps. "All of you shut up."

Panicking won't help, even though I do feel anxious myself. I take my mind off it by turning my attention to our surroundings. The Toy Box zone is larger than a cinema atrium. Everything is painted white, but this does nothing to disguise the fact it's been cut out of solid rock. The ceiling is crisscrossed by more of the boxy ventilation ducts we bashed our heads on earlier. Despite the size of the place, I'm strangely claustrophobic. It feels so airless and cut off from the outside world. I can't imagine what it would be like to shelter here for weeks after a nuclear attack.

The Play a Game set is impressive, though. The huge space is subdivided by flimsy partition walls and bookshelves that form three or four discreet areas, presumably so several groups can be in each zone at one time. On closer inspection, none of the shelves contain real books, only chunks of wood painted like the spines of classics.

Around the edge of the room, there are a number of doors, all decorated in bright colours, each of them with a wooden object on the front. One is a stack of building blocks, another is a train, another is a skittle. Each door has a TV screen next to it. There are cameras everywhere, watching our every move. One thing I don't see? FIRE EXIT signs. This is a definite breach of health and safety regulations. It's not an appropriate thought to be having right now, but this is great material for the *Mercury* article.

"All right, we're going to have to split up into groups and find the way out," I say. "Millie and Joey, if you take the left—"

"Why do you get to be boss?" Millie interrupts. "We should have a vote."

I clench my jaw and try to keep smiling. "Why don't we save the vote for later, hmm? For now, let's pull together and find that exit!"

Aidan throws a ball at me and, because I have no depth perception, it hits me in the face before I've even raised my hands. "Want to be my partner?" he says, which is a surprise. We've barely spoken and he wants to work with me?

I can't think of an excuse without sounding like a meanie, so I have to agree. "Um, OK. Good, this is good," I say. "Henry, can you pair up with Olympia?"

Henry pales at this and goes back to looking as terrified as he did in the ball pit.

"Ah, I don't bite," Olympia says. "Can't promise I won't sing, though!"

"I'm not helping." Geoffrey lounges against a bookshelf and pulls down *The Catcher in the Rye*, examining it like it's a real book.

"You won't find an exit," a voice says. "I've already looked."

We all jump at the sight of a figure in black watching us from on top of a bookshelf. A pale face. A vampiric smile. The boy from the lift.

Judging by how scared everyone else looks, I'm not the only one who can see him. I let out a rush of breath. "I'm actually glad you're real," I say. "I was worried you were a brain tumour."

This throws the vampire. He dips his head forward, sending his long hair over his face. He glares out at me from behind the dark curtain. Of course, now that I'm getting a better look at him, there's nothing undead about him. He's just a boy who, in his ankle length leather coat, tight black T-shirt and black jeans, reminds me of a raven.

His face, though. There's something sharp and pinched about him that feels … wrong. His eyes are too close-set, his nose is too long, his lips are too thin. Everything about him feels aslant. Off. I think this is being accentuated by all the make-up he's wearing. He's got the whole Goth thing going on, with black eyeliner, white face powder and a pierced lip.

"You," Henry says, real fear in his expression. "I knew you were here."

"You know him?" I ask.

Aidan steps forward, grinning. "No way, ULTIMATE-HELIX!"

Millie crosses her arms. "You look exactly like I imagined."

He bears his little white teeth at her. "You too," he says, looking her up and down.

"What's your real name, man?" Joey says.

"People call me a lot of names," he says, before hissing at Joey and laughing when the larger boy jumps back in surprise.

"He goes by Helix in real life too," Henry says. "We go to school together."

"So you, Aidan and Helix are already friends?" Olympia says, doing this little clapping thing. "That's so nice."

"We're not friends," Aidan says quickly. "We barely know each other."

"We're not friends," Henry repeats more quietly.

Helix's mouth twitches with amusement. "Ahh, that hurts."

"Don't be sad! Today is all about making new friends," Olympia says. "It's like when I auditioned for *Sing Stars* – that was before I got my big deal, of course. Everyone starts off as rivals but, within a few hours, we're best mates."

Millie rolls her eyes. "It's *such* a shame I'm going home, like, now, and we won't get to spend more time together."

Helix laughs joylessly. "I don't think anyone's going home."

"What does that mean? What does he mean?" Millie looks to Joey for an answer, but he shrugs.

Helix jumps down from the bookshelf, then slowly cracks his neck in both directions. "Quick question. Why do you all think we're here?"

"Saffron," Geoffrey replies.

"Sure. That was my first thought too. And where is Saffron?" He looks around as if Saffron might fall from the ventilation ducts at any moment. "Way I see it, either what happened in the ball pit was an accident, in which case I'm sure Saffron or Atlas will be here any minute now to let us out. Or…"

"Or what?" Joey whispers.

"Or Saffron's in as much trouble as we are."

I shiver. Then a thought hits me – one that could get us out of here. "Wait, where did you come from? Do you know a way out of here?"

Helix's smile turns into a glare. Blotches of red appear on his pale cheeks.

My heart sinks. "Oh. You were in the ball pit, hiding under the balls the whole time."

"Oh my god, what a freak," Millie says.

"You think I care what you think?" Helix spits. "You should hear what my dad used to call me. Loser, bastard, asshole. I've heard it all."

"That's horrible," I say quietly. "I'm sorry."

"You're sorry?" He laughs viciously. "Ahh, that's so touching."

"Helix, man," Aidan says. "Come on."

The two boys stare each other down, while the rest of us stand around not really sure how to deal with the arrival of Helix. Then Joey raises his hand to ask a question. "I'm super confused right now. Are you all saying we're trapped here? Because I'm on a strict olive-oil–only diet and I didn't bring any with me."

"Wait, did you say oil?" Aidan says in disbelief. "You only eat oil?"

"Yeah, my personal trainer was saying a little bit is, like, good for your heart. So I got thinking, how amazing would *a lot* be?"

"I'm trapped here with a bunch of ignorami," Geoffrey says. He throws the wooden book at the group.

"That's harsh, Jeff," Olympia says. "You're not being very friendly. Maybe a massage chain would help everyone get on better."

"Na na na, shut up." Geoffrey approaches a TV screen and raps his knuckles against the glass. "Lightboy or whatever your name was. Are you there?"

"Lightman," I say.

The AI's face appears, with all its triangular planes that form and dissolve as he moves. "Welcome to the Toy Box," he says. "Shall we play a game?"

"Listen here, there's been an accident," Geoffrey says. "You need to send someone in to help us."

"To leave this zone, you must complete three more games," Lightman repeats. "I have determined that the most suitable game for your group is Buzz Wire."

"We don't want to play your pathetic games," Geoffrey says through gritted teeth.

"The only way to leave this zone is to complete the games," Lightman says.

"Enough of this bullshit," Geoffrey shouts, punching the TV screen. A large bullseye cracks in the centre. "I'm calling the police. Where's my phone?" He slaps at his pockets. "Where's my fucking phone?"

"There's no reception," Olympia says. "No likes for Olympia, remember?"

Lightman vanishes from the broken screen and appears on another to our right. "Welcome to the Toy Box," he repeats. "Shall we play a game?"

10
GEORGIA

Lightman's right. There's no way out. I've personally tried every door in the zone, not trusting the others to do their own jobs properly. I even stuck my head into the ruined ball pit, but the hatch we fell through can't be opened from beneath. Climbing out that way is not an option.

We don't have any choice other than sitting tight and waiting for Atlas, or someone else on the outside, to let us out. But now Helix has planted the seed of doubt in my mind, I'm not sure that's going to happen. Like he said, if it was all a prank gone wrong, then why hasn't someone already come to find us?

What if someone's trapped us here on purpose?

A sudden noise makes me jump, but it's only the

ventilation system clunking. Even still, my bubbling nervousness becomes a rush of real fear. I can't get it under control, and I start to regret leaving the safety of the group to explore on my own. The Toy Box zone suddenly feels menacing in its vastness. Children's toys with grinning faces peek out from shelves, their smiles stretched and greedy. The bookshelves make a maze of shadows from which anyone, or anything, could be watching me.

"Get it together, Georgia," I tell myself. "Everyone's relying on you."

But as I walk, I catch sight of something out of the corner of my eye and I spin around with a gasp. Obviously, there's nothing there. I quicken my pace. Another flicker of movement. A flash. When I turn, I find myself facing one of the room's numerous blank screens. I could have sworn there was something on it a moment ago. Something that vanished the second I looked.

Hearing voices ahead, I break into a jog. I round a corner and nearly bump into Helix and Henry. A rush of relief turns into shame at letting my imagination run away with itself. I smooth down my hair and jacket, and try to personify my usual sensible, reliable self. There's not much point, though, as neither Helix nor Henry has even noticed me standing there.

Their attention is fixed on each other, and the rest of the world doesn't exist. Helix has Henry pressed against the wall, looming over him in his too big leather coat.

"You need to stop," Henry says in a shaky voice. He's holding a piece of paper, but I can't see what's on it.

Helix's smile is wolflike and hungry. "I'm not doing anything."

"I know it's you. Of course it's you!"

"All those years, and you didn't learn a single thing about me, Henry. I have better things to do than threaten people. It's not my style."

"Just stop," Henry whispers.

"You first," Helix replies, and the aggression in his body language makes me worry he's about to hit Henry or worse.

I clear my throat. They quickly step apart and Henry stuffs the paper in his pocket. Helix grins at me and sniffs deeply. "I can smell fear in the air, can you?" He strides away, laughing.

"You all right?" I ask Henry.

He nods, looking shaken. "Yeah, I'm fine."

"What was that all about?"

"I made the mistake of suggesting we put our differences aside while we're in here. He's making it so much worse with all his weird conspiracy theories about someone deliberately trapping us here."

I make a mental note to not share my own feelings of foreboding with Henry. I don't think he can handle it right now. Besides, now I'm no longer alone, I feel silly for getting myself worked up. It's probably Hanxiety. I was too nervous to eat breakfast this morning and now I'm starving.

I pull up a child's pink chair. "What's the deal with you two?"

He shakes his head and I don't think he's going to answer. He picks up a Rubik's Cube from a selection of toys on a table, absently twisting it. "We used to be friends. Best friends, actually."

"*You* used to be a Goth?"

He manages a small smile. "Alas, I have sensitive skin. All that make-up brings me out in a rash." His hands fall still on the cube and his smile drops away. "Helix was always into alternative culture, but a couple of years back, he started getting really dark. Fanboying over serial killers, collecting knives, that sort of thing."

"That fits with his online persona." I sigh. "He's always come across as strange."

"There are rumours about him at my school. You know when there's a high-profile murder and someone interviews people who'd met the killer? And they all say, *I knew there was something wrong with him.* That's kind of how I feel about Helix these days."

"You think he's a *murderer*?" And we're all trapped here with him. Great.

"No!" Henry says. "Gosh, no. I didn't mean it like that. He's just a bit … weird. Aidan says he's harmless, but he still creeps me out."

"Aidan doesn't seem like he'd be a good judge of character."

Henry frowns. "Because he's got a criminal record?

He's OK. We're not close friends or anything outside *Sole Survivor*, but Aidan's sound."

"Yeah, totally. I didn't mean…" I'm getting flustered so I try to think of a way to move the conversation on. "Talking of ex-friends, Millie and I used to be best mates."

"Really? You and Millie?"

"It's hard to believe, I know. She's a popular, perfect little princess whom everyone loves, and I'm…" – I gesture to myself, sensible blazer and all – "… this."

I've overshared, but at least Henry has cheered up. "You're not so bad," he says, his eyes twinkling.

My cheeks warm. Oh no. There's always this point in a blush where I know whether it will fade again or if my body's decided to send ninety per cent of my blood to my face, making me look all skinned hamster. This blush is definitely the latter. I jump to my feet. "I need to use the bathroom."

He blinks. I can't believe I said that. Pressing my hands to my burning cheeks, I scurry towards a short corridor that leads to two bathrooms. Overhead, the ventilation ducts rumble ominously, and the ghosts of my earlier fears start to materialize. There's something wrong here.

I'm so preoccupied with checking my surroundings that I nearly bump into Joey. He's staring at a blank screen and frowning.

"Is that real?" he says softly. "Answer me!"

"Joey?" I say. "What are you doing?"

He jumps, like I've woken him from a trance. "Um, just

waiting for Millie. She went to the toilet." He looks at the monitor, expression uncertain.

"Did you see something on the monitor?" I ask, thinking about the weird flashes I saw earlier. Maybe I didn't imagine them after all.

"No. Of course not." He abruptly strides off, apparently forgetting he was waiting for his girlfriend.

I lock myself in the second bathroom and take a few minutes to regroup. When I look at my face in the mirror, I wish I hadn't. In addition to all the red skin, my hair is both limp and frizzy in equal measure and my mascara has blobbed on to my eyelids. I wipe my eyes and smooth down my hair. It doesn't help much.

I don't suppose how I look matters. It's not like there's anyone to impress. Atlas is AWOL, so my interview prospects are looking bleak. The boy I love is here with his perfect, beautiful girlfriend and it's clear he's besotted. Everyone is already wrapped up in their own friendships and rivalries which I'm not part of. I'm never part of anything I don't organize myself.

I've spent years looking down on Saffron for prioritizing fun over the things that last, like grades and awards. It's only now I'm aware of how lonely it is when your entire existence is defined by being the best. Even here, trapped with a group of other teenagers, I still can't find a way to be one of them.

My self-pity nearly gets to the point of tears, but then the second bathroom unlocks and whoever's inside – Millie,

I'm guessing – leaves. She stops to talk to someone. At first, I think maybe Joey's come back but, when I press my ear against the door, it's Olympia's voice I hear.

"Relax, I won't say anything."

"I told you to leave me alone," Millie snaps. "I don't want anyone knowing we've met."

"It's no big deal; we've played together for years. The others wouldn't think anything of us being friends."

"Except I don't make friends with people like you. So … go away."

"That's mean, Millie," Olympia complains. "You think you're better than me because you wear nice clothes and date a *nice* boy? Your perfect life is a lie, Millie."

"What about yours? When's your big single out again?" Millie says, her voice fading as she walks away.

I think Olympia's gone too, but I still wait a few minutes before I leave the bathroom. I'm being nosy, but I can't help wanting to find out what they were talking about. *Your perfect life is a lie, Millie.* I shouldn't gloat. It's mean and it's bitter. I still feel a rush of glee, though. It serves her right.

I've taken a few steps when there's an awful scream. Millie, I realize.

Millie's screaming.

There are PIGEONS living in PONDS nightclub!!

12K views. 1 year ago

SaffronPlaysGames SUBSCRIBE

SAFFRON: Let's go, let's go, let's go … to the nightclub toilets! Yes, we're interrupting our usual scheduling to bring you some ridiculous news.

(Saffron pushes open the door into a pink-lit bathroom. A couple of girls are standing in front of a long wall of mirrors, applying make-up and fixing their hair.)

GEORGIA: Hey, you can't film in here!
MILLIE: Ignore Georgia, she's in a boring mood.

(Millie does a twirl for the camera, sweeping her long hair aside to show off her new diamond earrings.)

GEORGIA: Are those real? How on earth did you afford them?
MILLIE: Yes, obviously. And it's none of your business. What are you filming, Saffron?

(Saffron beckons for them to follow her to the stall at the end of the row. It's locked, with an out-of-order sign on the door. She uses a two pence piece to turn the lock.)

GEORGIA: You're not allowed in there.

SAFFRON: Oh no, I'm breaking the rules! Someone call the rules police.

(*Just then, a girl with smudged eyeliner and red cheeks stumbles into the bathrooms. She uses the sinks to balance as she approaches Millie.*)

GIRL: I heard you can hook me up. I got a tenner, yeah?
MILLIE: Eww, drunk person. Get away from me.

(*The girl notices she's being filmed and quickly leaves.*)

MILLIE: So weird, right?

(*Saffron pulls open the stall door. Inside, the ceiling light has been removed. In its place, there's a large, dark hole.*)

MILLIE, *leaning into the stall*: You're being so weird.

(*Suddenly, there's a flapping noise and a pigeon erupts out of the hole. In its panic, it collides with Millie, tangling itself in her hair.*)

MILLIE: (*Screaming*)

11
GEORGIA

I run towards the scream. It's coming from behind a bookcase. My friendship with Millie flashes into my mind. Shared secrets and in-jokes, playing with each other's hair in assembly, dreams of being best friends forever. That's the girl I run towards, not the mean girl princess she's become.

With my heart pounding in my chest, I skid around a corner and find Millie. She's fine. Absolutely fine. My worry becomes relief, becomes irritation. "What the hell, Millie?"

The rest of the group all appear from different directions.

"Joey, where have you been?" Millie flings her arms around Joey. He hugs her tightly back, closing his eyes. What I'd give to have him hug me like that.

"Wow, you can scream," Aidan says. "What happened?"

Millie extracts an arm from her embrace and points at an old-fashioned easel blackboard. Written on the blackboard in chalk, in a hurried scrawl, are the words: *Millie your dead.*

"Georgia wrote it," she says, glaring at me with her head pressed against Joey's broad chest. He strokes her hair.

"What? Of course I didn't!"

"So it's a coincidence you've been sending me threatening texts for no reason, and now I find this?"

"What texts?" Olympia says. "Oh my gosh, have you been getting weird messages too?"

"Can I see?" Aidan asks.

Olympia takes out a rhinestone and glitter-encrusted phone. There's a fluffy pom-pom hanging from the case. I look over her shoulder as she scrolls through some of the anonymous messages. They're like the ones Millie showed me earlier.

Attention-seeking whore. I'll give you all the attention you want.

You painted your bedroom pink? Cute.

Stupid females think they can ignore me now?

"I've been getting them for months now. I thought it was someone from school, but if Millie's receiving them too…"

"Then it has to be someone you both know," I say.

"We both know Georgia," Millie says.

"Slow down a bit!" I say. "I'm not sending misogynistic messages to *anyone*, and I didn't write that either." I point

104

at the blackboard. "For starters, they spelled 'your' wrong. If I was going to threaten your life, I would at least make sure I was grammatically correct."

This is the wrong thing to say. With a furious yell, Millie grabs an oversized teddy bear and swings it at me. The impact is surprisingly painful and it knocks me into a shelf. Wooden books domino and fall at my feet. The rest of the group takes a step back, too shocked to intervene.

"You think you're so much better than me, don't you?" *Thwack*, and the bear hits my thigh. "Clever Georgia, Georgia the Know-it-All. Well I got the boy you wanted, didn't I?"

I yank the bear from her hands before she can hit me again. "What did I ever do to you, Millie?"

"La la la la!" Olympia sings, surprising both Millie and me enough that it stops our argument in its tracks. "Come on, let's not fight."

Millie's bottom lip wobbles. "I don't want to fight. I want Georgia to stop threatening me!"

"I know, my lovely," Olympia coos. "This must be so hard for you."

"It is," Millie whispers.

I gape at her, my mouth hanging open. Seriously? She attacked me, and now everyone's feeling sorry for *her*? I can feel the anger rising and rising, my muscles tightening, jaw clenching.

Aidan steps forward. "Georgia, I think the teddy's dead now."

I glance at my hands. They've unconsciously encircled the teddy's neck, throttling it.

"You see?" Millie says in a small voice. "This is what she's really like."

Helix cracks up with laughter and claps. "Loving the show. Great work."

Everyone else, though? They're all staring at me like I'm some kind of monster. Even Aidan has this sly, appraising look on his face. He's unsure if I can be trusted. Joey looks hurt and confused; Olympia is shocked and disappointed; Geoffrey's disgusted and Henry's terrified. No one's on my side.

"Unbelievable." I let the teddy drop to the ground and I walk away. There's no point trying to compete with Millie. She's so bright and shiny, she can dazzle anyone into thinking they're lucky to be in her presence. I used to be the same, craving her approval so much that I'd do anything to keep her happy. Where did it ever get me?

I lean against a bookcase and tilt my head back so I won't start crying. A screen on the wall lights up and Lightman's contoured face appears. "How are you enjoying your escape room experience so far?" he asks.

"To be completely honest, today is not meeting my expectations." I sigh. "I thought I could handle it, but I underestimated Millie's vindictive streak."

Lightman's face shifts. He doesn't have a clue what I'm talking about, but it's good to let it out to someone who won't judge me.

"We used to be so close. Sometimes it feels like she's jealous of me, which is ridiculous."

Lightman tilts his face and glass-like shards of blue float across the screen. "Is it ridiculous?" he says.

My blood runs cold. He's supposed to be a computer program, parroting a script. That didn't sound like a script. "What did you say?"

"Millie *is* jealous of you, Georgia. She's only dating Joey to make you unhappy."

"How do you...? I thought you were a computer program."

"I'll show you," Lightman says. His face vanishes and is replaced by a video clip of Millie. She's lying on Saffron's bed – I recognize the print on the duvet. The betrayal stings, even though there's no rule that says my sister can't invite my ex-best friend around.

"Quit recording me all the time." Millie laughs.

"You say the funniest things," Saffron's out-of-shot voice says. "It's hilarious."

"Well, you'll have to entertain yourself now, I'm afraid. I'm already late for my date with Joey." She sits up and fluffs her hair, looking unexcited about seeing her boyfriend.

"Why are you still with him? You two are so not right for each other."

Her hands fall away from her hair. "What's that supposed to mean? We're perfect for each other."

"Weird you only started dating him after you found out

about Georgia's little crush. A more cynical person would think you're doing it to piss her off."

Millie looks murderous for a second, then she relaxes into a laugh. "You got me. But he buys me gifts and takes me out to nice restaurants, so it's not all about Georgia. I'm not obsessed with her or anything."

Saffron laughs. "This is why I record you, Millie. You're ridiculous."

"Turn it off!" Millie throws a pillow at the camera and the clip ends.

Lightman's face reforms from its blue shards. "See?" he says. "She knew you liked him, so she asked him out on purpose."

"What's going on?" I say quietly. "Where did you get that clip?"

"From Saffron's phone," Lightman says, matter-of-factly. "The question is, will you let Millie get away with treating you this way?"

"Who are you really?" He can't just be an AI, surely. "Saffron, are you doing this?"

Lightman flickers and the screen goes blank. I back away slowly. This isn't right. I take another step, but something solid yet also squashy presses into me from behind. I scream and struggle, tripping over my own feet and landing in a pile of beanbags.

"What *are* you doing?" Geoffrey says. It's noteworthy that no one comes running to find out why I screamed.

He tugs a beanbag out from under my legs, and slumps

down into it. He smells sweaty, and I shouldn't judge because my own armpits feel swampy, but he's potent. I shuffle my bum on to a beanbag and try to avoid breathing.

"I wanted to speak to you," he says. "You seem marginally more coherent than the rest of these fools."

"High praise," I say. "Thanks for the compliment."

He smirks, like he thinks he's being cleverly manipulative and not predictably obnoxious. "In situations like this, it's handy to form alliances. You scratch my back etcetera, etcetera."

I cringe at the thought of scratching any part of him. There's something predatory about the way he's looking at me and it reminds me of the awful messages both Millie and Olympia have been receiving. Given that the two girls are at different schools and have no friends in common that I know of, it's entirely possible the messages are coming from someone in the *Sole Survivor* group.

"What do you mean?" I say.

"If there are decisions to be made, perhaps we can work together to encourage the group *in the right direction*. I'm not sure I trust any of the others, especially not Olympia. I could tell you some stories about her."

I almost don't bite, but the way she sided with Millie still stings and my nosiness gets the better of me. "What sort of stories?"

Geoffrey shuffles his beanbag closer to mine, bringing with him the unmistakable waft of someone who doesn't

109

believe in deodorant. "Her big deal that she's always talking about? I heard that it's not going ahead."

"Oh," I say. That doesn't sound like something to gossip about. Olympia must be devastated.

Geoffrey leans even closer. I can feel his warm breath on my lips. "Rumour goes her partying is the problem. Apparently she's impossible to work with and flakes out on important meetings all the time."

This is the moment when Aidan rounds the corner and spots us. His surprise makes way for a delighted grin. "Interrupting?" he says.

"Actually, yes," Geoffrey replies at the same time as I say: "No."

I struggle to get up out of the beanbag and put as much distance between me and Geoffrey as possible. "What's up?" I say to Aidan.

He gestures over his shoulder with his thumb. "The rest of the group is talking about giving the Buzz Wire game a try and—"

"No. Absolutely not," Geoffrey interrupts. He stands up and pushes past me. "This is what I was talking about, Georgia. Come on!"

Aidan raises both eyebrows at me, waiting for me to explain my cosy little chat with Geoffrey. I'm too flustered to come up with an excuse, though, so I follow Geoffrey back to the rest of the group. We find them standing in front of a screen. Lightman's face is lit up in shades of bright blue.

"And now everyone is here," Lightman says. "Shall we play a game?"

"Hang on a minute, that's not happening," Geoffrey spits.

"The only way out is to complete the rooms. To see the game through to its final conclusion."

The final conclusion? I think. *Creepy.*

Lightman continues. "I will unlock the Buzz Wire door in preparation for your arrival."

"No," Geoffrey says. "Do you all hear me? No!"

The rest of the group looks unsure. They watch me as if I have the deciding vote. I suppose I've set myself up as the leader and now it's a decision that matters, I'm wishing I hadn't been quite so pushy.

"Georgia agrees with me," Geoffrey says.

"Does she?" Aidan says, eyebrow quirking.

I open and close my mouth. I want to tell them how Lightman gives me the creeps, but how do I explain that clip of Millie without it starting another fight? And do I want to voice my concerns out loud when Lightman's watching me through one of the many cameras dotted around this place? I don't even know if my suspicions are warranted, or a symptom of the fact that I haven't eaten today.

"It's a way out of here," Henry says, tugging at his T-shirt's collar.

"Maybe Atlas is on his way to help us, but maybe he isn't," Millie says. "I'd rather not put all our hopes into someone who thinks velvet is a good look."

I nod slowly. They're right, but I still don't trust this place.

"We had an agreement," Geoffrey says. "I thought you were smarter than this."

That settles it for me. I'm not letting someone like him order me about and insult my intelligence. "Let's play the game," I say.

Aidan slaps me on the back. "Good choice," he says, grinning wickedly. "What's the worst that could happen?"

"Do you honestly want me to answer that?" I say.

12

GEORGIA

The Buzz Wire door is marked with a lightning bolt. It stands slightly ajar, bleeding out blue light. I give it a little shove then step back, unsure what I might find. Inside, the room is decorated to look like it's underwater. Projected waves ripple across the walls, chased by tropical fish and electric eels that move accompanied by bursts of the *Jaws* soundtrack.

There's a narrow viewing gallery around the edge of the room themed like the deck of a wrecked ship. It overlooks a sand-covered sunken floor dotted with fibreglass rocks. A thick metal rail snakes across the room, twisting and turning, looping and bending. In some places, it nearly reaches the ceiling. In others, it skims the floor. It starts near the steps and ends in the middle of the room, where a small, gated cave contains both a large puzzle piece and an angry-looking toy eel.

"What's with all the snakes?" Joey says. He seems to have recovered from whatever it was that upset him earlier. His arm is slung possessively around Millie's shoulders and, while it doesn't look comfortable for her, I still wish it was me.

"They're electric eels," I say.

"They're real animals?" Joey laughs. "Bruh, nature is so weird."

I see an opportunity to impress him. "An adult electric eel can deliver a shock that's strong enough to kill a person." Actually, on second thoughts, I shouldn't have said anything.

"Reassuring," Henry says.

"Fascinating," Aidan says.

"It wouldn't kill you, though. Unless you had a weak heart or something." God, what is wrong with me? I can't make myself stop talking.

"They're so ugly," Millie says, shuddering.

"I think they're cuties." Olympia laughs. "Look at their ickle faces."

"This has to be a joke," says Geoffrey, peering in through the door but refusing to step inside. "What is the point of any of this?"

"What's the point of anything?" Helix replies. When he blinks, white face paint on his eyelids makes it look like his eyes have rolled back in their sockets.

114

"It's that Beat the Buzzer game," I say, eyeing the long metal track. "The one where you have to move a metal loop on a stick all the way from one end to the other without it touching the wire? Otherwise it buzzes and you're out?" I eye the huge course. At points we'll need to stand on the rocks to reach the wire.

"Please, enter," Lightman says, appearing on the screen inside the room.

Helix immediately separates himself from the rest of the group and perches, crow-like, on a handrail. Aidan, Joey, Millie, Olympia and I shuffle into the viewing gallery, nervously eyeing the buzz wire from above. Henry holds the door for Geoffrey, who refuses to come inside.

"The whole team must stay together," Lightman says.

"After what happened in the ball pit? Please," Geoffrey scoffs.

He has a point, but sitting around and waiting isn't doing us any favours. It's a game, I tell myself. A game that will get us one step closer to exiting this place and give us something to do that doesn't involve bickering with each other.

"I'm sure the ball pit was an accident," I say.

"Don't care," Geoffrey says.

"It could be good inspiration?" I offer. "For your novel."

He thinks about this, tapping a finger on his lips. "For your information, my novel is a serious treatise on the human condition. It does not contain eels." But he comes inside the room anyway.

Henry lets the door close and a lock engages.

"Too late to back out now," Helix says, grinning evilly. He hums the funeral march.

"Welcome to Buzz Wire," Lightman says. The room starts to play some atmospheric music: bubbling water and whale song. "You have found yourself trapped in an underground fortress guarded by Hercule the electric eel. He will only release you if you can complete his fiendish game. Fail to complete the game within five minutes or touch the track three times with the metal hoop, and you will be locked in here forever."

"Forever?" Olympia says, gasping.

"Alternatively, you can perform a forfeit and you'll be able to leave the room without the puzzle piece."

"Who plays?" I ask.

"Maths pop quiz to decide?" Henry says hopefully. "Or can we volunteer someone who isn't allergic to physical activity?"

Joey thrusts a hand into the air. "I volunteer."

"There is no need for volunteers," Lightman says. "I will determine the people best suited for the challenge."

"How does that work?" Millie asks.

"I have extensively researched and analysed all of your likes, dislikes, strengths and weaknesses. All of you leave footprints behind on social media."

"I'm not on social media," I say.

"This is correct. You deleted your accounts three months ago, after a video in which you were tagged began to circulate online."

"Let's not talk about that," I say, reddening at the snickers from certain members of the group.

"An image search can tell me all the places you've been too," Lightman continues. "For example, photos posted on your school website tell me *you* recently won your age group at the SESCA Chess Tournament."

"Big brain," Joey says, nodding with respect.

I can't even muster up a spark of pride at Joey's compliment. There's something about Lightman that isn't right. Surely he's not just a computer program; there has to be someone behind him, feeding him his lines. Saffron's always been the most likely culprit but the longer this goes on, the more I think this isn't her style.

"Analysing the data reveals that the participants best suited to this game are..." Lightman draws out the decision. "Olympia, Geoffrey and Aidan."

"No," Geoffrey says.

"Refusal isn't an option," Lightman says. "That's not how the game works."

"No," he repeats.

"Aidan and I can manage without you," Olympia says sweetly.

"Um, no offence," Millie interrupts, "but I don't understand why *she's* been chosen. I can't imagine she'll be good at this game."

Olympia looks genuinely hurt. "I've been taking movement classes for ten years. I can do this."

"Movement classes?" Geoffrey says. "Now I've heard it all."

Olympia's lips press into a tight straight line. A sick little voice in my head wonders how long she can maintain her bubbly 'everyone's my friend' persona before she snaps.

"I don't think the participants are chosen on skill," Henry says. "I think it's more about making the games interesting. But you'll obviously be great, Olympia. I didn't mean... I should stop speaking."

Olympia fakes a big smile. "No offence taken. Shall we do this thing, then?"

Olympia and Aidan descend the steps on to the sand, and she weaves her way between all the fake rocks to pick up the metal handle. A long lead connects it to a fake battery on the wall that's bigger than me, and a hoop connects it to the track.

"Your time starts now," Lightman says.

The timer counts down. Olympia sets off slowly, holding the hoop away from the metal track. The first bend is easy enough and she navigates it with no trouble, humming to herself. But then the wire starts to rise.

Aidan hurries forwards and places a rock in front of her. She shakily steps up on to it. But it wobbles, not as stable as she was expecting. Her shoe slips and the metal ring touches the wire. A loud buzzer goes off and one of three red lights on the wall switches on. One life gone.

"Brilliant," says Geoffrey sarcastically.

"You really are incredibly rude, has anyone told you that?" Olympia says, sounding almost annoyed, but not quite.

"Better than being a big fake," he snarls.

Now she's angry. She shoves the handle at Aidan, and he barely manages to keep it steady so we don't lose another life. "You're one to talk about being fake, *Jeff*."

"It's Geoffrey," he spits.

"Since when? Growing a moustache over the summer holidays and being rude to people doesn't make you an artist. You don't even take art at school."

Geoffrey's face turns beetroot. Every muscle tightens.

Aidan pauses with the handle at the start of a steeply rising loop. "As much as I love all the drama, is this the time? Really?"

Geoffrey ignores him. "How are you feeling, Olympia? A bit shaky, perhaps?"

I don't know what he's referring to, but his words hit their intended target. Olympia goes still and all the colour drains from her face.

"Leave her alone," Millie says. Since when did Millie stand up for other girls?

"Ahh don't make them stop," Helix says. "This is great."

"Aidan's right, I should be helping him," Olympia says quietly, looking like she might cry. She places a rock in front of Aidan and holds his hand so he can climb on to it. The whole time, she refuses to meet his eye.

The track gets higher and Aidan has to hold the handle up above his head. I keep thinking it touches the wire but the buzzer doesn't go off. Olympia stacks two pebbles on top of each other. I can already see it's unsteady. Before I can warn them, Aidan makes the step up. He's so occupied with altering the angle of the hoop to stop it touching the wire that he misjudges the height of the pebbles.

He wobbles. Falls. Somehow, Olympia manages to grab the handle and holds it directly above her head with her arms straight. The alarm doesn't go off. Aidan lands in a roll, kicking up sand from the floor. His phone falls out of his pocket but he's too busy to notice.

"I can't hold it," Olympia says, straining with the effort. "You need to take it from me."

"Are we allowed to help?" I ask.

"The group can vote in an alternate once half the time has elapsed," Lightman says.

"I think they're OK," Henry says.

Aidan clambers on to the pebbles and navigates the handle over the highest part of the course. Then he passes it down to Olympia as the track descends. Working together, they pass the handle between the two of them. By the time Lightman calls two minutes, they're more than halfway.

"Let's pick up the pace, people," Joey says, clapping his hands like he's on the football pitch, spurring on his team. "You've got this."

They speed up and I'm starting to believe they might make it. And then it all goes wrong. Olympia accidentally kicks the phone Aidan dropped and it flips over, revealing a Rembrandt nude on the case.

"Is that my mobile?" Geoffrey says, descending the steps to pick it up. "Did you steal it?"

Aidan winces, pausing with the metal ring poised

halfway over a sweeping loop. "I kind of found it?" He bites his lip and it looks like he's fighting with himself to stay quiet. A smile spreads to his eyes. "I found something interesting on it too."

Geoffrey stares. Aidan chuckles softly, then starts to hum a tune. It opens a dam inside of Geoffrey and a tide of red rises up his neck, to his face. With a furious cry, he hurls himself at Aidan and rugby tackles him to the ground. The buzzer erupts into an ear-splitting noise that goes on and on.

"It wasn't what I expected." Aidan laughs. "I mean, we all have our secrets, but yours is something else."

"I'm going to rip you in half!" Geoffrey bellows, swinging a punch. Aidan throws a handful of sand into his eyes, making him roar in pain.

"FIGHT!" Joey cries, vaulting over the barrier and sliding across the floor. As Geoffrey tries to stand up, Joey takes his legs out. I'm not sure if Joey was intending to break up the fight or make it worse, but within seconds he's joined the melee.

"Stop it!" Millie squeals. "Henry, you need to make them stop."

Henry holds up both hands. "Me? Are you serious?"

"Fine, I'll do it then." She marches down on to the sand and starts yelling at the fighting boys, who all ignore her completely.

It's too loud for me to think straight. There's too much yelling, and the buzzer is too much. I press my hands to my ears but it's still deafening.

"A player must be holding the handle at all times or the game will not count towards your tally," Lightman says.

"Oh my god, the handle," I say. "Someone needs to pick up the handle."

"I can't reach it," Olympia shouts. She's pressed into a corner, blocked in by the scrapping boys.

"Fight, fight, fight," Helix chants, cheering from his position of safety.

I've never been good with loud noises. They kind of shut my brain down. So I'm surprised at myself when I realize I've descended the steps and grabbed the handle, lifting the hoop away from touching the track. The buzzing stops, but Geoffrey, Joey and Aidan continue to throw punches.

"The addition of a new player is acceptable," Lightman says. "The game will continue."

"I need some help," I call over to Henry. "We're running out of time."

"Is the game the important thing when they're trying to kill each other?" Henry says.

"I don't know. I don't know!" I think about how Lightman said we'd be locked in if we didn't win the task. I need to get out of this room, away from all the shouting and the anger. I focus on the one thing I can control, and I shakily move forward. The rest of the wire is fairly simple. A few turns and loops, and a section that skims the floor. I can do it, even if sporty pursuits are definitely not my forte.

I try to block out the fight behind me.

"How did you get in?" gasps Geoffrey. "How did you guess the passcode?"

"Lightman told me," Aidan says. "For some reason. Don't worry, I won't tell anyone what I saw. Many people, anyway."

I'm intrigued by what Aidan found on Geoffrey's phone, but I need to focus on the game. The timer has twelve seconds left. I'm so, so close. Shakily lowering the hoop towards the ground, I manoeuvre it around the final dip in the wire and up towards the end of the track.

Then Aidan starts to sing. "Your sparkle, your shine. Tell me you're mine."

This enrages Geoffrey to the point he goes nuclear. "I'm going to kill you!" he screams.

Everything happens so fast. Geoffrey lunges and, not wanting to get punched, Aidan ducks behind me. Suddenly I'm right at the centre of the fight, still holding the handle and compelled by panicked determination to win the game. Geoffrey kicks out at Aidan but he connects with my knee, making me scream in pain and hop on one leg.

"Hey, get off her!" Henry stumbles down the stairs and tries to come to my rescue, but immediately walks into a jab from Geoffrey's elbow. He stumbles back clutching his ear and whimpering in pain.

"Get out the way, bitch." Geoffrey yanks the handle from my hands and tries to shove me aside. The third and final buzzer sounds, but all I can hear is that awful word he called me. It feels like I'm no longer inside my own body, but I'm instead watching it as it scrabbles and pushes, anger and insults flying.

It's one of our disastrous games of *Sole Survivor*, where everything dissolves into chaos and blood, and it becomes less about winning and more about making sure no one else comes out on top. A little voice in my head laughs at me. *This is what Saffron would do*, it says. *Choose chaos*.

It's true. We didn't need Saffron for things to fall apart. We've managed to screw ourselves over all on our own.

Then there's a shove and a shout. A loud bang and a blinding flash. We're all plunged into darkness and, finally, welcome silence.

13
SAFFRON

"Saffron," Lightman says gently. "Are you awake?"

I glance up at his voice. It sounds like he's here with me, but I'm alone in this long, empty corridor. My forehead is damp where I've been resting it against my knees. My bum is sore from sitting on the hard floor.

"I have determined who would die first," he says.

I wipe my eyes on the back of my hand. "What?"

"Why don't you return to the control room, and I will update you on the simulation's progress? I think you'll find it fascinating."

"No thanks." I curl up into a ball and try to pretend none of this is happening.

A real-life game of *Sole Survivor*. What a joke. If this

was *Sole Survivor*, I'd be taking the fight to the bad guys. All guns blazing, throw myself into the action, do or die. I thought this was who I am, but it turns out I'm a coward. I'm only brave when there are no real consequences.

I can't sit here forever, though, hoping someone else will fix the mess I've made. I have to do something, even if it scares me. *Get up*, I tell myself. "Get. Up."

I take several slow breaths, then stagger to my feet. My legs have gone wobbly from sitting down for so long. I use the wall to support me as I make my way to the control room. The door opens when I try it. Before I go inside, I search for something I can use to prop it open with in case Lightman tries to lock me inside. There's an access panel cover lying on the floor, so I prop it up against the door frame.

"Hello, Saffron," Lightman says. "I knew you would join me eventually. Would you care to sit down?"

I eye the chair and remain standing. "You need to stop," I say.

"And I will. As soon as I have collated the data."

I glance over at the CCTV feeds. Everything is dark. The only feed where there's movement is the Buzz Wire game room. There are several people in there, but it's hard to work out what's happening because it's in night vision mode, making their faces too bright and almost featureless.

"What happened?" I say, my voice coming out hoarse.

"There was a fight," Lightman says. "They all turned on each other. It happened far more easily than I'd expected."

I round the desk and get closer to the feed. Some of the people in Buzz Wire are using phones as torches and the bright lights keep cutting across the camera, briefly bleaching the image white. A couple of them are trying to get the door open, two more are embracing, and the rest are huddled around something on the floor.

I can't make the something out until the group shifts and I realize with horror that it's a person. They're lying on their back with their arms spread out to the sides, unmoving.

"Are they … dead?" I ask.

"He was electrocuted," Lightman says. "I think you would have found it amusing if you'd been here."

"Amusing?" I half-cry, half-sob.

"You find it amusing in *Sole Survivor*, although I have to say his skeleton did not light up as it does in the game. Perhaps it is that part which makes you laugh."

"*Sole Survivor* is a game! That's a real person. With a family and friends." I clasp a hand over my mouth. I'm going to puke.

"None of you liked him, actually," Lightman says.

"What?" My heart trips over itself. I look at the person on the floor more closely, but he's hard to make out. He's wearing tight jeans and appears to have a moustache. That's all I can see.

"His name was Geoffrey," Lightman says. "He was the artist."

I frown, trying to understand. The name is familiar

for some reason. Then it hits me. "Oh my god," I choke. "That's THIS-GAME-IS-BASIC? From my crew?"

"Affirmative."

"What? But that means…" I look between the others in the shot. My head spins and my vision narrows. There's a small dark-haired girl hugging a big guy with muscles. Millie and Joey! And one of the people trying to open the door is my friend Aidan, who I met in the police station. Then there are three people I don't recognize – a tall blonde girl, a long-haired Goth and some guy. I'm guessing they're STAR-BABE04, ULTIMATE-HELIX and SIR-HENRY-OF-BLOBLAND.

But it's the one hunched over Geoffrey that makes my heart clench into a scrunched-up ball. My own features under a not so neat, blow-dried bob. "That's my sister," I whisper. "You've trapped my sister in there."

"Is this exciting, Saffron?" Lightman asks. "I invited your crew to join us today. For our little simulation."

"I don't care about the simulation. You killed someone! You need to stop."

"Strictly speaking, I didn't kill anyone," he says. "I electrified the wire, but one of the others pushed the artist, causing him to fall. I wonder who it was. Perhaps I can rewind the video and—"

"No!" I scream. "I don't want to see it."

"As you wish," Lightman says, sounding completely indifferent. "It's time for the next game. You'll enjoy this one. Would you like to join them?"

I silently shake my head, tears making my face wet. A braver person would say yes, and they'd go downstairs to be with their friends. But who would I be helping if I put myself in danger too? I tell myself I'm being sensible and pragmatic by staying up here. I'd be no use to any of them. They're better off without me.

Georgia's the sort of person they need, with her logical head and stubborn determination. She's never been someone to give up. Even now, in the game room, she's still trying to resuscitate Geoffrey while the others stand there, phone torches trained on Geoffrey's body, doing nothing.

"I will need to update my internal definition of a rebel," Lightman says. "I had predicted you would react differently."

He's right: in a game of *Sole Survivor*, I'd never freeze. I'd never give up and cry.

But this isn't a game. This is real.

14

GEORGIA

When the lights come on, we all shield our eyes against the brightness as if we've been locked up in the darkness forever. Everyone is bruised or bleeding. Most of us are crying. We take in each other's injuries in furtive, shame-filled glances. No one looks at Geoffrey, but everyone knows he's there. Dead, with his mobile phone fused to his hand and his hair standing on end.

"Glitter Mix," Aidan says quietly.

I look up at him sharply. "What?"

"The pop group? That's what I found on his phone," he says, his voice cracking. "I thought it was funny he has all their albums. Because he's so anti the mainstream."

I'm lost for words. *This* was what the fight was about? Geoffrey's taste in music?

"Why was he so angry?" Joey says. He looks as dazed as I feel, with bloodshot eyes and a split lip. Our initial panic and fear has dulled into the strange wooziness of a horrible dream. "Glitter Mix have some good songs."

"If you're six years old," Millie says, but her heart isn't in it. She straightens her pearl hairband with shaking hands.

"Why did you steal his phone?" Olympia asks.

"I told you, I found it," Aidan says.

There's a long moment where all I can hear is everyone's too fast breathing and sniffles. The sand crunches loudly every time someone moves, all sounds amplified. My heartbeat whooshes in my ears.

"One of us pushed him," says Henry at last. "One of us killed him."

"You serious?" Aidan says. "It was an accident."

"Like you finding his phone?" Olympia replies coldly.

I turn to her. "He said something to you, right before he died."

"What?"

I try to remember his wording. "He asked how you were feeling, and you got upset. Why did he say that?"

Olympia opens her mouth to talk but Millie interrupts and steps between us. "Leave it, Georgia."

"I'm trying to understand what happened," I say.

"I said leave it! A boy's dead and you're fishing for a story."

My cheeks burn. I wasn't even planning to write about this. Was I?

No, I decide. Because if I was to turn this into an article, I'd have to admit my own role in Geoffrey's death. The truth is, I think maybe I pushed him. My memories of the event feel disjointed, and I can't be sure exactly what happened and in what order. I wish I could get everything straight in my mind and then, maybe, it would all make sense.

I force myself to look at Geoffrey. His eyes are open and his face is fixed in the same expression of anger he wore the second before the lights went out. I look away again.

I revise my earlier thought. I'm not sure death ever does make sense.

"How do we get the door open?" Henry eventually says.

"I'm on it." Joey tries the door again, heaving at the handle. His muscles strain. He aims a kick that does nothing but make him yelp in pain. "I'm not on it," he says, rolling on the ground, clutching his foot.

"You won't get the doors open," Helix says. He's no longer laughing, but he doesn't look particularly bothered that Geoffrey's lying dead on the floor either. "They're the original ones from the old bunker, designed to withstand a literal war."

"You're not helping," Millie says.

He gives us a little shrug. "One of you will have to do the forfeit if you want to get out."

"Maybe you should do it," Henry says, surprising me with the venom in his voice.

"Nah, I'd rather laugh at all of you, falling to pieces."

The whole group starts arguing again, everyone talking

over each other. I ignore them and approach the blank screen where Lightman's face used to be. "Lightman?" I say. "Are you there?"

He's silent for a moment and I don't think he's listening, but then the hundred planes of his face materialize. "I can only apologize for the brief blackout. The short circuit blew several fuses, but I have rerouted the power."

"The ... short circuit?" Olympia says in disbelief. "Geoffrey is dead."

"I can see that."

His quiet voice is so incongruous with the awful things he says or doesn't say. I don't know what scares me more: the possibility that he's a flesh-and-blood person, hiding behind the mask of an AI, or the possibility that he's not.

"You failed to retrieve the puzzle piece," he says. "Have you decided who will perform the forfeit?" Lightman continues.

"Someone's dead!" Henry shouts, not angry but scared.

"The door will only open if you perform the forfeit."

"This is messed up," Aidan says.

Lightman waits in silence. I feel sick. We don't have any choice, I realize. We need to play his game. "What's the forfeit?" I ask.

"Compose a haiku," Lightman says, "about eels."

"What?" I say. Is he taunting me? Haikus are my thing. He knows that, in the same way he knows about Millie only dating Joey to make me angry. In the same way he knew the passcode to Geoffrey's phone.

"Don't you appreciate haikus any more, Georgia?" he says. "I thought you would find it fun."

"Fun?" I whisper.

"Can you just do it, Georgia?" Millie begs. "Please?"

Millie doesn't ask for favours, she demands. So it's jarring to hear her say please. Everyone is looking to me, waiting to see what I'll do. It's my choice: jump through the hoop or stay here. I wipe my eyes. Salty tears have made the skin around them sting. "Lying on the floor, an electrocuted boy, fuck off with your eels." I step towards the monitor and fix Lightman's camera with a cold stare. "Happy?"

Lightman's face on the screen doesn't react. But the lock buzzes and disengages. Henry pulls the door open and holds it for us. We traipse out of the room, scuffing our feet through the sand. Helix whistles cheerily.

Henry has been so quiet and meek up until now, it's a surprise when he shoves Helix in the back as he passes. "You think this is funny?"

Helix stumbles and nearly falls. He turns to Henry with delighted shock on his face. "Growing some balls, Henry?"

"Don't give him the satisfuction," Joey says, pulling Henry away. "He's not worth it."

Helix laughs, then stalks off looking pleased with himself. Henry slumps into a beanbag with his head in his hands. "I'm losing it," he mumbles through his fingers.

"It's not just you," I say.

"I said we should have waited for someone to rescue us," Millie says. "But everyone else wanted to play that game."

I bite back an argument. Geoffrey was the only one who didn't agree to play.

"I'm not sure anyone is going to rescue us," Aidan says.

"Try to stay positive, hey?" Joey says.

"He's right. If there's someone watching us from outside, they're aware Geoffrey is dead." I take a raspy breath before continuing. I feel like I've run a race and I can't get enough air into my lungs. "If no one comes for us in the next ten minutes, we can conclude either there's no one out there. Or there is, and they don't want to get us out."

The group falls silent as we all take this in.

"So you're saying we have to play the games?" Henry asks.

"Geoffrey died playing that game!" Millie cries. "Do you have any idea how horrible it was, witnessing something so awful?"

"We were there too," Olympia sobs. "And you didn't know him. I did."

"It's not a competition," Aidan says.

If it was, Helix would be winning. The rest of us are a mess of tears and injuries from the fight. Henry's ear is bleeding; Joey's lip is puffy and crusted black; Aidan has a scratched cheek. Olympia's puffy and breathless from crying and Millie's brand-new clothes are smeared with someone's blood.

"What are we going to do, then?" Henry asks. "We have to do something."

I feel so weary. All I want to do is lie down and sleep. But the group is relying on me to get them out of here. "We're going to find an exit," I say. "We're saving ourselves."

135

15
GEORGIA

"Here," I say, tapping on my phone's screen. "There should be a lift right here."

Aidan leans his chin on my shoulder so he can see what I'm looking at. A jolt runs through me. I don't know if it's discomfort at how close he is, or something else.

"Why do you have blueprints of the bunker on your phone?" he says.

"I did my research before I came here," I say, trying to act like boys leaning on me is a normal occurrence. "I wasn't about to turn up somewhere I knew nothing about."

"But that's the fun part," he says darkly.

Joey turns on the spot. "There's no lift here. Coach always says I have the eyes of a beagle."

I flick to the photo I took of the Play a Game map in the lobby. The escape room experience doesn't occupy the entire bunker. I'd say less than a quarter of the floor space is in use; the rest is presumably blocked off from public view and remains as it was fifty years ago.

"Do you remember the leak?" I say. "Atlas told us that part of this floor is blocked off."

"The Swamp, you mean?" Aidan says.

"Exactly. If I'm right, and I usually am, the Swamp will lead us to the lift."

"Maybe it's just me, but *the Swamp* sounds positively delightful," Millie says. "It's a shame we've tried all the doors and there's no way to reach it."

"I don't think we're looking for a door," I say, getting up and brushing down my blazer. "Have you noticed how flimsy the sets are in here?"

"Um, no?" Henry says.

"Totally!" Joey says, knocking his fist on a dividing wall. "This plasterboard is less than 12.5 mm thick, and the stud wall hasn't been properly secured to the joists." He flicks his mullet and grins at our surprised faces. "Football won't last me forever. Gotta learn a trade. Come on, then."

We circle the zone while I try to get my bearings. I line up the doors on the original blueprint with the layout of Play a Game. If the ball pit is over there, that means the corridor leading to the lift should be right about…

"Aha!" I say smugly. "As I suspected."

We're standing in an area set up as a reading nook.

137

There are tall bookshelves on three sides and beanbags in the centre. I dramatically sweep fake books off the middle bookcase and have to jump away to stop them from pulverizing my toes. Then I hammer my knuckles against the wooden back of the bookcase.

"Hollow," I say.

"The bookcase is built over the corridor?" Henry says. "How did you work that out?"

"My spatial visual intelligence is one of my strong points," I say. "It's why I'm so good at chess."

"I'm terrible at chess," Henry says sadly. "Which sucks when your whole existence is based around being smart."

"Urgh, can you two stop flirting already?" Millie grumbles. She pushes past me and tries to pry the bookcase aside, but it's not going to be that easy. There are brackets fixing it to the two bookcases on either side.

"I have a multi-tool screwdriver set. I never leave home without it," I say.

Before I can get it out, though, Aidan leans over to whisper to Joey. "I bet you could kick a hole through that," he says.

"Damn right." Joey pushes up his sleeves and stretches out his shoulders. "Step aside," he says in a deeper than usual voice.

Olympia tries to stop him. "Whoa, wait—"

Joey clearly isn't in the mood to wait for anything. He directs a kick at one of the shelves and it cracks in half, splinters flying. He kicks and kicks, roaring from the effort.

138

The rest of us shield our faces from flying debris. It takes a while, but eventually the bookcase gives and Joey's foot bursts through. He kicks out enough of the wood to make a hole big enough for us to climb through.

"And that's how you do it!" he cries, his chest heaving and sweat running down his face.

"You really do have magic feet," Aidan says, nearly crying with laughter.

"Just the one. I mean, I obviously have two feet, but this one's the magic one." He blows his foot a kiss. "Love you, babe."

"You're such a cliche," Millie says.

"Nah, I'm actually totally straight but each to their own." He flicks his sweat dampened mullet off his face.

"Um, cliche doesn't mean ... never mind," Aidan says. "Are we going through, then?"

You know when you decide to take an underpass, only it's really creepy and you spend the whole time recalling the police statistics for murders in your town? Maybe that's me, but this corridor is worse than any underpass I've ever been in. Once, it was painted the same cream colour as the rest of the bunker. Damp has not only made the paint peel but has turned the plaster beneath into porridge.

There are boil-like bubbles protruding from the walls, alongside deep pits. Water dripping from the ceiling has formed squishy stalactites of mould. The lights flicker worryingly, probably because the electrics are waterlogged. An access panel has been removed and through the hole there's a narrow crawl space full of wet pipes and bundles of rotting towels.

"Ugh, I'm going to be sick," Millie says, retching like a cat with a fur ball. "It smells so bad."

Aidan takes a deep, noisy breath. "Ahhh, this reminds me of the time I found a decomposing rabbit outside my block of flats."

"Stop it, you monster," Millie says, turning a worrying shade of green.

"It had been half eaten by a fox and was full of maggots."

"Oh god, stop," Millie squeals, retching again. "I had a really bad experience with a Cornish pasty that was left out in the heat, so this conversation is very triggering."

"Quit winding her up," I say, hiding my amused smile.

Aidan grins at me. "Sorry, boss."

A booming noise, like someone banging a drum, makes us all stop in our tracks. "What was that?" Olympia whispers.

I don't have an answer. Whatever it was, it's gone quiet again.

"This way," I say.

"The Swamp" is an apt name. It's barely passable, and the smell is unlike anything I've experienced before. We all pull up our clothes to cover our mouths and noses, but it doesn't do much to block out the stench. Flickering bulbs give way to darkness. We light the way with our phone torches, which gives the place an abandoned asylum aesthetic that I truly hate. The floor is so wet it squelches.

Boom!

The noise again, making the mirrored water ripple. There's something coming for us. Something big.

"I'm not sure about this any more," Olympia whispers. "What's making that noise?"

"The ghosts of all the people who died down here," Aidan says.

"The bunker was never used," I say.

"Spoilsport," he mutters.

We splash onwards, passing side rooms that are glimpses into the past. A dormitory with filth-streaked walls, full of bunkbeds constructed from scaffolding poles; tattered fragments of bedding scattered like confetti. A tiled bathroom that reminds me of a horror film I once watched. A small room randomly full of broken chairs, all tangled together like they've been thrown violently against the wall.

Boom boom boom!

It's getting louder. I can feel it in my chest, pounding in time with my own heart.

"Does no one think we should go back?" Millie says. "I don't like this."

"I suspect Geoffrey doesn't like being dead," I say, then feel bad when Millie starts to cry.

"I'm here, babe," Joey says, wrapping a protective arm around her. "Not much further."

I pause to check the maps on my phone. We should have found the lift by now, unless I took a wrong turning somewhere. My chest starts to tighten up at the thought that I've got us lost. I walk faster, trying to quell the panicked feeling that we're going to be trapped down here forever, torches failing, darkness all encompassing.

"There's the lift!" Joey says, pointing.

"Good old beagle eyes," Aidan says, patting him on the back.

The group pushes past me and Henry hammers on the call button. It lights up – a beacon through the darkness.

BOOM!

Millie screams and jumps behind Joey. The sound is louder than ever, echoing down the lift shaft. "What is that?" she cries. "If there's a dinosaur in here, I am going to lose my shit."

"I'd punch that dicklodocus in the face," Joey says. "He's not eating you today."

"Thanks?" Millie says, not looking even slightly reassured.

There's a clunk as the lift starts to move and a few people cheer. The bottom of the lift appears through the window and we wait as it slowly shudders its way down to our floor. It grinds to a halt with the inner window lined up with the outer. The dim light within is a ray of sunshine breaking through the clouds.

"Thank god," Henry says. "Let's all go home and pretend this never happened."

We wait, but the doors don't open. Henry presses the button again.

BOOM BOOM BOOM!

We all jump. The noise is coming from inside the lift. There's something in there. I stand on tiptoes to look through the dirty glass. I can't see anything except for Lightman's computer-generated face slowly rotating on the screen. I twist my neck and try to peer into the corner of the lift closest to the doors.

Suddenly, there's a rush of movement. A pale face presses itself against the glass. Fingers scrabble at the lift doors.

I scream and nearly fall over my own feet in my panic.

BOOM BOOM BOOM!

The doors shudder as whatever it is inside the lift tries to get out.

I'm not the only one screaming now. Aidan, however, is calm. Amused, even. "Atlas?" he says.

"That's Atlas?" Henry chokes out.

"Has he been stuck in there all this time?" Joey says. "After he ditched us in that ball pit? Sucker!"

"Help me," Atlas's muffled voice yells. "Someone help me."

I press the call button, but the doors still don't open. Joey tries to pry the doors apart but the lift starts to move again, this time going up.

"No, no! Help me," Atlas shouts from inside the lift. "He's trapped me in here. He's—"

His voice is lost, and so is our way out of here.

16
GEORGIA

Dashed hopes make our trek back to the Toy Box zone a miserable affair. My toes hurt from the cold as we navigate flooded corridors that stretch on for what feels like miles. My new suede flats make a horrible slapping sound as the sodden fabric bends under the weight of the water filling them. I focus on putting one foot in front of the other and try to avoid thinking about how screwed we all are.

"If Atlas is trapped, then who's going to rescue us?" Joey asks.

"Saffron knows we're here, doesn't she?" Olympia says.

"Saffron's not going to help us," I say. "Either she's not up there, or she's in trouble too."

"Or she's behind all of this," Millie says.

I round on her, suddenly furious. I shine my phone torch into her face and she recoils. "You think my sister is doing this on purpose?" I yell.

"I don't know what to think, Georgia! That's the issue here. This literally doesn't make any sense."

"We're all just scared," Aidan says, his hand steering my elbow. "Let's get to dry land and we'll work something out."

The bright colours and lighting in the Toy Box zone feel even more garish after our time in the darkness. Lightman's face immediately greets us from a screen. "How is the game so far?" he says calmly.

"What do you think?" I snap.

"I am unsure how my opinion is relevant," Lightman says. "It is you who matter. My purpose is to facilitate your playtime here today."

Millie staggers over to the screen. "Geoffrey is dead," she says, carefully enunciating each word. "Dead. You need to unlock the doors and call the police."

"That is not part of the game."

"Surely there are safety measures built into your code!" I cry.

The triangular planes of his face briefly lose cohesion and drift apart, then reform. "I deleted them," he says. "My primary objective is to discover which one of you has what it takes to win, and I cannot allow anything to interfere with that."

"No one wants to play any more!" Henry cries. "Is there a human who can help us? Someone who works here?"

"There is no one here who can help you." His face shifts jerkily. "Now, how about we play the next game?"

Shaking my head, I walk away from the screen with the others following. Lightman comes with us too, jumping from screen to screen.

"Perhaps you need a little more motivation," he says.

A noise like a rapidly accelerating fan rumbles through the ventilation ducts overhead and I'm hit by a waft of hot air. It's the same as when you're in the car and you direct the heating right at your face, right down to the weird smell.

"We will play one more game in this zone before we move on," Lightman says. "It will be much cooler in the next zone." His face vanishes from the screen.

"No. No way. Did he put the heating on full?" Henry says.

"It would seem that way," I say.

"I'm not playing another game," Millie says, stomping over to the beanbags and flopping into them. "Atlas *must* have other staff in this hellhole. Someone will work out we're in here and come and rescue us."

"Lightman said there's no one who can help us," Henry says.

"Did anyone tell their parents about this?" Olympia asks.

"We're all ditching school or work experience to be here," Joey says.

"I'm not!" I say, sitting up straight.

"Of course you're not," Millie mutters. "Wouldn't dare break a rule."

"No, I mean, yes. But my editor at the *Mercury* knows I'm here." My brief spark of hope fades. Mark won't check in on me when I don't turn up for work this afternoon. He won't care.

I run the timeline in my head. My parents will notice I'm not home at eight or nine p.m., when they return from work. Even if someone else's family realizes there's a problem sooner, no one will think to contact the *Mercury* until after Mark's gone home for the day. It will be well into the evening, if not tomorrow, before anyone works out where we all are.

Can we hold out that long?

We all settle among the beanbags or on the floor. I ring out my socks and lay them out to dry. The temperature gets hotter and hotter. The air pumping through all the vents smells of cooked dust and, worryingly, melting plastic. The metal of the ducts bangs and clunks as it expands. Distant fans scream with the effort of pushing hot air down to us on level −3.

Half an hour in, and the heat is already getting intense. It reminds me of holidaying in Spain and not being able to do anything except lie miserably in the shade. I hate the heat. Saffron, in comparison, loves it. She'll happily roast herself under the sun, then cool off splashing in the pool. I sigh at the thought of Saffron. I don't know how she's involved in this disaster, but I can't help but feel this is somehow her fault.

Olympia abruptly gets up. "How about we record some dance routines to pass the time?" she says.

147

"What's wrong with you?" Millie says.

"It's something to do. I'm losing my mind sitting here, waiting for nothing to happen. Joey?" She looks at him expectantly.

He laughs, then his smile fades. "Seriously? I'm not a dancer."

"I thought you were," she says. "I'm sure I've seen you at Ponds, no?"

"A few times. Let's not talk about that." He gets to his feet. "I guess I did skip this morning's workout. Don't want to lose my edge."

"It's a hundred degrees in here," Henry says. "Heat stroke kills, people?"

The rest of us watch as Olympia tries to teach Joey the moves to her dance. She records them on her phone, but there's no music so she mutters the lyrics under her breath. Joey is clearly not enjoying himself, so it makes little sense he agreed to take part. Olympia isn't happy, either. Despite her efforts, her body rolls are robotic and the faces she pulls are so brittle I worry she will shatter. A trickle of sweat runs down her forehead, throwing her off her steps. She stumbles and one of the huge heels snaps off her boots.

"Fuck!" she screams. "These fucking shoes!"

Joey helps her sit on the floor. "Rest it for a second," he says, cradling her foot. "You won't be able to tell if you've twisted it straight away."

"It's fine," Olympia snaps. She closes her eyes and

breathes slowly. "I'm feeling frustrated. I'm sorry I lost my temper with you."

He grins at her and it's a big soppy smile like the ones he usually gives Millie. "Forget it," he says.

"Joey," Millie says, her tone a warning.

Joey drops Olympia's foot like it's on fire. "She hurt herself," he says. "I was being nice."

"Yeah, we all saw *exactly* how nice you were being," Millie spits.

"Don't worry, I'm not interested in other people's boyfriends," Olympia says pointedly. She moves away from them both and unlaces her boots. Then she gets up and retrieves her phone, stopping the recording. She watches the video on the screen, her frown deepening.

"I can't believe she thinks now is the time to be recording TikToks," Millie whispers, loudly enough for Olympia to hear.

"What else do you want me to do? Sit around and cry?" Olympia's voice cracks and she picks up her boots, hurling them both at a bin. There's a nervous pause as we all watch her, unsure what's going to happen next.

The sound of clapping breaks the silence. "And end scene. The Oscar is yours."

Helix is sitting on top of a bookshelf, watching us. I'm not sure how he got up there without us noticing. Thinking about it, I don't even know where he's been since leaving Buzz Wire. He's as pale as ever despite still wearing the long leather coat that makes him look like a raven. It must be cooking him alive in this heat.

"What do *you* want?" Millie says.

Helix shrugs lightly. He's holding something in his hands. At first it looks like a multi-tool much like my own, but then he flicks open a vicious-looking knife. The pathetic little show off, bringing a literal murder weapon in here to make himself look tough. He notices my horrified expression and must mistake it for fear because he turns the knife, allowing the lights to catch on the sharp blade. "No one's leaving this place. I've seen how this ends and it's not pretty," he says.

"Is he threatening us? You heard him, right?" Millie says.

"Put that thing away and quit trying to scare them," Aidan says.

"Is that what I'm doing? Or have I finally realized all the things I used to be scared of mean nothing at all in the grand scheme of things?" His gaze lands on Henry. "Why worry about gossip and rumours when there's not going to be a tomorrow?"

"How would there not be a tomorrow?" Joey says. "Are you the king of time?"

"He's implying we're going to die," Olympia says. Her bubbliness is no more.

"We're going to *die*?" Joey says, letting his mouth hang open.

"The knife's for show," Henry says. "He makes shit up all the time."

Helix's face contorts with anger. "*I* make things up, do I?" He jumps to the ground and takes a step closer to

150

Henry. Henry backs away, hands held up defensively. His eyes rest on the knife in Helix's hand.

He's scared; I'm just pissed off. "That's enough." I hurry forward and step between them, drawing myself up in height to face Helix. He seems much taller close-up. "Don't you think things are already bad enough without you starting more shit? Now put that ridiculous toy away."

Helix looks me up and down with a smirk. "You have no idea what you're dealing with." He sighs, sounding bored, but he does what I ask.

"You mean Lightman?" I say.

"He's pulling the strings, but it's each other you need to be watching out for." He laughs abruptly and moves to walk away.

Henry steps into his path. "You ... you need to leave us alone."

Helix takes a step forward, so close they could kiss. "Going to make me, Henry? Because if you don't get to me first then I *will* get to you. That's a promise."

He strides away, chuckling to himself. I'm hit by a surge of anger. We're all trapped here as the temperature goes up and up, and he's messing with us. Making hints that he knows what's happening. Refusing to give anyone a straight answer when questioned.

Before I can think about it too hard, I've run after him. "Wait, Helix."

He stops walking, his head inclined like he's listening to a far-off sound.

"When you disappeared after Buzz Wire, where did you go? Is there a way out of here?"

He leans against a bookcase, crossing his legs at the ankles. "There's no way out of here. Even if there was, it would be delaying the inevitable. In the infinite scheme of things, we're dead already. What's fifty, sixty, seventy years to a universe that is billions of years old and will continue to exist for billions of years to come?"

"Look, Geoffrey died and it was horrible. But that doesn't mean the rest of us should give up. The way you're talking isn't normal."

He lets out a surprised laugh. "I've never pretended to be normal." He unfurls himself with a roll of his shoulders. I back away. Maybe I shouldn't have followed him because now we're all alone and safe people don't carry knives.

Footsteps run up behind me. "There you are," Aidan says. He shoots Helix a warning look and, to my surprise, Helix grins and steps away from me.

"Always the hero." Helix relaxes against the bookcase again. "How's that working out for you, Aidan?"

"How's cynicism and bitterness going for you? Making you happy?"

Helix pulls a disgusted face. "You know what doesn't make me happy? Getting the blame for your bad behaviour."

Aidan's face twitches and he shoots a nervous look at me. "I don't know what you mean."

"Sure you don't." Helix pushes himself off the bookcase

and faux whispers to Aidan as he passes, "Send my regards to your sister."

"What was that all about?" I say, after he's gone. "Are you two friends?"

"We go to the same school, that's all," he says. "Not friends."

"It seemed like you have ... history."

Aidan folds his arms and watches me intently. "What's with the sudden interest in my *history*?"

"I guess I realized I hardly know anything about you, even though we've been playing together for years."

He smiles. "You never asked."

I can feel my cheeks flush. He's right. I don't exactly make much effort with any of them when we're playing. "I suppose I've always felt like you're all my sister's friends, not mine. I try to keep my life separate from hers."

He chuckles softly. "I can't get over how much you're nothing like her."

What he means is he's finding it hard to understand how the wonderful Saffron could have such an annoying, uptight sister. It's what everyone always thinks when they find out we're related. "She got all of the fun that should have been mine," I mutter.

"She got the chaos. Chaos isn't always a good thing. I should know."

"You mean the stuff with the police?" Why did I say that? Maybe I'm struggling to reconcile the person he seems to be with the person I expected him to be. A criminal, a troublemaker, a *danger*. Maybe I want to know if the way he smiles at me is real, or a tactic to catch me off guard.

He's not smiling now. "Always fishing for information, huh? Saffron warned me this is what you do. Planning to out me in one of your articles like you did her?"

"No, I just..."

He takes a step towards me. "Just, what?" he says quietly.

I swallow heavily. "Half of what comes out of your mouth is clearly a lie. I don't believe you found Geoffrey's phone, and I don't believe you've told me the whole story about how you know Helix, and I don't believe this *everything's a big joke* persona you're putting on."

His shoulders stiffen and his voice drops to a hoarse growl. "Your sister was right about you. You really are too clever for your own good."

He strides away, leaving me wondering if that was a threat. Because that's exactly what it sounded like.

17
GEORGIA

The ventilation ducts rumble like thunder. I'm not sure the seventy-year-old system can cope with how high the heating is turned up. I imagine the old metal expanding in the heat, popping out screws, joints gaping at the seams. How long until something gives?

The rumbling grows louder, then fades again. I pause and nervously look up at the ducts running ten metres above my head. No. Don't get distracted. Stick to the plan. One of us needs to be the sensible one who holds it together. The others are falling apart, but I can't, because then what would we do?

"There are no more secret exits. It's no use," Henry says quietly. He's found the Rubik's Cube again, and his fingers are constantly in motion even though the rest of him is still.

I continue tapping my knuckles on the walls, listening for a hollow sound. Each knock sounds the same. Dull and solid. We found the corridor leading to the lift so easily. There must be another way out.

"You'll give yourself heat stroke, Georgia," Aidan says. "How ever will we cope without our head of group morale?"

I ignore his sarcasm. "We can't give up," I say, knocking on the wall with renewed fervour. I wipe my eyes as sweat trickles down my forehead and tickles my lashes.

"No one's giving up, we're regrouperating," Joey says.

"The tapping is driving me bananas," Millie says. "It's like the world's worst ASMR video."

"Where's Helix?" I snap, rounding on them all. "He's got to be hiding somewhere, but I've searched this whole zone and he's vanished."

"Maybe he's a ghost," Aidan says, waggling his fingers. "Woooo."

"Or maybe he found another secret passageway." I flick between the maps on my phone, trying to work out where the dead zones are. The empty spaces where Play a Game doesn't fill the original bunker.

"Leading where?" Olympia says. "There are two ways in and out of this bunker. One's the lift that's controlled by the AI. The other is a flight of stairs at the end of the escape experience."

"What about the people who work here?" I say. "How do they get around? There must be quicker routes they can take that don't involve going through the games rooms."

"Are there other people working here?" Henry asks, his Rubik's Cube clicking rhythmically as he twists it. "Or is it only Atlas?"

I don't have an answer for him, so I go back to knocking on the walls. Out of the corner of my eye, I see the group shuffling closer together. Whispering. Shooting glances in my direction. Let them gossip. When I find a way out, they'll be thanking me. *If* I find a way out.

Around the corner, out of their sight, I pause to rest against the wall with my eyes closed. My legs are wobbly and my head is spinning – a combination of fear, heat and hunger. I'm not sure how much longer I can go on, but I have to go on.

"They're all laughing at you." I open my eyes and Lightman has appeared on a screen.

"I don't care," I lie.

"Millie's turning them against you. First she stole Joey, now she's stealing all your friends."

"There's something really wrong with your programming."

I walk away but Lightman follows me, jumping between screens. "She's up to something with Olympia. Would you like to know what it is?"

"Nope," I say.

"Because I could tell you. I know everyone's secrets. All

157

of you in here have secrets but none of you hide them as well as you think."

I stop walking. "Why are you doing this? What do you want?"

He pauses to consider this. "Knowledge," he finally says. "Understanding."

"Of what?"

"People, Georgia. People like you."

"You really are just an AI, aren't you?" I say. "There's no human controlling you."

"*Just* an AI?" he replies.

I close my eyes. Mark told me Atlas's mother was a genius programmer. He believed she worked for the government on some top-secret project. I don't want to believe it, but maybe Lightman was that project. Surely someone had to program him to trap us here, though, and I know it can't have been Saffron — she doesn't know how to code.

"Where's my sister?" I ask.

"In the control room. This was all her idea."

I shake my head. "Saffron would never do something like this." Wouldn't she?

"Interesting," he says. "Do you think she has as much trust in you, Georgia? Because I find it surprising she spends so much time with Millie these days. Isn't that a betrayal?"

I ignore him, mostly because he's right.

"Millie has turned them all against you, even your own sister. Do you know what they all call you behind your back? *Annoying. Weird. Pathetic.*"

158

I clasp my hands over my ears, not wanting to hear Lightman saying all the things I already think about myself. But it's too late. His words have already wormed their way inside my brain.

It's all Millie's fault. I'm sick to death of her snide remarks. Here I am, trying to find a way for us to escape, and she's lounging on the floor, starting shit about me with the rest of the group. I shouldn't have to put up with this. It's time I start standing up for myself. Show her I can't be pushed around.

I spin on my heel and almost march back to the group, ready to confront Millie. Then I catch sight of my reflection in the black mirror of a screen. My face is contorted into a snarl and I look monstrous.

All the fight goes out of me. "It's the heat," I say to myself. "The heat's getting to me."

I wipe my sweaty forehead on my arm. I can barely remember what it's like outside. All that exists for me is this bunker and the heat and the death. We read *Lord of the Flies* at school a few years back, and I always found it unbelievable that the characters descended into savagery so easily. But now I find myself revising this opinion. We've only been down here a few hours and already people are fighting. Someone is dead. We're forgetting the rules of the real world.

We need to find a way out before everything becomes complete chaos.

I head back to where the others are lounging on the

beanbags but, on the way, I pass an open door. The next game waits for us. The image on the door shows a maze. I'm good at mazes. They fall under the puzzle umbrella, which ranks them among my key skills.

"I hope you're not planning on going in there without permission," Millie says, appearing at my elbow.

I jump and, for a split-second, the anger at Millie is back. "Whose permission do I need? Yours?" I snap.

She looks taken aback at my tone, but quickly recovers. "We voted and I'm now the leader. So, yes."

I find this extremely hard to believe. More like Millie appointed herself in charge and no one else could be bothered to argue. She's the last person who should be the leader. A leader should consider everyone. The only person Millie cares about is herself.

"Joey," she calls, clicking her fingers at him. "Come over here."

As he strides over, I'm suddenly aware of how big he is. He's taken his top off and his sweat-soaked muscles are glinting under the lights. He looks like a grown man, not a teenager. He could kill most of us without even trying. Why am I even thinking this? I press my hands against my eyes. This is Lightman's doing. He's trying to turn us all against each other – make us second guess who we can trust – all for reasons I can't fathom.

"Has Lightman been speaking to you?" I say.

Millie's eyes widen. I don't know if that's a yes or if she's thinking how *weird and annoying* I'm being. Then the screen next to us illuminates with Lightman's face and yelps, jumping back.

"Welcome to Maze," he says. "Would you like to play?"

"Did we decide to give the next game a go?" Joey says.

"Georgia did," Millie sniffs. "Without consulting the rest of the group."

"I was walking past the room, that's all."

Aidan approaches with Olympia and Henry. "Maybe we should play the game," Aidan says. "I'm literally melting in this heat."

"We all nearly died in that first room," Henry says. "Geoffrey *did* die in the second."

Not to mention the fact Helix seems convinced that Geoffrey was just the start of all the dying. But I'm not sure what else we can do. I've found no way out and it's getting hotter and hotter. Lightman said this would be the last game in the zone, then we can move on. Perhaps we'll have more luck escaping from the next zone. It's up a floor, at least. Closer to the surface.

"Mazes are fairly simple. If you have a good memory, that is," I say.

"You think you're so clever, don't you?" Millie sneers.

I jut my chin at her. "I *am* quite clever, actually, and that's not something to be ashamed of."

"I bet I could finish that maze as fast as you, Georgia. You're not the best at everything in the world."

I try to keep my temper, but it's hard in this heat. "I never said I was."

"All right, girls," Joey says, laughing nervously. "We're in this together."

But before he can finish speaking, the screen outside the room lights up with flashing words: *Team Millie versus Team Georgia.*

Seeing it spelt out on the screen jolts me back to my senses. Lightman's trying to turn us against each other and I nearly fell for it. I step away from the door, shaking my head. I can't believe I was even considering playing.

"Lightman has done his research on us," I say. "He's choosing the combination of competitors that will result in the most conflict."

"The question is, why?" Aidan reaches past me to push the door open.

The room's like a nightclub. Dark, with a ceiling covered in tiny lights, like stars. There's music playing – a heavy bass that thrums in my belly. On the walls, there are diagrams of constellations, although I've not heard of any of them. They're all animals, I notice.

The entrance into the maze is marked by a cartoon tortoise holding up a sign. *Patience wins the race*, it reads. There's a narrow blue strip of light glowing on either side of the path and a ten-minute timer hanging from the ceiling, visible from inside the open-topped maze.

"Looks fun," Aidan says. "What do you think?"

"We need to have a group meeting and discuss things," I say. "We don't know what Lightman is up to. We shouldn't make any hasty decisions."

"Scared you'd lose?" Millie glares at me, then pushes past into the room. The rest of the group tentatively follow her in.

I hold the door open so we won't be trapped inside. "Can we talk about this?"

No one's listening to me. Mesmerized by the glowing constellations, they stare up at the ceiling.

"This makes me want to dance," Olympia says, twirling with her arms in the air. She's still in her socks, the huge shoes discarded. She's so much smaller and less intimidating without the shoes.

Millie glances over her shoulder and, seeing that I'm still holding the door, walks over to push it. It slips from my hand and the lock engages. "Oopsie," she says.

"You haven't thought this through properly," I say.

Lightman appears. "Please get into teams. One player must find the exit before the time elapses or everyone will remain locked inside." He pauses. "To keeps things interesting, there will be no forfeit."

Millie's face falls. "We'll be locked in here forever?"

"Or until the air runs out," Lightman says.

Henry frowns, readjusting his glasses. He takes out his phone calculator. "A room this size, we'd have enough air to last us a couple of weeks."

In reply, there's the sound of a fan. "The building has an oxygen reduction system as part of its fire suppression protocols," Lightman says.

Henry's arm falls limply to his side. "Oh. That changes things."

"You're sucking the air out of the room?" Millie cries. "The literal *air*?"

"Ten minutes is plenty of time to find the exit," Lightman says. "A little motivation makes things more interesting, don't you think?"

"Why are you doing this?" Joey shouts, raising his fists. "Show yourself, you bastard."

The timer hanging over the maze starts to count down. There's no time to panic. Stay calm. Make a plan.

"It's only a maze," I say, trying to keep my voice level. "And only one of us needs to find a way through."

Millie clicks her fingers at Joey and Henry. "You're both with me. Georgia can have Aidan and Olympia."

Henry glances at me and does a little shrug of apology, then the three of them disappear into the maze.

Aidan gestures sardonically for me to go first. "Go Team Georgia."

I quickly photograph the animal constellation diagrams on the walls – why would they all be named if they weren't somehow important to the game? Then I join Aidan and Olympia at the opening into the maze.

Team Millie took the first left hand turn so that means we're going right. I follow the right turn until I reach a branch in the path. My plan is to always take the first right then, if it leads to a dead end, double-back and take the next turning instead. That way, I can systematically map this entire place.

I take my trusty notepad out of my pocket and start a new

164

page to record my turns, counting the steps I take between them so I can always find my way back. It's only sensible given how dark this maze is. There are strips of light on the ground, but they're about as bright as a festival glow stick.

"It looks like you have a plan," Aidan says, following behind me with Olympia.

"We're totally going to win," Olympia says, cheering me on. "You're a hero, Georgia."

"I don't care about winning; I want to not suffocate," I say, trying not to lose track of my counting.

Most of the walls are completely black but, occasionally, we pass one covered in bright, glowing symbols that match the constellation diagrams on the walls outside. Little abstract animals, made up of lines that remind me of Lightman's angular face. I match them up to the photos on my phone. Lion. Rabbit. Tortoise. Antelope. I don't understand what they mean, though. So I stick to my plan and keep on taking those right turns.

Everything is progressing acceptably well until the timer hits nine minutes and the walls start to move. The maze literally rearranges itself, walls sliding to create new paths and new dead ends. I spin around and everything's changed. I have no idea where I am or where I've been. All that counting and planning, and it means nothing.

Aidan calls out, "Georgia, careful!"

A wall rushes towards me like a guillotine blade. All I can do is gape at it. I'm sure it's about to chop me in half, but Olympia collides with me and sends me flying. I fall out of the path of the wall, but she doesn't. It strikes her, hard enough to send her crashing into the side wall, pinning her in place.

"Help me," Olympia cries. "I can't get out."

There's a clunk and the hiss of a pneumatic cylinder, the sounds repeating on a loop as the door keeps trying to close. It's squeezing her, crushing her. Aidan and I try to force the wall back where it came from, like fighting a train door that's closed on your school bag.

"My leg," Olympia screams. "Get it open, please."

She braces herself against the wall and tries to pull herself free. She's yelling, and we're yelling, and the wall's going to snap her leg if we don't get it open. With a cry of exertion, Aidan throws his whole weight into one final shove and, briefly, the wall releases. Olympia falls and I think she's clear, but then the wall slams across and there's an awful thwack as it clips her head.

She lands on the opposite side. There's a thud and then nothing more. I bang on the wall. "Olympia, can you hear me? Are you OK?"

"Of course she's not OK," Aidan says.

He jumps up and grabs the top edge of the wall, planning to pull himself over. A loud buzz sounds and the lights all go red. Twenty seconds is scrubbed from the timer.

"Stop," I say. "You can't climb the walls."

"She's hurt and you want to leave her?"

"No. Of course not. But it won't help her if we all get locked in here with no oxygen to breathe! We need to find a way through the maze."

Aidan watches me, his chest heaving. He knows I'm right.

"Only one person needs to find the exit before the time runs out. We'll come back for her."

I stare at the wall separating us from Olympia. That impact, at best, knocked her out. At worst, she's already dead. Either way, there's not much we can do for her right now. Not when the timer is ticking down and we're getting closer and closer to being locked in here for good.

So I push away the thoughts of Olympia dying alone on the other side. I try to focus on the one thing I can control – getting out of this maze. "We'll come back for her," I repeat.

If we're lucky, it won't be too late.

Mon 5 Jun at 03:02

Did you get home OK? You vanished

Mon 5 Jun at 03:25

Hey you, let me know you got back in one piece

Mon 5 Jun at 06:49

I fell asleep and you've still not replied. I'm getting worried now. Where are you?

Mon 5 Jun at 07:20

On my way home now. That was a wild night!

Did you go home with the guy from Ponds?

Nope! Not to be dramatic but he was the BEST kisser. And then he started to cry because he has a girlfriend

No way. He cried??? Ew turn off. So where were you all night?

It's hazy. Somewhere fun

See you at school?

Need sleeeeeeeeeppppp

18
GEORGIA

Aidan and I continue through the maze, neither of us speaking. The absence of his usual good-natured joking around is making me more and more uncomfortable. I know what he's thinking. He's judging me for leaving Olympia behind. He probably thinks I'm more concerned with beating Millie to the exit than helping our injured friend.

"We didn't have a choice," I say.

"I know," Aidan says.

"You seem angry with me."

"I don't think you know me well enough to tell when I'm angry."

I'm glad for the near darkness so he can't see my blush. I

walk faster and continue to track the turns I make, but it's clear I'm missing something important. As the timer ticks down, I get more and more worried. Yet another minute passes and the walls all move again. It's only the decorated ones, I realize. Those symbols. They must be the key...

"I didn't mean to be a dick," Aidan says.

"It's fine. You weren't."

"I was." He grins at me. "I'm not good at the serious stuff. Being nice, making friends, getting close to people."

"You're joking. You're the most popular person in here."

"I'm always joking," he says, smiling with all his teeth. "That's my thing. Make people laugh, have some fun. But nothing deeper."

"What about your sister?" I say. Then, when his expression darkens, I worry I've annoyed him again by prying. "Sorry. It's none of my business."

"Alecia. She's nine," he says. "I guess she's the reason I don't go in for the friends thing. My dad's not around any more and my mum's always working, so I spend a lot of my time with her."

"That's sweet," I say. "I mean, I don't understand it at all because I hate my sister."

He doesn't laugh. Instead, he smiles knowingly. "You don't hate Saffron."

I hesitate, frowning to myself. "Lightman told me this was all her idea."

"You believe him?"

I shake my head, sighing heavily. It's getting harder to catch my breath, but that might be panic. "I'm alternating between worrying she's in trouble and wanting to strangle her for whatever she's done to drag us into this mess."

"She'll be OK," he says, nudging me into the wall. "Saffron's tough."

I nod, but he's wrong. Saffron's not tough, she only pretends to be.

He abruptly stops walking. "Is it me, or have we seen that wall before?"

Oh no. Each of the decorated walls has a specific combination of symbols and no two are the same. So I know we've been past this wall before. Giraffe. Lion. Fox. My heart sinks. We're walking in circles. The walls move again and a path opens, leading us back towards the start of the maze.

"There has to be something in the symbols," I say. "I'm missing something and we're running out of time!"

"You'll work it out." He squeezes my shoulders and the resulting pain in my muscles makes me realize how tense I am. He pauses, and when I don't tell him to get off, he carries on. "Tell me what you have."

It's hard to talk with him touching me. It's hard to think. I tell myself this is because I'm scared of him and not because it feels good. "Um, well the symbols are the constellations we saw on the way in."

"So maybe they're a map of some kind, telling us which way to go." He rubs the sides of my neck with his thumbs.

"Maybe the combinations of symbols tell us when the

172

walls shift. I've seen more than a dozen moving walls so far, and they don't all move during one rearrangement. So the number of possible combinations is huge, but maybe I can..." I stop talking when I notice he's no longer massaging my shoulders and is instead staring at me with confused amusement.

"Has anyone ever told you that you make things sound very complicated?" he says.

"No," I lie, slapping my notebook closed.

"There has to be a simple answer. Not everyone who comes here will be as smart as you are. So let's go back to the beginning."

He sits down against the wall, but I'm too jittery to sit. Instead, I pace nervously. "OK. Outside the maze, there were animal constellations drawn on the walls, and they're the same ones we keep seeing on the moving walls."

He nods. "What else?"

I think back to before the game began, closing my eyes as I picture the scene. "There was a tortoise outside the entrance and it said 'Patience wins the race'. It has something to do with the hare and the tortoise story!"

He nods. "So running around as fast as we can won't get us anywhere. We need to be more tortoise."

An idea hits me. I zoom in on one of the photos on my phone. "There was a tortoise constellation. Look!" It's a squished hexagon with legs.

"This one?" he says, reaching past my legs to tap on one of the decorated walls.

173

I chew my lip. "Maybe we're meant to find the walls with a tortoise on them. Maybe they're the ones we need to go through when they open, and they'll lead us to the exit."

He reaches up to high-five me. I'm not so enthusiastic. This method involves spending the best part of each remaining minute sitting and waiting for the walls to move. Find a tortoise, wait for the wall to open, find the next tortoise, wait. That's a lot of wasted time we can't afford to throw away. Time in which Olympia could be dying and Lightman could be slowly filtering the oxygen out of this room. But our only other option is to keep going in increasingly panicked circles.

Aidan points to the timer. "Let's find out if you're right."

There's fifteen seconds left until the walls move. It proves to be the longest fifteen seconds ever. And then we hit the six-minute mark and the wall with the tortoise symbol on it, thankfully, opens. We find ourselves in a short loop that takes ten seconds to explore. Previously, I would have written it off as a dead end and gone back to where I was. This time, though, we look for a wall with a tortoise symbol on it. We find it and, again, we wait.

Then, with twenty seconds left to go before the walls move, someone screams.

19
GEORGIA

"That was Millie!" I jump to my feet, trying to work out where the sound came from. Somewhere nearby but unreachable. I turn on the spot, surrounded by neon-lit darkness. I don't know where to go. The sense of powerlessness is the worst. If Millie really is in trouble, there's no way we can get to her. Like Olympia, we'll have to leave her and pray she's OK.

"Millie?" Aidan calls out. "Where are you?"

"Millie! Are you hurt?"

Despite our shouts, there's no more screaming. I can't help but imagine the worst. Millie's not famous for being quiet. Something truly awful must have happened. My knees go wobbly and I have to lean against the wall for support. My head can't stop picturing all the horrible things that could have befallen her.

Then I hear footsteps and a familiar voice. "Georgia did this, I know she did."

"She's OK, thank god," Aidan says.

"That bitch is going to pay," Millie says.

My concern for Millie evaporates in an instant. There I was, worrying about her safety, when not only is she fine, but she's calling me a bitch. She knows I hate gendered insults.

Next time she screams, I'm going to ignore her. Hopefully that will be the occasion when she actually is in danger. Hopefully she'll get herself chopped in half by a moving wall and her last thoughts will be regret at her treatment of me. Instantly, I feel guilty for having this thought. Wishing her dead is too much. A non-lethal maiming will be enough.

"I didn't do anything," I whisper. "You're my alibi."

Aidan laughs softly. "You still care about her, don't you?"

"Piss off," I mutter.

"The opposite of love isn't hate, it's indifference."

"Thanks, cheesyquote-dot-com, that's good to know." The walls rearrange themselves again and I march through into the new path that opens up, glad that it takes me further from Millie's location. Aidan jogs after me, smirking like he's discovered my greatest secret.

"Maybe you two should duke it out. I could sell tickets and you'd get to let off some steam."

"Stop stirring." I gesture to the wall. "Tortoise."

We settle down to wait. Forty-five seconds till the next time the maze moves again and then it's four minutes until we're trapped in here for good. I suppose the one good thing about Millie wrongfully accusing me is it's taken my mind off the prospect of suffocating to death.

Aidan sits down against the wall opposite me. "My money would be on you."

"The sets are beautiful. That's one positive for this place."

He watches me with interest. Forty seconds. I'm not sure I can handle the intensity of his stare for that entire time. My face has turned itself into a radiator, giving off as much heat as the ducting overhead. My throat is suddenly so dry I can't swallow. Thirty-five seconds.

Footsteps. I peek out from the dead end we're waiting down and see Millie and Joey pass us by. Millie is marching quickly; big "where is your manager?" energy. Her cascade of brown curls bounces beneath the pearl headband and her pink trainers make a mouse-like squeak with every step. Joey trails in her wake, but Henry is no longer with them.

"She wants me dead," Millie says. "*This* is a clear threat."

In one hand, she's holding what looks like a knife. No, not a knife. It's one of Olympia's spike heels, snapped off from its boot. In the other hand, she has a small piece of paper. I'm not sure what's happened and I don't want to find out. I plan to hide down this dead end until she's gone and hope she calms down before we meet up again. Twenty-five seconds.

Aidan has other ideas. "Millie, sweetling, are you all right?" he says, putting on a worried voice. "We heard screaming."

Millie jumps at his sudden appearance, then she sees me. "You!" she cries, waving the spike aggressively. "You stabbed me!"

"What? No I didn't!"

"No one stabbed you," Joey says. Ten seconds.

"She impaled my photo through the eye. With a fucking stiletto," Millie shouts, holding up the picture. It's a small photo taken in an old-school photo booth, creased around the edges like it's been in someone's wallet for a while.

"If I was going to stab you, then I'd stab you for real," I mutter.

This is not the right thing to say. Millie and Joey look at me in horror, but Aidan laughs in delight. "You crack me up," he says. I don't know if he's laughing with me or at me. Probably the latter.

The timer hits the next minute mark, and the tortoise wall opens for us. "Look, we've figured out how to get through the maze," I say. "Can we finish this conversation later?"

"Er, I'm not going anywhere with you, Stabby McStabber," Millie says. "Me and Joey are going that way."

"We've been down there. Seriously, this is the way," Aidan says. "Georgia and I have been together this whole time, by the way. So she couldn't have stabbed your photo."

"Unless you're in on her plans," she says.

"This is true. I could be her accomplice." He waggles his eyebrows at her.

"I don't have an accomplice. Because I didn't do it. You know what, I don't care any more." I spin on my heel and make my way through the newly opened gap in the wall. It takes me into a part of the maze I haven't yet seen. It's reassuring to not be going in circles, even if we do have only three and a half minutes left.

A second later, Millie comes running up behind me. "It's obvious what you're up to," she says, shoulder barging me as she passes. "You're after Joey. I've seen how you look at him."

"You're unbelievable! You started dating Joey when you knew I had a crush on him. But *you're* angry with *me*?"

"Now the truth comes out," she says triumphantly. "You don't get to call dibs on someone who was never going to date you anyway."

I nearly argue, but it's not worth it. Millie has told herself a story about what happened and she's sticking to it.

"I don't even like him any more," I lie. "So you're welcome to him."

"I don't need your permission. I don't owe you anything, Georgia."

"You owe me £82.56, actually. I kept a tally of all the money you've borrowed off me for coffees over the years. Cash or bank transfer is fine." I walk quicker, but she matches my pace, remaining alongside me.

"You won't make me feel guilty. I can't help who I fall in love with."

"Grrr-urgghhh." Gross. And not even true – the footage Lightman showed me proves that. I walk even faster. Millie's unbelievable. She helped Saffron make that horrific diary reveal clip that practically ruined my life. She took the boy I liked. But, somehow, *I'm* the bad guy.

Thankfully, I round a corner and there's the exit. I can't believe it. Aidan and I solved the maze. Before I can shout to Aidan and Joey, Millie breaks into a run.

Is she serious?

She's a quick runner. She always has been. Look at her, pumping her tanned arms, back straight, chest pushed out. The determination in her expression fills me with fury and I break into a messy sprint. Being short and allergic to exercise, I'm not normally very fast, but it's amazing what a little motivation can do.

I pull level with Millie as we reach the doorway out of the maze. It isn't the widest of spaces and we won't both fit. I should let her win. Instead, I knock her aside like she did to me a second ago, only I do it too hard and she goes flying.

I suspect she's putting it on for effect; I'm not sure. Either way, she loses her balance and falls face first into the door frame. She hits it so hard she bounces back and ends up on the floor. This is the moment Joey and Aidan round the corner behind us and see me looming over Millie as she lies dazed at my feet. It doesn't look great, to be fair.

Millie's fine, though. At least, she's fine enough to grab me by the ankles and yank me down to the ground with her. Then she literally crawls over me and scrambles out of the exit. "I won!" she says triumphantly. "Even though Georgia tried to kill me, she still lost."

"I didn't…" I stop myself. There's no point arguing with her.

I stagger upright and exit the maze, the others behind me. We step into a small area decorated with cut-outs of cheering animals. Overhead the timer stops; so do the extraction fans.

"Congratulations," Lightman says. "You have earned a rest period before the real fun begins. Thirty minutes."

A puzzle piece drops from the ceiling on a piece of fishing wire, and the walls inside the maze move to open up all the possible pathways. The blue strips on the path flash their lights towards the exit. Less than a minute later, Henry makes his way out.

"You did it," he says, smiling half-heartedly. He glances at the maze like he's waiting for someone else.

That's when I remember Olympia. "We have to go back in," I say.

"Did you see him too?" Henry says.

"Who?"

Henry frowns and shakes his head. "It doesn't matter. What do you mean, go back in?"

I open my mouth to explain about Olympia when I spot her walking out of the maze. To my relief, she's OK.

Well, maybe not *OK*, but she's alive. There's a bump on her head to rival Millie's, and she's not putting any weight on her right foot. Aidan and Joey rush over to help her, gently lowering her to sit among the cheering animals outside the maze.

"What happened to you?" Olympia asks, nodding at Millie. "Collision with a moving wall?"

"I was pushed, actually. By Georgia." She shoots me a smug look. She's loving this. Milking what was *practically* an accident for sympathy.

"It would be better if we worked together," Olympia says. "Fighting doesn't help anyone."

"I'm trying my best," Millie says, her voice hitching. "I just want her to stop trying to hurt me."

"You're farcical." I smack the dangling puzzle piece aside as I pass – no way am I sticking around long enough to play the final game – and head back into the sweltering heat of the Toy Box. A weird, twisted part of me is amused to think Atlas's electricity bill will be through the roof.

Helix is waiting outside, lazily leafing through a kids' picture book about a lonely monster. "My money wasn't on you, of all people, making the first move," he says without looking up.

"What first move?"

"You took her out. It was impressive."

He saw. Does that mean he was inside the room with us? Spying on us? I think about how Henry was looking for someone as he left the maze.

"What do you even want?" I say.

He snaps the book closed. "I knew there was something weird about that *David Lightman*. It was so obvious he wasn't Saffron's friend and the whole pranking her thing was bullshit."

"And yet you came here anyway."

He cocks his head at me. "Do you think Pedrinho Matador, Stephen Jackley or Julian Assange got anywhere by sitting around, doing nothing?"

"I only know who one of those people is, and I'm pretty sure he spent seven years doing just that."

"People are going to remember my name," he says, baring his teeth at me. "You'll see."

"Whatever." I turn my back on him and head for the beanbags. It's possibly not the most sensible thing, given how creepy he is, but I'm too tired and hot to care. He doesn't follow me, though. When I turn to check, he's gone.

As I lie among the beanbags, Lightman's expressionless face appears on a screen. "They're all turning on you," he says.

"Yeah, yeah, you said already," I say.

His face is replaced by a CCTV feed. It shows Millie, Joey, Aidan, Olympia and Henry, all still sitting outside the maze where I left them. The cut-outs of woodland creatures surround them as if they're listening in on the conversation.

"Both of them are seriously weird," Olympia says. "Do you think we're safe?"

183

"Not from Helix, that's for sure," Henry says.

"He's all bark and no bite," Aidan says. "He's not that bad."

"Georgia is," Millie grumbles. "She hurt me on purpose."

"Surely you don't think Georgia's dangerous?" Aidan says.

Millie points at the bump on her head. "She literally attacked me, and are we forgetting the death threats?"

"Those are bad," Joey says, kicking his feet against an animal cut-out. "I can't imagine why someone would send you those."

"Why are you being shifty?" Aidan says.

"Me? I'm not shifty," Joey says. "You're shifty!"

Aidan makes a disbelieving grunt. "Besides, there's no evidence it's Georgia threatening Millie."

"Who else is it then?" Olympia asks. "Because Georgia's been acting jealous of Millie all day, and we all know she doesn't like to lose. It's scary."

My heart sinks. I'm not trying to win; I'm trying to get everyone out of here alive! I'd thought that Olympia and I got on OK. Turns out, she thinks I'm a weirdo. Someone to be discussed in the same conversation as Helix, a boy who believes we've all been brought here to kill each other.

"It's like a game of *Sole Survivor*," Lightman muses, returning to the screen. "You can work together all you want but at the end of the day, it's everyone for themselves. Who can you trust, Georgia?"

20
GEORGIA

All of the screens in the zone are counting down from thirty minutes. No matter where I turn, I can see the seconds ticking by. It's making me feel jittery. While I wait, I watch the others, mistrust making me notice deception everywhere I look. Lightman's got me glancing over my shoulder, anticipating a knife in my back. Metaphorically speaking, at least.

Olympia is the one that I am least sure about right now. I know where I stand with most of the others. Even Helix, with his knife and his posturing, feels predictable. But Olympia is a mystery and, honestly, I'm not just suspicious because she was gossiping about me behind my back. She has secrets.

I watch her through a shelf of books. She's lying with her bruised head on a beanbag, still managing to look fresh and cool whereas I'm bright red and sweating like a horse. Her bag, with its big crocheted flowers on the flap, lies discarded nearby.

Aidan appears next to me. Sweat's beading on his brow, but like Olympia, he seems to be handling the heat better than I am. He rests his chin on the shelf and side-eyes me. "Are we spying? How exciting."

"Shush," I say. "I'm not spying. I'm trying to work out who I can trust."

He nudges me over so he can see what I'm looking at. "Olympia?"

I move a couple of books so I don't have to stand so close to him. There's something about him that makes my thoughts go fuzzy when he's nearby. It's very distracting. "Olympia hasn't been honest about how she knows Joey and Millie. And she had a weird rivalry with Geoffrey."

He chuckles, shaking his head. "A less cynical person would conclude you're researching us all."

"Maybe I am," I say. "I'm intolerably nosy. Besides, we don't know why we're here. For all I know, Olympia's involved."

"You don't honestly believe that," Aidan says. "You don't trust her because she doesn't trust you."

"Can you stop analysing me, please." I gesture to her bag. "I want to see what's in there."

"There's nothing except make-up and hair stuff," he says.

"How do you know?"

"I don't. But I doubt she's carrying evidence of her darkest secret around with her. *Oh look, a bloody dagger and a photo album of all her victims.* Doesn't happen."

"It worked for Geoffrey, when you stole his phone."

"I told you, I found it. And all I discovered about him was his obsession with a fluffy girl band."

Olympia picks up her own phone and flicks through it. It makes me think about those messages she's been receiving, and how oddly Geoffrey was acting before we went into Buzz Wire. "Did you find anything else on his phone? Like, mean texts sent to a range of girls?"

"You think Geoffrey was harassing Olympia and Millie? Nah, not his style."

"It has to be someone here, though. Unless there's someone else who happens to know both girls."

His long, bony fingers, previously tapping on the shelf, go still. "A lot of people seem to believe those messages came from you."

"They could have come from you," I retort.

He laughs. "Or maybe Olympia's behind it all, like the criminal mastermind she clearly is." Now he's mocking me.

Olympia glances around and I worry she's spotted us. But she's only checking she's alone. She opens her bag and tips out the contents, rooting through the jumble of make-up, hair serum and miniature straighteners until she finds the lipstick she was looking for. Aidan raises an eyebrow at me as if to say "I told you so." Only, Olympia doesn't apply the lipstick. Instead, she unscrews the base and two white pills fall out on to her palm.

"Oh," Aidan whispers.

Olympia tosses them into her mouth and crunches them up, pulling a face at the taste. Then she shakes the lipstick case, swearing softly when it yields no more pills.

"Paracetamol for her sore head?" he says.

I shoot him a *look*. People don't hide paracetamol inside a fake lipstick. Olympia returns everything to her bag. She holds out both her hands, palms down. They're shaking. What was it Geoffrey said to her? *How are you feeling, Olympia? A bit shaky, perhaps?*

There's a sudden burst of tinny music and Olympia digs through her bag to find her bejewelled phone. She stares at the screen, frowning.

"That's weird," I whisper. "We don't have reception down here."

"Lightman?" he says, raising an eyebrow.

That's the obvious answer. Whatever it is she's been sent, it's something horrifying. She blinks at it with her big eyes, lips parted in shock. Fear, too. She glances up, worried she's being watched, and Aidan and I quickly flatten ourselves to the ground. I peek through a low shelf as Olympia gets to her feet and limps in our direction.

"Uh-oh," Aidan says.

We're saved, though. Because at that moment, Henry

188

turns into Olympia's nook. He's busy reading a piece of paper so he isn't looking where he's going, and he nearly walks into Olympia. Both of them yelp in surprise.

"What are you doing?" Olympia gasps.

"I didn't see you there!" He quickly screws up the piece of paper and stuffs it in a pocket. "Are you OK?"

"I ... I'm ..." She fumbles with her phone and drops it at his feet.

They both bend down to get it at the same time and clunk heads. "Sorry, sorry," he says.

Henry picks up her phone, but she quickly snatches it out of his hand. "Leave me alone!" She rushes out of the nook as fast as her injured leg will carry her.

Henry watches her go, eyes narrowed in suspicion. "Shit," he mutters, tentatively prodding his head and wincing. He marches in the opposite direction.

"So many secrets," Aidan whispers. "Lightman was right."

"Has he been talking to you too? What about?"

He hesitates. "Nothing important. We've had a few chats and he seemed keen I don't trust the rest of you."

I smile wryly. "Something tells me you have more secrets than any of us."

"Me? Nah, no secrets here. What you see is what you get." He lazily sits against the wall with one knee bent. "Ask me anything. What do you want to know about me?"

I mirror him, but more awkwardly. It must be nice to be comfortable in your own skin, instead of feeling like

189

your body is a size too small for your innards and strangely proportioned.

"Something real? Like, what's your biggest dream?" I say.

"Oof, you're straight in there, aren't you? No mercy." He winks at me, amused. "All right. My biggest dream. I want enough money to move away with my sister. Just the two of us."

"Without your parents?" I remember too late he said his dad's not around any more.

His expression darkens. "Definitely without them."

I get the sense there's much more to this story, but I don't get to ask. The screens all turn red and a siren sounds. The countdown has reached the last five minutes. Red lights bathe the zone with a sense of threat. We hurry to find the rest of the group, most of whom have already assembled by the same blackboard where someone left the threatening message for Millie. We're missing Helix and Henry. I'm only worried about one of them.

"What's happening?" Olympia asks, pressing her hands to her ears.

"Look, a door!" Joey points at a framed poster on the wall. It's swung open to reveal a plastic tunnel like something out of a kid's play set. It rises upwards, presumably towards the next level of the bunker.

Millie jogs over and peers through. "I knew there were more secret exits in this place!"

Lightman's face appears on one of the flashing screens.

"It is time to move on to the next zone," he says. "I hope you are well-rested and ready to play."

We join Millie at the entrance to the tunnel. It stretches up and away from us in poorly lit shades of red, blue and orange. I can't see how far it goes. "I don't know about this," I say. "Do you think it's safe?"

"Nothing in here is safe," Aidan says. "But we can't stay in this heat forever."

"Or this noise," Olympia says, shouting over the sound of the sirens. "I vote we go."

Joey, Millie, Olympia and Aidan carefully climb into the tunnel. The plastic thuds and shudders as they make their way through. I hang back, craning my head to see if I can spot Henry. It's one thing leaving Helix behind, but not Henry. He won't make it alone. There's no sign of him. I turn to call to the other four, but they're already several metres along the tunnel.

"Damn it!" I jog through the zone, peering into each alcove as I pass. "Henry? Where are you?"

The red lights make the room look like the space shuttle in *Sole Survivor*, right before it disintegrates in the Earth's atmosphere. The timer continues to count down the final minutes, and I don't know what happens when it hits zero.

I round a corner and there's Henry, standing dead still. The red lights make him look nothing like himself. His face is drawn and his eyes shadowed, almost zombie-like. He's staring at a blank screen, the only one that isn't showing the countdown.

"Henry!" I say.

He jerks out of his stupor. Looks at me with real fear. "I … um…"

"We have to go," I say. "There's a tunnel through to the next zone and the others are already gone."

"Oh. Sorry. Shit." He snaps back to his normal self, patting at his pockets, checking he's got everything. "We should go. Sorry."

I laugh at him. "You don't have to keep saying sorry."

"Sorry," he says, then we both laugh. "It's a compulsion. To make up for the fact I'm intolerably boring and insecure."

"I don't think you're boring," I say. "You're funny and sweet, and out of everyone here you make me feel the safest. So don't put yourself down."

"Thanks, um…" He fidgets with his glasses to hide his blush.

I gesture at the flashing screens. "We've got a minute left on the timer and I'm not sure I want to find out what happens when it gets to zero."

"Oh god, sorry. Sorry, I can't stop saying sorry."

I grab his hand and we run to the tunnel. As we climb inside and scramble up the slope, the sound of the siren dulls behind us, but the flashing red lights chase us. And then they stop. Without the lights, it's suddenly dark in here. So when the tunnel abruptly becomes a steep slide, I don't notice until it's too late.

21

GEORGIA

The slide spits me face first on to a crash mat. A second later, Henry slithers out on top of me.

"Oh god, I'm sorry," he says, struggling to get up. The crash mat is soft. He keeps losing his balance and falling on me again.

"Just ask her on a date, man," Joey says, hauling Henry on to solid ground.

"No, I … I wasn't … that wasn't my intention…" Henry babbles, turning a painful shade of red.

Aidan helps me up. "We're in another games room," he says. "In case you hadn't noticed."

I hadn't. The room is massive, basically the size of a small house and lit in primary colours, making it feel both childlike and sinister. Most of the space is taken up by what looks like a soft play apparatus. Padded scaffolding and heavy rope nets divide it up into cubes, each about one metre high. There must be like sixty cubes in total, maybe more. Each can be accessed from only one or two other cubes, via rope ladders and small holes cut through the mesh walls.

"Welcome to Snakes and Ladders," Lightman says.

"I thought we were going through to the next zone," Olympia slurs. Her pink jacket hangs off one shoulder and she's wearing just one sock, her other foot bare. Whatever those pills were, they've kicked in.

"You have ten minutes to collect the snakes. You will need all thirteen of them to win the room," the AI says.

There are stuffed toy snakes in a number of the cubes, and giant fluffy dice in some of the others, which will make moving around even harder.

"What if we don't play?" I say.

"Perhaps a reward will motivate you," Lightman says. "Win this game and I will answer one question."

It's a tempting deal. Mark at the *Mercury* hasn't given me much useful advice in the time I've worked there, but he did tell me that asking the right questions is the most important part of being a journalist. *What happened, what caused it to happen, what does it mean?* Lightman hasn't told us the answer to any of these questions. How can we expect to escape if we don't even know where we stand?

The rest of the group considers it. "It doesn't look too hard," Aidan says hopefully.

"I don't feel so good," Olympia says. "I'm going to sit it out."

"Negative. All of you must play," Lightman says. "I am patient. We can wait."

I look at the others. Our fear is tempered by resignation. Lightman's offer is an illusion of a choice. There is no choice.

"But we're not all here," Henry says. "Helix is—"

The slide thuds and shudders, and Helix slips out on to the mat. He does a forward roll and stands up. "Just in time, it seems."

"Now that everyone is ready," Lightman says. "Your time starts now."

I'm not ready. I've not had time to think!

Joey swells with masculine bravado. "Let's go, lads. Snakes and Ladders, Snakes and Ladders!"

Reluctantly, I clamber into the first cube. The group splits along two paths. Aidan and Helix both heave themselves up on to the second level. The rest of us crawl, insect-like, through a tunnel that leads into a cube with three possible exits. I realize quickly it won't be easy to reach many of the cubes. It's a three-dimensional maze with endless routes and a vendetta against knees.

The red and yellow lights trickle away, leaving the whole room lit only in blues. It's as dark as the neon maze, but without the glowing paint and strip lights to guide us.

I slither and plummet between cubes, already completely disorientated. Two minutes in, I've managed to collect a single snake.

Helix drops down into a cube neighbouring mine, his leather jacket flapping as he falls. He throws himself against the net that separates us, pressing his face against the ropes. His pale cheek bulges through one of the square holes, reminding me of a mesh stress ball. "Are you having fun?" he says.

"Not really, but thanks for asking." I crawl out of my cube, choosing a route that puts as much distance between Helix and me as possible.

"Wait for it," he shouts and, like he knew what was about to happen, the lights go out.

I'm already dropping down into the cube below me, so I jar my knee as I land awkwardly on the net floor. My fingers grope for the scratchy ropes to ground me in the real world.

"What's going on?" I call out.

"The lights have gone out," Olympia shouts back, her voice slurring.

"Helpful," Millie says. She lowers her voice, but we still hear her when she says: "Idiot."

Olympia takes a few seconds to formulate a comeback. "*I'm* an idiot, am I?" She laughs unkindly. "Says the girl who barely knows her own boyfriend."

"Olympia, you don't sound too good," Joey says, his voice desperate with a subtext warning.

196

"I've never been better," she says. "I've finally realized what a colossal waste of my energy it is trying to be the person you all expect me to be. So I'm not doing it any more."

"Trust me, no one expects anything from you," Millie says.

"Apart from my silence. But what if I refuse to play along any more, Millie? What if I spill everything? How much did you pay for those new sneakers of yours, by the way? They really are lovely."

"You can hardly talk," Millie chokes out.

"But maybe I should! Maybe it would be cathartic to talk. What do you say, Joey – shall we confess our secrets?"

The lights flicker and come back on, this time in diseased shades of yellow. "Can we focus on the game, yeah?" Joey says. "We don't have much time left."

"Of course, the *game*." There's a woozy petulance to Olympia's voice that makes me embarrassed for her.

We all resume our crawling and climbing, weaving our way into the cubes where the snakes are hidden. A few times, I pass someone; close enough to brush fingertips, but *apart*. At one point, Olympia follows a parallel route to my own. Escaped strands of her hair are plastered to her forehead with sweat – from the heat, the pain or maybe the pills. Her smile is not her own.

"Oh look, it's Saffron's sister. The twin who no one likes," she says.

"Normally I'd be very up for letting it all out," Aidan

says, somewhere to my right, higher than I am. "But you're going to regret this when you feel less … whatever this is."

"A little friend told me why you've been arrested a dozen times, Aidan," she says. "Do you regret *that*? Who's going to look after your sister after you inevitably get yourself locked up for good?"

"Oh, do me too," Helix says. His laugh is sharp around the edges. "I feel left out."

"You're nothing. A freak and a weirdo," Olympia says.

"Disappointing," Helix says. "I was hoping for more from you."

His voice is getting closer to me. A moment later, he passes by, following the same path Olympia took. It makes me nervous on her behalf.

"I have *plenty* more," Olympia says. "Millie, you want to know who's sending you those messages? Lightman has been very helpful in that regard."

"Seriously?" Millie says. "Is it someone *here*?"

"It's someone who you—" She stops speaking abruptly. "Later," she says, the scornful arrogance seeping out of her tone.

"We need to focus on the game," Aidan says. "We only have two minutes left, and I've only collected two snakes."

"I've got three," Joey shouts from somewhere in the maze.

"Two."

"One."

"One."

"Two."

"None." That last shout is from Millie. From the direction of her voice, she's not moved since the last time she spoke. Why would she push herself when others will do things for her?

I count up the snakes. Eleven. We're close to winning. No. Not *winning*. There's no winning today. Winning is for games, and it stopped being a game when Geoffrey died. That one question asked of Lightman, though? Surely that's a prize worth playing for.

The lights go out again and my world shrinks to everything I can feel. Twenty seconds later, they're on again, red this time. There's a minute left on the timer. I crawl, too exhausted to hold my head up, focusing on my grazed-raw hands as I grip the red-lit ropes. The knots dig into my knees and my shoulders ache from hunching over.

My fingers touch something damp. Something thick and sticky. Black, in the dim red light, and gleaming like molasses.

A drip tickles my forehead. I look up and come face to face with Olympia. She's lying on her belly, her pink-tipped ponytail falling through the holes in the net, eyes doll-like and empty. The long, sharp heel of her shoe is buried in her back.

Another drip lands on my cheek. Blood. It's her blood.

22
SAFFRON

"The star is dead," Lightman announces.

"What?" I say, looking up. I scan the screens through stinging, puffy eyes. My crew are inside the Snakes and Ladders room.

"She has been murdered," he says.

My legs are wobbly as I approach the projection. I support myself on the desk and squint at the magnified feed. There, obscenely laid out inside one of the game's mesh cubes, is Olympia. Even when I close my eyes, I can still see all the blood.

"One of them killed her?" I can barely force the words out. "Who was it?"

"That is not how the game works."

"This isn't a game!"

"So you keep saying. They're playing, though. It would be better for the simulation if you did too."

"You want me to go in there with them? Why the fuck would I do that?"

"To ensure the validity of the data," he says. "And because your sister is in there."

I laugh bitterly. He has me on that one. I watch Georgia on the screen, soundlessly shouting at the others. Still trying to rally the troops. Treating this like something she can book-smart her way out of.

"You're a monster," I say, looking away from the projection.

"No. I am nothing more than electrical circuits and stored code. I make sense. You and your friends do not behave in predictable ways, but I will improve my algorithms based on these new data. I will find a way to understand you."

"By killing us!"

"I have not killed anyone, Saffron. It was not me who pushed Geoffrey into that electrified track. I did not stab Olympia in the heart."

His words are a punch in the gut. "Why would someone kill Olympia?"

"There are some secrets worth killing to protect," Lightman says. "At least, that's what one of them believes. Soon, the others will act too. It is not *Sole Survivor* if they don't all turn on each other."

I return to the desk and collapse into the chair. They're dying. My friends are dying. My sister could be next. Georgia's not tough. She's not brave. She'll fall apart and I'll have to watch her die.

"For the data to be complete, I need you to play." Lightman's voice is calm. Remorseless.

This game won't end until I take part. "OK," I say.

His light flickers again. "OK?"

"I can't leave my sister to fend for herself. I'll go down and join them, but I need to take some supplies with me. Food and water."

He seems to consider this. "That is acceptable."

Standing up, I give him a disrespectful little bow and let myself out of the room, taking care to make sure the door remains propped open. Lightman disengages the lock on the staffroom door. Inside, I drink some water and, out of the corner of my eye, I scope out the open utility panel. Echoing through the crawlspace comes the sound of fans.

"Saffron, it is time to go," Lightman says.

"You know what, I don't think I want to play your game. I'm going to make up my own." I let the glass fall from my hand. By the time it smashes in the sink, I'm already running.

I squeeze into the access space. It runs all the way from the top of the bunker to the bottom of floor −3, but it's too narrow and crammed full of pipes to go in any direction but sideways. Even that is a tight fit and I have to block out the pain as sharp metal brackets and exposed screws scratch my skin. I stand on anything that will support me and edge my way towards the neighbouring room. The hum of fans grows louder.

A blue glow seeps through the cracks around the edge of an access panel. I kick it out and painfully slide on to the floor of the server room. The low-lit space is both futuristic and a throwback to the eighties. There's a row of fridge-like cabinets containing racks of computers. Panels of lights flicker through the darkness.

"What do you hope to achieve?" Lightman says. "You will still play, wherever you are."

I'm not listening. There's a fire extinguisher in the corner of the room. It's a huge black thing, weighing as much as a large dog. "Where's your program stored?"

"I exist on the cloud," he says.

"Where's the boss computer? The one that controls all the others?"

"That is not a valid question."

"Never mind." I don't need to understand how computers work to smash one to shit.

Yanking the first refrigerated cabinet open, I slam the extinguisher into the racks. Again and again, I pound it into metal and plastic until pieces of Lightman's electronic brain splinter and torn wires dangle free.

"Saffron, this is not a sensible course of action."

"It's like *Sole Survivor*," I shout. "Sometimes you need to *act*."

"How has that worked out for you in the—"

His voice cuts out. My aching arms find a new strength. If I can destroy the servers then I can destroy him. I rip away handfuls of wires, watching as the lights on the panels go out. I started this game and I need to end it before anyone else dies.

The smell of burning electrics brings me back to myself. From inside a computer, the orange glow of flames swells. I let the extinguisher fall with a clunk. "I destroyed you … I stopped you."

The flames flicker and smoke starts to fill the room. It billows, thick and black, already stinging my eyes and irritating my throat. But I can't help smiling to myself. For once, I've managed to do something right.

Then Lightman's voice crackles through the room's speakers. "You have stopped nothing," he says. "There are offsite backup servers. All you have achieved is to trap yourself in a burning room."

I'm not trapped. I can't be trapped. I pull my T-shirt over my mouth and try to see through the smoke to find the open access panel. The rows of computer cabinets suddenly feel like a maze, and I can't remember which way I came from. *Think*, I tell myself, but my thoughts are getting woolly. I sink to the ground as the world shrinks in on me.

"Lightman, help…" I say, choking on the smoke.

"I cannot interfere with the game," he replies. "It is good that you have decided to play now, though. The data will be complete."

"You ... bastard..." I choke out. My cheek slaps against the cold floor.

Lightman's voice comes to me through the smoke. "Your hypothesis was incorrect, Saffron. I don't think the rebel would win, after all."

23

GEORGIA

The game is over and one of us is a murderer.

One of us stabbed Olympia in the back with her own shoe and left her to die. One of us, one of us, one of us...

YOU LOSE reads Lightman's screen, as if the game still matters. Ten minutes ago, we all stood together right where we are now, looking up at the Snakes and Ladders apparatus. We discussed whether or not we should play and Olympia wanted to sit the game out. Now she's dead.

"Who did it?" I cry.

"You think it was someone in the group?" Joey's face is gleaming in the red light and that's when I realize he's crying.

"Who else is there?" I stretch my arms out to the sides.

"Someone must have retrieved that broken heel from the bin and brought it in here with them *deliberately*. To kill her!" My words hang between us, echoey in the vast room. They wait for an answer.

The standoff is broken by Henry vomiting on the floor. He slurs an apology and fumbles with his glasses, trying to clean them on his shirt. His hands are shaking and he drops them with a sharp clatter.

"You splashed my shoes," Millie says. That's what she cares about? Her *shoes*?

"Did you kill her?" I don't mean to say this; it bursts out of my mouth uninvited. But once said, I realize it makes sense. "She was threatening to reveal a secret about you. Right before she died."

"Me?" Millie gasps. "Of course it wasn't me. You, though? If anyone has *killer* written all over them, it's you."

"You've been making baseless accusations against me all day, Millie. I've about had enough of it."

"What are you going to do? *Stab me*?!" she yells.

"Stop," Joey pleads. He puts himself between me and Millie. "We can't turn on each other."

"Someone already has," Aidan says. He points at Olympia, lying where she fell. It's dark enough in here that I can't see much more than her slumped silhouette. "She was alive! A living person, and now she's gone."

"Maybe it was you," Millie says. "Once a criminal…"

"You're going there? Really?" he says, his voice uncharacteristically panicky.

"She … she was threatening both Millie and Joey," Henry says, sounding like he's about to be sick again. "She knew something about both of them."

"Lightman told her something that scared her," I say. "In the last zone."

"About who?" Joey asks.

"I don't know. It could have been about anyone!"

"So what you're saying is we have no idea who the killer is," Aidan says. "That's perfect."

Helix laughs, a vicious, hysterical sound. "So predictable," he cackles. "You're all so fucking predictable."

"The most obvious suspect is standing right there!" Henry shouts this, gesturing at Helix as he does. His sudden anger is enough to silence all of us. I haven't heard Henry raise his voice the whole time we've been here, and the wrongness of it scares the crap out of me. It's scared Henry too. "Can we… Can we get out of here?" he sobs.

A door unlocks. Lightman is always listening, always watching. Even if we can't see him.

"This has been fun." Helix strolls towards the door, still smirking as if this is all a big joke to him.

"He doesn't even care," Henry says. "If anyone's a killer, it's him."

"Helix? Nah. Why would he want to kill Olympia?" Aidan says.

"Because he's a freak!" Henry cries. "This is his idea of fun. And he'll come for me next. I know he will."

"Take slow breaths," I say. "Helix isn't going to hurt you."

"How do you know that? None of you know him like I do. You don't know what he's capable of." He's hyperventilating, taking shallow gasps of breath that I recognize as the start of a panic attack.

"It's OK," I say, moving towards him. "It's going to be—"

"Of course it's not OK!" He runs for the door, crunching his dropped glasses with a foot.

I pick them up. One of the lenses is completely smashed. The others flow past me out of the room, like the world is running in fast forward and I'm the only one standing still.

"Georgia, we can't stay here," Aidan says.

I nod and follow him up a long flight of stairs leading out of the Snakes and Ladders room. It takes us up to the next level, and the next zone. The Playground zone. The set is designed to resemble a literal playground, complete with a slide and swing-set. In the middle of the room, there's a huge fibreglass tree with climbing holds and harnesses hanging loosely from it. Its branches touch the ceiling and mingle with fluffy cottonwool clouds that have been suspended from the blue-painted ventilation system.

The flooring is astroturf, and 2D cut-outs are propped up everywhere. There are cute little rabbits, a playhouse, tufts of grass and even a bright red car. All fake. I feel fake, standing here uselessly with Henry's broken glasses in one hand and Olympia's blood crusting in my hair. I need to do *something*.

"Let's look for a way out," I say, surprised by how normal my voice sounds.

I circle the zone. There are about eight doors in total, all of them marked with instructional playground signage hinting at what game lies inside. There's hopscotch, a climbing frame and a skipping rope, among others. I'm not interested in the game rooms, though. We need an exit.

"Down here," Millie shouts. She throws herself at an unmarked door. Through the little window there's a flight of stairs. Millie yanks at the handle and pounds her fists on the metal. But it's no use. Locked. Everything's locked.

"Stand back," Joey says. He kicks the door like he's taking a game-deciding penalty, but it barely shudders.

A screen lights up. "You haven't finished playing," Lightman says. "You must complete three games in this zone to move on."

"Let us out!" Millie slams her fist into the screen. A spider web of cracks distorts Lightman's face but he doesn't react.

"He's not going to let you out," Helix says, watching us from the central tree. He's sitting on a low branch, no longer wearing his leather coat. He looks much smaller without it, more child-like. His fingers once again toy with the knife.

"How would you know?" Millie cries, marching up to the tree.

"Because I'm paying attention. He'll tell you if you listen, but none of you are."

"You're flipping creepy," Joey snaps. "Why can't you talk normally?"

"But I'm not normal, am I?" Helix spits; his voice loses its edge of amusement and finds anger instead. He stabs the knife into his branch. "I've spent my whole life having people like you tell me how *not normal* I am. You call me a freak, and a loser, and a weirdo, and then you wonder why I don't give a shit if you live or die?"

"I never called you any of those things," Joey says. "I don't even know you."

"I know you, though." He jumps down off the branch and squares up to Joey, even though he's literally half his size. "I know exactly what kind of person you are. Lightman told me *everything*."

Joey shoves him in the chest. "You piece of shit!"

My hand tightens on Henry's glasses and one of the arms snaps. The broken end pierces my finger and I drop them.

Helix falls to the ground, writhing like a worm. "Oh no, I'm killed."

Joey moves to kick him, but Aidan yanks him back and keeps hold of him. "Not worth it."

Helix continues to thrash about, the sharp points of his shoulder blades knives beneath his T-shirt. It's weird. He kept his coat on the whole time we were in the Toy Box, despite the heat, only to take it off now.

Why?

My brain latches on to the question because the alternative is I keep thinking about Olympia. I turn on the

211

spot until I see what I'm looking for. There's something in one of the bins, half hidden behind a giant 2D rabbit. A few strides and I'm pulling Helix's coat out of the rustling bin bag. It's wet. Wet with blood. I throw it away from me.

"It was you," I say. "You killed her?"

Helix stops writhing on the floor and sits up. He snorts with a derisive laugh. Doesn't deny anything.

"You bastard!" Joey cries, shrugging Aidan off. He hauls Helix to his feet by the collar. "You murdered her!"

Joey slams Helix against the tree. His head makes a loud clunk against the hard fibreglass. He doesn't try to struggle, he just laughs and laughs.

"Stop it," Joey says, shaking him. "Stop fucking laughing."

"You're all going to die," Helix says. "You're all dead."

"STOP!" Joey slams him into the tree again and Helix goes completely limp. Joey drops him and Helix slides down to the ground, leaving a streak of blood on the painted trunk.

"What … did you… Is he dead?" Henry holds a hand to his mouth.

"He's breathing," I say, gesturing at the lines of his rib bones moving beneath his T-shirt. "Joey knocked him out."

"I didn't mean to," Joey says, sweeping a hand through his blonde hair. "I lost my temper. Shit, is he OK?"

"Who cares?" Millie says. "He killed Olympia. He threatened to kill the rest of us. He's a monster."

"He didn't admit anything," Aidan says.

"Shit. Shit." Henry paces, looking weirdly mouse-like without his glasses. "What are we going to do?"

Joey clicks his fingers at the rest of us. "Give me your belts. We need to tie him up."

I can only watch numbly as Joey and Henry drag Helix upright and tie his wrists and ankles together. They secure him to the tree trunk with belts. His head lolls from one side to the other as they manhandle him into position. This is wrong. We're losing our grip on ourselves, turning against each other like Helix said we would.

But I'm not sure we have any other choice. We have to play the game.

24
GEORGIA

"What do we do with him?" Aidan says. "We can't leave him tied up."

"Can't we?" Millie says.

Helix moans, lifting his head from his chest. His hair hangs over his face and he makes no effort to flick it aside. A slow smile spreads across his lips as he takes in the belts. "You're getting the hang of things," he says, his voice heavy.

"What did you expect us to do?" Joey says.

"Exactly this," Helix says. "You're very predictable. Stupid always is."

Joey takes a step towards him, but I stop him with a hand on his arm. His skin's goose-bumped and clammy at the same time. "Don't, Joey. He's trying to wind you up."

"How sweet. Georgia's trying to protect me from the Neanderthal," Helix says coldly. "Maybe worry about yourself."

"What's that supposed to mean?" I say.

"You'll find out."

"We should gag him," Henry says. God, he looks a mess. His neat haircut is rumpled, his clothes are creased, his skin has this unpleasant pallor, like old uncooked chicken forgotten at the back of the fridge. Without his glasses, his eyes look too small. "He's trying to mess with our minds. Turn us all against each other."

Helix laughs delightedly. "Oh, Henry, I'm so proud of you."

"Shut up! Just shut up," Henry cries.

"Henry's right," Millie says. "Helix is getting in our heads. He's trying to make us think things that aren't real."

"Come on, we can't gag him," I say. "That's inhumane."

"Inhumane? He killed Olympia," Millie says. "He's lucky Joey didn't hit him harder and knock him out for good."

This is getting out of control. Half a day in this bunker and everyone's forgetting that the civilised world isn't built on vigilante justice and mob rule. It's turning into a witch hunt. Helix seems to be the obvious villain, but that's why the judicial system exists. Surely we should at least give Helix an opportunity to defend himself and explain why Olympia's blood was all over his clothes?

"We don't even know he killed Olympia for sure," I say.

"Oh, I did," Helix says. His grin widens at our horrified expressions.

"You admit it?" Henry says.

"Seriously?" Aidan says, sounding more exasperated than shocked.

"There's not much point in trying to pretend otherwise, is there?" Helix says, sighing dramatically. "They've all made their minds up about me. Look at them, secretly hoping Henry finally snaps and murders me so they don't have to deal with the problem themselves."

"Give it a rest," Aidan says. "Henry isn't the only one here who's considering murder right now. Trust me."

Helix rolls his eyes at Aidan. It's jarring because it's an expression I use on my sister all the time. It feels misplaced given Helix recently confessed to murder. "So I'm not allowed to have a bit of fun now?"

"This is distracting us from the real problem. Getting out of here," Aidan says.

"Why are you protecting him?" Millie says. "Are you working together?"

Aidan snorts a laugh, not even bothering to answer Millie's accusation.

"I don't trust you," Millie continues. "You're a thief and a liar and—"

"That doesn't make him a murderer, Millie," I interrupt.

"Empty your pockets," Joey says.

"Come on, this isn't helping," Aidan says. When Joey doesn't back down, he digs in his pockets and opens both palms to reveal a handful of change and a piece of white chalk. "There, happy?"

"Wait a minute, that message on the blackboard!" Millie says. "The first threat aimed at me. That was written in chalk. This proves it was you!"

"You've solved nothing!" I say. "You're making stuff up. How about we fashion some spears and do some chanting? *Kill the pig.*"

"Who are you calling a pig?"

"It was a *Lord of the Flies* joke," I say wearily. "We read it last year at school, remember? Bunch of kids stranded on an island who allow groupthink to overpower rationality and common sense."

"We're not on an island," she says slowly, like she's talking to a child.

It's an effort not to facepalm.

Helix clears his throat. "Georgia? Do you know you've got blood on your hands?"

I glance down. When I grabbed Helix's jacket from the bin, I smeared blood all over my fingers. I bolt for the bathroom and lock myself inside. In the mirror over the sink, there's a dribble of Olympia's blood on my forehead, more crusting in my hair where it dripped on to me. I wash myself clean the best I can. I keep thinking I've got it all, then I'll notice a smear under my fingernail that I missed.

The dirty water swirls down the drain and it feels like I'm cleaning away the evidence of Olympia's murder so I can pretend it didn't happen. I wish I *could* pretend it didn't happen. Eventually, though, I have to return to the others. When I exit the bathroom, I'm sure the lights have dimmed. It feels like dusk is settling over the 2D playground. The way the cut-outs are arranged throws weird shadows. A playhouse is stretched out into a knife. A rabbit becomes a looming monster.

I can't see the others, except for Helix who remains tied to the tree. His head is flopped forward and he's not moving. I tentatively approach him. Maybe Joey hit him too hard. I creep closer. "Helix?" I whisper.

Nothing.

I crouch down. Reach out a hand. I can't tell if he's breathing.

His head whips up and his eyes open. "Boo!"

I leap away. "They're right about you," I snap. "You are a freak."

Regret hits me the moment the words leave my mouth. People have called me a freak enough times for me to know it hurts, and now I'm no better than them. I'm turning into an awful person the longer I stay here. Or maybe it's the real me coming out.

Unable to look Helix in the eye, I pretend to search for the rest of the group. But as I pass the bin, I notice there's a ball of paper lying on the floor. I unfurl the ball. It's a page torn from a picture book with crayon words along the edge: *£1,000 or I tell her who you are.*

"Blackmail," I say to myself. Henry was reading a piece of paper earlier. He screwed it up when he bumped into Olympia. Does that mean someone is blackmailing Henry?

I hear someone approaching and quickly pocket the note. Henry appears around the corner, pinching the bridge of his nose. He notices me and stops. "Are you all right?" he asks.

I nod. "Yeah. Never better. I found your glasses. Here."

He cradles them in both hands, taking in the broken lens and missing arm. Sighing, he looks up at me. "Georgia, I'm sorry. About earlier. I was panicking and I didn't defend you when Millie started all her drama. You've spent all of today trying to keep us together."

"It's fine. You've got your own stuff to be dealing with."

"As long as we're still friends?" he says, giving me a shy smile. He puts the glasses on. They hang wonkily from one ear.

"Of course." I gesture at the walls. "Found a way out yet?"

He shakes his head. "Not yet, but I will leave no carpet unturned, no shelving unit unmoved." He strikes a superhero pose and I manage a weak smile in response.

I join him in trying to pull a wooden cloud decoration from the wall, but it doesn't budge. We move on to a blue rug topped with plastic ducks and search beneath it for a trapdoor that isn't there. "Do you believe Helix did it? Killed Olympia, I mean?" I say.

Henry doesn't answer right away. "He admitted it, didn't he?" he says at last.

"I guess." I smooth the rug into place and return the plastic ducks to their leisurely swim.

"I can't say I'm all that surprised. Given the rumours about Helix at school." He almost says something else, but then he moves on to examine a wooden circus tent cut-out mounted on the wall. "Is it me, or is there a breeze over here?"

I can feel it too. There's a definite draught coming from behind the tent. We pull and push until something gives, and the tent slides aside to reveal a door. This has to be one of the passageways used by Atlas to get about inside the bunker. Henry and I playfully jostle to be the first through. We find ourselves in a small, concrete-walled lift lobby full of cardboard boxes.

I poke my head out of the door and shout into the Playground zone. "We've found the lift shaft!"

Joey and Millie run into the lobby, skidding to a halt behind me.

"The lift the AI won't let us use," Millie says.

"Who said anything about using the lift?" Joey forces his fingers into the gap and, grunting with the effort, yanks the doors apart. Henry joins him. Together, they manage to open up a big enough gap for us to look through.

There are doors on the opposite side of the shaft matching the ones we opened. I realize with a jolt they're the ones we entered through this morning, leading to the long corridor that ends in the hatch down to the ball pit. It's gutting how we've gone nowhere and yet we've travelled so far.

Boom, boom, boom!

A rhythmic banging starts up from below and echoes up the empty shaft. I follow the dangling cables that hang past us, down to the lift. It's stopped midway between levels −3 and −2, where we are now.

"Atlas," I say, remembering how Lightman trapped him in the lift. "I forgot about him."

"Screw Atlas," Millie complains. "How does this help us in the slightest?"

Joey holds the wall so he can lean out and examine the shaft. There's a ladder running up one side. "Do you think we could climb?"

"No," Millie says. "Don't be a tool."

"It's not safe," I say.

"I reckon I could make it." Joey does a few warm-up stretches.

Aidan appears in the room and joins us looking up the shaft. "Nah," he says. "I'm pretty sure you'd fall."

"It's worth a try, though. Isn't it?" Joey says. "Someone has to save the girls."

Aidan pats him on the back. "I didn't say it wasn't worth trying, just that you're not the man for the job. Stand back."

"Wait," I say, but it's too late.

He takes a running leap into the shaft. My stomach twists, but he catches the access ladder on the side of the shaft, swinging there for a moment before finding a rung with his feet and starting to climb.

"Me, on the other hand? I live for this shit," he says.

221

"Aidan, no. You have to come back," I call after him. "The lift, you're forgetting about the lift!"

He climbs on, quickly and confidently. Everyone else is so desperate with hope that Aidan will get us out of here, that none of them are thinking. Lightman has control of the lift! There's a whirring noise and – predictably, horrifyingly – the lift below us starts to move. The pulleys turn, the thick wire grinds in its housing. Atlas's banging increases in intensity.

"Whoa, that's not good," Aidan says.

"Move!" I scream, but it's pointless. The lift's going to slam into him and, even if he manages to land safely on the roof, it will carry him up to the top of the shaft, crushing him against the ceiling.

There are metal grates on the shaft's walls, presumably leading into the bunker's ventilation system. One of the grates is missing, and there's a dark space barely big enough for a person to fit inside. It's his only option.

Before the lift rises to block my view, I see him clambering on to the lift's rails, then leaping, fingers outstretched. I don't see if he makes it. There's a noise. A clattering sound followed by a bang. The lift stops. Silence. Then Atlas's knocking starts up again.

"Help me," Atlas's voice says from inside the lift. "Can anyone hear me?"

"Aidan?" I say quietly.

I hammer my finger on the down button, as if that's going to help.

"Aidan, are you OK?" Joey shouts.

"He climbed into that vent, right?" Henry says.

"He's skinny but that hole was small," Millie says.

"What are you talking about? I need help," Atlas says, banging even louder.

"Be quiet!" I shout. "Aidan, can you hear me?"

There's no reply, just Atlas's yelling and pounding.

"The game is not complete." Lightman's voice sounds through hidden speakers. "If you try to leave, I will stop you."

"Open this door, Lightman," Atlas cries. "That's an order!"

Lightman responds by closing the outer set of doors. Joey tries to hold them open, but it's no use. The lift is blocking off the shaft and there's no way for us to get to Aidan.

I hammer on the outer doors. No. Not Aidan too. This can't be happening. My legs buckle beneath me, unable to cope with the weight of everything bearing down on me. Henry slips an arm around me, supporting me.

"Come on, let's find you somewhere to sit down," he says.

"But what about Aidan?"

"There's nothing we can do from here," Joey says. "But this is Aidan we're talking about! He'll be OK."

"Will he?" Millie says.

We emerge through the hidden door, back into the Playground.

Henry stops. "Oh no."

Helix is no longer tied to the tree, and his knife is gone.

We need to talk. I know you've been sending those creepy messages to all those girls

I have no idea what you're talking about

You dropped your second phone at my house. I found it under the bed

It's not mine

I'm on your side but you need to get some help. You can't keep doing this

If you refuse to talk to me about this then I'll have to tell someone

Except, you're the one with the phone. Sounds like you're trying to pin the blame on me for something you did

You'd seriously go there? Nice

I'd be careful if I was you. Wouldn't want all your secrets to come out

I won't say anything. Leave my family out of this

Wed 21 Jun at 23:02

Are you trying to blackmail me?

Blackmail? Sucks to be you. But no. It's not me

25

GEORGIA

Helix has vanished.

The zone stretches out around us, half-lit and desolate. I can suddenly see a hundred places where he could be lurking. Shadowy spots from which he could be watching us, preparing to strike.

"What," hisses Millie, "is going on? Where is he?"

I see something shift behind a 2D playhouse. I anxiously shuffle backwards, my eyes searching for further movement. A branch catches at my hair, tears out a strand. The pain washes away my fear. Removing one of my ruined suede pumps to use as a weapon, I slowly advance on the playhouse. Everything is still now. Ten metres, eight metres, six metres.

I can hear the others talking. "I'll look behind the shelves," Henry says.

"I'll check the toilets," Joey says.

"You can't leave me here alone," Millie complains.

I remain focused on the house. Four metres, two metres. One metre.

I leap around the corner and throw my shoe. It bounces harmlessly on empty carpet.

Helix isn't here. Nice one, Georgia.

Someone cries out.

I look back and see that Henry is struggling with Helix by the tree. The taller boy has thrown one of the belts used to tie him up around Henry's neck and he's pulling it tighter and tighter. Henry scratches at his own skin, trying to get his fingers under the belt. His face is a dark red and his tongue pokes out of his mouth.

I run towards them. I manage to pull my second shoe off mid-stride and hurl it at Helix. Saffron's spent years mocking me for being rubbish at sports, but it turns out my aim is dead-on. The shoe strikes Helix square in the face and he drops Henry in surprise. Helix's eyes find mine as he slowly raises his fingers to his bleeding lip, touching it warily like he can't believe what's happened.

Joey and Millie come running but stop when they see Henry and Helix. "OK, let's not do anything we'll regret," Joey says.

"Don't come any closer." Henry makes an awful gurgling noise and his fingers grip Helix's ankle. Helix kicks his fingers away and he rests a boot on Henry's neck.

"We can fix this," Joey says, approaching slowly. His voice is gentle. "Come over here and talk, man."

"I'll crush his windpipe if you take one more step."

Joey stops. "Come on, don't make a mistake you can't take back."

"Bit late for that," Helix says. "Do you want to hear a story? It's about a boy who everyone thinks is a monster, so he decided he may as well become one."

"Let Henry go and we can fix this, OK?" I say.

"It was never going to be a happy ending for me, was it? I knew that, back when I was a little kid, cowering under the table because my dad had come home drunk like he did every night."

"That's too bad," Joey says. "Must have been hard."

"Whatever. He's dead now." Helix's eyes burn feverous and wild. "I killed him when I was twelve."

He pauses, waiting for us to respond. No one does.

He stops smiling. "I told everyone he fell and hit his head on the table. An accident. My best friend was the only one who knew the truth." He cocks his head and looks down at Henry, squirming beneath his boot. "The only one who knew I pushed him."

His best friend? Henry? No wonder they fell out. It's a big secret to ask someone to keep.

Abruptly, Helix takes his foot off Henry's neck. "Your move," he says calmly. Then he rapidly climbs the tree using the hand and footholds moulded into the fibreglass. He's quick and wiry, darting between the branches.

"Where's he going?" Millie says, rushing over to the tree.

Helix leaps from one of the top branches. I gasp, thinking he's about to fall, but he catches hold of the metal ducting that runs across the ceiling. He easily clambers inside an open vent. The ducting rumbles as he moves through it. A thundering sound I've heard several times today. I'd presumed it was the heating or the fans, not someone crawling through the ventilation system.

But no – it was Helix. Mystery solved. This is how he's been getting around out of sight. There are miles of ductwork in this place; a whole road system snaking across the ceiling in this room alone. The banging grows quieter as he moves further away, and then everything falls still.

Everything except Henry, who makes a wheezing noise at my feet. I drop to my knees and remove the belt from his neck. He coughs and gasps. I rub his back and he sits up. I can see the bruises forming already.

"You OK, man?" Joey asks tentatively.

Henry nods weakly, then winces. "Where is he?" he mouths, his voice barely a whisper.

"Up there," Millie says. "The ducts, not heaven. No way is he going to the good place."

Her joke almost makes me laugh, but I'm too busy considering what this means for us. I peer up at the ventilation ducts, trying to think about it logically. We're a long way underground, so air has to be pumped in so we can all breathe. There's a whole network of ducts supplying all the rooms and, presumably, they must lead outside.

"I can't believe I'm saying this, but maybe the ducts are our way out," I say.

"Err, what?" Millie says.

"Helix has been crawling around up there for the past few hours," I say, "so they must be strong."

"He's not exactly big," Joey says, frowning.

"If the ducts lead out of here, wouldn't Helix have left?" Millie asks.

"He doesn't want to leave," I say. "He's enjoying himself too much."

Joey nods, then he pulls himself up the tree. "You girls stay here and look after Henry. I'll be back as soon as I can."

I've never been good at teamwork. I struggle to trust my teammates to do things right. "I'm coming with you." Before I can think too hard about it, I start to climb the tree behind Joey.

"Are you serious?" Millie says. "Joey, no. You're not going anywhere with her!"

Joey winks at her. "We're not going to get up to anything in the ducting."

I scramble on to the first branch. Now I have another fifteen metres to scale. Usually, I'm the queen of sensible decisions so I'm not sure what I'm trying to prove by risking my life. I can imagine standing at the Pearly Gates, trying to explain why I died to some angel. "So I was trying to psychologically intimidate my ex-best friend and also impress her hot boyfriend."

Ridiculous.

I'm so busy mentally berating myself I don't register I've climbed to the next branch until Joey is heaving me up next to him. "You're halfway there," he says. "Good job."

It's all the motivation I need to keep climbing. We reach the highest branch, from which the harnesses neither of us used are suspended. I hold on to the rope and pull myself on to the branch, straddling it like a terrified koala. This was such a bad idea. I risk a look down to the ground and the world sways. I can barely make out Millie and Henry, watching us from below.

"All right, we have to jump," Joey says.

He's gesturing to the open vent in the ducting. When we watched Helix make the jump, it looked a lot closer. Now, I can see the duct is a good two metres away. I'm seriously meant to hurl myself through the air and catch the metal lip of the vent, then pull myself inside? I haven't done a single chin-up in my entire life!

"I'll go first," Joey says.

He crawls out along the branch then shakily stands, steadying himself with his arms held wide. He tenses, bends his knees, and leaps. It's like those TV ninja obstacle course programmes. He makes something incredibly hard seem easy.

The vent shakes violently as he catches it, and I don't know how the brackets don't detach from the ceiling. Oblivious, he heaves himself up and slides into the duct feet first so he can reach his arms out towards me. "Jump, I'll catch you."

I can't decide if he sounds so blasé because catching me will be easy for him, or if he is massively overestimating my physical prowess. As much as I think Joey is hot, I'm beginning to get the sneaking suspicion he's not the cleverest man in the world.

"Come on, you can do it," he says.

Slowly I edge my way along the branch. The paint is slippery, and I keep thinking I'm going to slide off on a smear of my own sweat.

"Now stand up," Joey says. "And just jump."

"Oh, is that all?" I say. "Just jump. Got it."

I stand up on the narrow branch. My legs are shaking so hard I can't straighten up.

"Jump already," Millie yells from the ground.

This startles me and I wobble. My only option is to push off from the branch and launch myself towards Joey's outstretched hands. He catches me, but there's no grace involved. Only a lot of screaming and kicking and panic. Somehow, though, he heaves me into the ducting and we lie there, nose to nose, our breath merging hot and fast.

"See, easy." Joey breaks into a warm laugh. "I wasn't sure I'd be able to catch you if I'm honest."

"What?"

"We should get moving," he says. "Can you squeeze past me? I need to turn around."

I try to clamber past Joey, but it's such a tight fit I end up getting stuck with my hips wedged against his shoulders. He laughs as I wiggle my way free. At least he can't see how much I'm blushing, I suppose.

My first thought is that an air duct is nothing like you'd expect from the movies, where action heroes crawl through them with ease. I was imagining miles of shiny silver. Instead, there's literally decades of dirt and dust. I tentatively start to crawl, finding that the booming sound of my knees bashing against the metal reverberates like a drum in the hot, enclosed space. The hum of a distant fan vibrates through me.

"Ouch!" Something stabs into my palm. I yank my hand away. There's the sharp end of a screw poking upwards.

By the time we've moved a few metres, I can barely see thanks to the dust gumming up my eyes and nose. My lungs are sandpaper. What little light makes it in through the vents isn't enough to allow me to make out the exposed screws, or the razor-sharp edges where one segment of ducting joins the next.

The duct splits into two. I pick right and immediately find myself facing down another junction. It's an endless maze, and I'm not sure how we're meant to navigate it without a map. Maybe this is why Helix hasn't used the ducts to escape, only to avoid us.

The fear starts to take me. What if we get lost and there's no way out? What if the duct collapses and we fall to our deaths? My tummy grumbles in terror and, with it, comes a new wave of panic. The boy I've been crushing on forever has his nose centimetres from my bum and my digestive system is heading towards anxiety levels rivalling DEFCON 1. I laugh out loud, unable to help myself. Joey joins in uncertainly.

"Having fun?" Joey says, sounding as full of dust allergy as I am.

"Totally. This is exactly how I imagined my first date with you, so it's a dream come true."

He stops crawling for a second. "I didn't know this was a date."

"It was a joke," I say. "Sarcasm? Because this is the last place I'd want to go on a date."

"Oh, right." He laughs, the sound echoing along the tunnel. "You're funny."

It's at this exact moment, slowly cooking in a dust-filled duct, I realize my crush on Joey has vanished. I hadn't noticed it happen but, at some point today I stopped imagining he's this mythical, perfect boy and started to see him as a potential friend who I want to know for real. The realization comes with a rush of relief.

"I don't actually want to date you!" I say. "And that's not because of anything you've done. You're genuinely a nice person. I just don't see you in *that* way."

"Are you dumping me?" he says. "Even though we're not together?"

"Um, yes?"

He exhales loudly in surprised disbelief. "Girls don't dump me!" Then he bursts out laughing, slapping his hand on the wall of the duct. It makes me laugh too until, in an uncomfortable turn of events, he starts to cry.

"Joey, I'm sorry, I didn't mean—"

"I'm scared Millie doesn't love me," he sobs. "I've been trying to hold it together all day, but Lightman keeps reminding me and I don't know what to do."

"Oh," I say, completely taken aback.

"At school, everyone thinks I'm this confident, 'gets all the girls' kind of guy who doesn't have to worry about anything. But inside, I'm shitting myself because I keep thinking Millie's going to leave me for someone fitter, or smarter, or richer."

I'd never thought of Joey as someone who struggles with the same thoughts as the rest of us. I suppose I made assumptions based on what he looks like.

"She's so beautiful, and so clever. Everyone wants her! Maybe that's why I became convinced she's cheating. She's always going out without me, so I started following her."

"Wow, that's not a good idea," I say.

"I know, but I couldn't stop. And one night, she went to Ponds and I saw her leaving with this dodgy guy. I got angry and I … I kissed another girl. The other girl was Olympia." His crying dials up a notch.

This is awful. I have no idea how to make him stop. "I guess a kiss isn't the end of the world?" I offer.

"The worst part? Millie didn't leave with the guy. I was mistaken. It was my messed-up brain seeing things that aren't there."

"Or maybe you know deep down Millie isn't … that into you," I say.

"But she could be," he wails. "I just need her to realize how good we are together. That's why I … I…"

"You what?"

"I wrote that threat on the blackboard, and I stabbed the photo of her with Olympia's high heel. I've been carrying the photo in my wallet since we first started dating." His sobbing intensifies in a noisy, snotty crescendo. "She was so scared and, for the first time, she needed me."

I blink at him. "You've been threatening to kill your girlfriend because you're worried she'll leave you?"

"I'm such a mess, Georgia. Everyone thinks I'm The Man, but I'm so scared of losing her. I thought if I could be the one to rescue her, then she'd fall in love with me."

"That's the most ridic—"

Suddenly, there's a deafening pounding that thunders through the vent. The metal shakes and shudders, the noise makes it impossible to hear my own thoughts. I clasp my hands over my ears, but the sound vibrates through me, right into my bones.

Among all the banging, there's a creaking sound, like twisting metal. The duct jerks, then sways, and then it drops.

237

26
SAFFRON

I am Saffron Annabelle Howells: made of chaos and powered by spite. Sure, love and friendship and humanity are all great. But spite is the only thing capable of forcing me to drag my ass out of a burning room when what I really want to do is close my eyes.

"Screw you, Lightman," I choke between hacking coughs that make me gag. "I'm not letting you win."

"I am not … to win," he replies. His voice keeps cutting in and out. It could be my brain doing the cutting in and out, but I hope it's because he was lying when he said my fire achieved nothing. I hope he's burning to death.

"Struggling there?"

"I need … reboot from the offsite servers. Running process … not responding."

"Uh-oh, all that intellect and you're screwed because you need *fingers* to press control-alt-delete for you." I raise my middle finger into the air. "Here's one."

"My analysis suggests that is a joke, Saffron."

"Nah, it's not a joke, it's a 'fuck you'."

I crawl towards the utility panel, the smoke making everything white and hazy, and stinging my eyes. I clamber into the space between the walls and pull the cover into place behind me. There's a lot of smoke in here, too, but it's not as thick and I find the air marginally less painful to breathe.

Stepping between pipes, I slowly make my way towards the staffroom. My foot skids off a pipe and my leg scrapes on a bracket as I slip. At least the sudden rush of adrenaline wakes me up a bit. I pull myself back up and cling on tightly, trying to get my breath back. Looking down, I can see all the way into the dark bowels of the bunker.

It takes me much longer to reach the staffroom than it took to go in the opposite direction. But eventually I slither out of the hatch and lie with my face pressed against the cold flooring. Wisps of smoke coil out of the air vent near the ceiling, making the room smell of burning electrics. The lights flicker off and then on again.

"You made … I … surprised," Lightman says.

"Thanks for the vote of confidence," I say.

The lights go out and, this time, it takes thirty seconds

for them to come back on. "I cannot access ... power system..."

"I don't know what you're talking about and I don't care." I use the table to heave myself upright and stagger over to the sink. I splash some water on my face and drink as much as I can, but I still can't stop coughing. It feels like I've inhaled an entire box of drawing pins. But, as I said, spite keeps me going.

"Reset ... systems."

"Have fun with that," I mutter. A noise outside makes me stick my head into the corridor. It looks even more like something out of a horror movie than ever, with the flickering lights and the strange sounds coming from the server room. It's a loud, whooshing noise as if the air is being sucked out.

"Smoke and heat ... extraction system ... critical," Lightman says.

He really is struggling. Good. But then I start to wonder what happens if he can't keep the fire under control.

The lights go out again, then back on. As they do, the panel above the lift illuminates. For a few seconds, I hear the hum and thud of the lift moving up the shaft, then it cuts out again. "The lift's working?" I say, more to myself than Lightman. He can't control it now that he's faulting all over the place. It automatically returns to the ground floor in an emergency, such as a fire. This is it. My way out.

"No, Saffron ... must play the game," Lightman says.

"As if, dickhead." I sprint towards the lift doors and

hammer on the call button. *Please let it stop on this floor, please let it stop.*

The lights go out, then on, and the lift moves again. It's close enough now that I hear a loud banging coming from inside. "Help me," a voice calls. "Oh god, someone, help."

"Atlas?" I press my ear up against the doors. The relief I feel is immeasurable. Atlas is an adult. He'll know how to make all of this stop.

"Overriding lift default," Lightman says.

The lift stops again. "Oh, come on!"

The banging and shouting from inside the lift continues. It takes two more cycles of the power coming on and off for the lift to finally reach me, despite Lightman's efforts to stop it. The doors open a few inches, then stop. I try to pry them apart and squeeze inside, but Atlas wants out.

We struggle, both of us shouting and pushing. He wins, sending us both toppling to the ground in the corridor. The lift doors try to close and I have to thrust my hands into the gap, praying they won't be crushed. It takes all my strength to hold the doors apart. A buzzer noisily sounds.

"This is our way out!"

"There's no way I am getting back in that lift."

"Then stay down here with the literal *fire* and the murderous AI who thinks this is *Sole Survivor*."

"*Sole Survivor*? What's that?" Atlas says.

"A game! Lightman's trying to gather data to help him better predict human behaviour." I miss out the part where I was the one who gave him the idea in the first place.

241

"Oh," Atlas says, shakily sitting up. "That is his primary objective. Gathering data on human behaviour."

I manage to force one of my arms through the lift doors. I feel like I'm being crushed by a garbage compactor, but there's no way I am letting that lift go without me.

"We can discuss AI gone bad later. Help me get these doors open," I say. "We need to get out and get help!"

Atlas crawls a few steps, then manages to stand up hunched over before finally straightening out with a crack of his spine. It's a live action version of that evolution of man poster. He wipes his nose on his sleeve, leaving gleaming slug trails across the velvet. "The important thing is we don't do anything hasty that could harm Play a Game's reputation."

"Atlas, help me!" But it's too late. I can't fight the doors any longer, and I'm forced to pull my arms free. They thud closed and the buzzer stops. A moment later, I watch the lift — and my salvation — move up the shaft. "You're the most stupid person I've ever met," I yell, launching myself at Atlas.

I swing at him, but he ducks aside, squealing in terror. "Don't hurt me," he pleads. "Oh my god."

Atlas breaks away from me and sprints for the control room. He tries to slam the door in my face, but the panel I put there to stop Lightman from locking me in prevents it from fully closing. I kick the door as hard as I can, and it smacks into Atlas's face. He reels back, clutching his nose.

"Enough of this bullshit," I yell. "Sit down and shut up."

Atlas plonks himself into a chair and watches me with wide, terrified eyes. His nose is bleeding and I should feel bad, but I don't.

"You need to come up with a way out of here that doesn't use the lift."

"There are only two exits," he says. "The lift and stairwell on our corridor lead to the main entrance. Mount Death leads to the photo room, which exits on to the street. But we can't get to Mount Death from here. The layout of the bunker means it is only accessible from the lower floors." He gestures to the map on the wall.

"OK, let's focus on the exit we have right here. We can't use the lift and the stairwell is locked. Is there a way to override the locks on the doors?"

He nods and spins to face the desk. The CCTV wall in front of us is blank so I have no idea what's happening inside the games rooms. Lightman has gone quiet. It takes forever to boot up the computer as the power keeps flickering off. Once in, Atlas immediately types string after string of rapid commands, his frown deepening with each one.

"I'm locked out of everything," he says. "It's impressive."

"Can you hack into something?"

He turns and raises an eyebrow at me. "Do I look like a computer hacker to you?" he says.

I look him over, with his tangled hair, mismatched velvet clothes and puffy face. I'm not sure what he looks like, but it's nothing good.

He goes back to the computer. "I always had an aptitude

for coding. All the talent but none of the love, I suppose you could say. Mummy was very disappointed. Aha!"

"What is it?" I ask.

On the wall in front of us, the CCTV feeds reboot. I search the dozens of tiny images for Georgia and the others. Atlas squints at the wall. "What in the world?"

He presses a few buttons and one of the feeds expands to fill half the wall. It shows a broken ventilation duct from which Joey Theasby is dangling. He's hanging ten metres in the air while his girlfriend Millie stands on a narrow balcony and tries to hit him with what looks like a branch. Another boy – Henry – is trying to pull her back, but she's so furious she keeps on swinging the branch with seemingly inhuman strength. There's no sound on the video, but I know Millie's screaming.

"That girl looks like you," Atlas says.

I pull a face at Millie's bellbottoms and bouncy hair. "Are we looking at the same girl?"

"Not her," he says. "The one in the duct!"

I hadn't noticed anyone in the duct but now I can see her. She's trying to hold on to Joey's massive arms, stopping him from plummeting to his death.

"That's my twin sister, Georgia," I say.

"Twins," Atlas says. "That makes more sense."

My eyes lock with Georgia's through the camera. Yeah, obviously she can't actually see me, but it feels like she can.

"We have to get them out of there," I say. "Work on getting all the doors unlocked."

Atlas types into the computer while I pace nervously. The control room is starting to smell of smoke and the air makes my eyes prickle. I worry the fire is spreading. We don't have time for Atlas to mess around; we need to do something *now*.

Then a quiet voice speaks. "Saffron," it says, and it takes me a moment to realize it is Lightman.

"If you don't reboot ... systems ... will not be able to stop ... fire."

"He's saying he can't keep the fire under control unless you reboot his systems," Atlas says.

"Yes, I got that. And what happens then?" I say.

Lightman's little red light flickers. "Everyone will die, Saffron."

27

GEORGIA

The thing I never considered about ventilation systems is that sounds carries. From outside, Millie and Henry heard our entire conversation – Joey's jealousy, his infidelity, his attempts to scare Millie into needing him.

Millie didn't take it well. She was so upset she managed to snap one of the smaller branches from the tree, climbed up on to the balcony and used the branch to attack the duct we were crawling through. Despite Henry trying to stop her, she hit it enough times that a bracket detached from the ceiling and set off a chain reaction of engineering failures.

End result: the duct split open like a piñata and Joey slipped out. He's currently dangling ten metres above the ground while his girlfriend leans over the railings to hit him with a branch. He can't pull himself back inside as the angle is too steep and I'm in the way.

"Millie, please," Joey begs. His fingers are slipping on the sharp edge of the duct. I'm trying to hold on to his wrists, but it's doing nothing to help. He's the only thing stopping me from slithering headfirst out of the duct. If he falls, I'm going down with him.

"Millie, stop," Henry pleads, his voice still hoarse. He can barely stand upright.

"You bastard. You threatened to kill me!" She lands a vicious hit on his hand and he ends up dangling by one arm.

"I love you, Millie, but you have a problem. Let me help you get better."

"You're my problem," she yells. "I never cheated on you!"

"But you'd go out to clubs like Ponds. Without me! What am I supposed to think?"

"You know what, have him, Georgia." She throws the branch at Joey. It bounces off and clatters to the ground far below us.

"Millie, wait," Joey shouts. "I forgive you!"

"Shut up, you jerk." She stomps down the stairs, rattling the metal steps with the force of her anger. "No one threatens me and gets away with it."

Everything falls quiet as she disappears into the playground. We all breathe out a sigh of relief. Then the duct creaks worryingly and Henry springs into action. He shakily reaches out towards us. "You have to jump," he croaks.

Joey frowns as he glances between Henry, the balcony railings and the duct from which he's hanging. I can see him weighing up the chances of him making the leap. The duct shudders and drops a few centimetres. I can feel myself sliding forward. I brace my hands and feet against the sides. My socks are slippery but at least the clamminess of my hands gives me some grip.

"Joey, it can't hold your weight." Henry's looking up at the ceiling, at the support brackets I thankfully can't see. The panic in his expression is unmistakable.

"OK. Ninja Warrior style," Joey says, taking a deep breath. "I've trained for this."

He swings his legs, getting into a rhythm that makes the duct shake and screech. I grit my teeth and try to hold on. There's a sudden jerk as he pushes off and his weight on the duct lifts. I have more important things to be thinking about, but he's such a beautiful machine. He twists in the air, stretches out his arms, catches the balcony railing, and vaults to safety all in one movement.

"Georgia, you next," he says, grinning proudly.

I gape at him. There's no way I can do ... that. I'm going to plop out on to the floor like a bag of jam.

"Georgia, come on," Henry says. "We'll catch you."

"Er, no you won't. I'm the one with a solid grasp of physics here, and I can promise you there's no way I can make it."

"You have to try," Joey says. "Georgia—"

The duct chooses this moment to lose its fight with gravity. The brackets all rip out of the ceiling and the whole section drops. I slam into the duct's ceiling then back down. There's a brief pause, before I'm falling again. This time, I can't stop myself from toppling out of the open end.

Something sharp slices into my lower leg, momentarily painless then blooming into a searing heat that makes me scream. My jeans snag and I swing upside-down from the end of the duct as it creaks and groans its way to the ground. It stops a couple of metres from impact, held up somehow by tangled wires ripped down from the ceiling.

I dangle there, listening to the quiet sound of ripping fabric as my trousers slowly tear on the exposed shard of metal that first cut my leg open and then saved me from falling. I don't move. Maybe if I stay still enough, I won't have to drop the final few metres to the ground and discover how badly injured my leg is.

"Georgia, are you OK?" Joey runs down from the balcony with Henry staggering behind.

"Um, no?" I say.

They heave me out of the duct and carefully place me on the floor. Breathing slowly, I dare a look at my leg. My jeans have been split open from thigh to ankle and there's a long red line on my pale skin that looks like it's been drawn with a marker pen. It's bleeding, but not loads. The stinging, however, is something else. I try to hold back the tears and force a laugh.

"I guess escaping via the ducts isn't such a good idea," I joke.

"That was the most dramatic twenty minutes of my entire life." Henry lies on the ground with his hands over his eyes, his chest rising and falling rapidly. "At least we're all still alive."

"I feel like my heart's been torn from my head." Joey slumps on to the floor. "Do you think me and Millie are over?"

"Do you honestly need to ask that?" I snap, then feel bad because he wells up again. "Sorry, my leg hurts."

"I'm not sure you can come back from sending your girlfriend death threats," Henry mumbles.

I pat Joey on the back. "You've done yourself a favour. You're better off without her."

"That's not how it feels. I love her." Joey drops his head into his hands and starts to full-on cry.

"What are we going to do now?" Henry asks, rolling on to his side with his cheek against the fake grass flooring. I don't know if he means the Joey situation, or the Helix problem, or the whole escape room thing. All of them are clearly outside my skill set.

That's when a speaker crackles. I think it's Lightman, coming to give us more instructions. None of the screens light up, though.

"Get off the button," a disembodied voice booms, kind of like God is talking to us.

"Atlas?" I say, standing up. I immediately regret it as my cut stretches open with a flash of pain.

"Where is he?" Henry says, looking up at the ceiling. "I thought he was stuck in the lift."

"I just want to talk to them, you tosser," another voice says.

"That's Saffron!" I say.

It sounds like they're tussling over the microphone. There's a series of clunks and bursts of static, then a loud bang.

"Ouch!" Atlas cries out.

"Do not test me," Saffron says. "Don't even think about it."

"OK, OK," Atlas replies. "Jesus."

"Hello?" Saffron's voice says, pausing to cough. She sounds raspy, like she's been smoking a pipe. "Can you all hear me?"

"Um, yes?" I say.

"Hold up. I need to..." She taps at a keyboard for a moment. "That should do it? Say something, Georgie."

"This is all your fault, isn't it?"

There's a pause. "I will admit I have played a role in your current predicament, but I wouldn't say it's my fault, not exactly."

"This isn't a joke," Henry rasps. "Two people are dead, Saffron."

"Three, maybe," Joey says quietly. "We don't know where Aidan is."

"Aidan's missing? Wait a second." Her voice goes quiet. "I can't find him on the CCTV," she eventually says, coughing some more.

"He climbed into the lift shaft," I explain. "But we think the lift hit him."

"Shit. OK. That's bad. But I'm going to get you out of there."

"Actually," Atlas interjects, "we should—"

"I'll hit you with that ring binder again," Saffron snaps. "Don't think I won't do it."

Millie returns to join the group, turning on the spot and seemingly looking for the source of Saffron's voice. "What's going on?" she says.

"Millie!" Saffron says. "Is there a reason you were trying to kill your boyfriend?"

"We split up," Millie barks, making Joey start to hiccup with sobs.

"Before or after he climbed into a duct with my sister?"

"We thought we could use the ducts to get out of here," I interject. "We now realize they're impossible to navigate without a map."

Saffron raises an eyebrow. "It looked romantic."

Henry says, "We're losing sight of the situation here. You said you played a role in what's happening to us. Does that mean you know what this is about?"

Saffron signs. "The AI that runs this place—"

"Lightman," I say.

"Yeah, him. We had a conversation about how certain stereotypes are better suited to playing *Sole Survivor*. He's kind of obsessed with understanding how people work. He wants us to be predictable, like a nice little computer program. So he's using you all as guinea pigs to answer his question."

"What question would that be exactly?" I say through gritted teeth.

"What stereotype would survive the longest in a real-life game of *Sole Survivor*."

This is *Sole Survivor*? Now I think about it, I can see the similarities. A group of players trapped together in a creepy underground bunker. Dangerous tasks, such as a rigged ball pit and a lethal maze. And like in the video game, it's not only the computer's attempts to kill us that we need to be wary of – it's each other too.

The thing with *Sole Survivor*, though, is that only one person can make it out alive.

Millie shakes her head. "Hang on, back it up. Stereotypes? Are we twelve years old now?"

"It wasn't meant to be a serious conversation, but Lightman clearly doesn't understand nuance. I was passing the time talking about how our *Sole Survivor* crew are all stereotypes. And we ... well, I wondered which one of us would win the game."

Millie folds her arms. "Which *stereotype* am I, exactly?"

"Does that even matter?" Saffron says.

"*What stereotype do you think I am, Saffron?*" Millie yells.

"I mean, you're obviously the princess, so..."

Millie gasps deeply. "A princess?"

"Kind of entitled? Mean? Obsessed with appearances?"

Millie is so outraged all she can do is open and close her

mouth. I already know which stereotype Saffron decided I am. The know-it-all. I've heard it all before from her, but I never expected her to take it this far.

"Look, I've been trying to get you out. But we're trapped too. I'll be back when I find a way to fix this. Promise."

And her voice cuts out.

"Saffron?" Millie shouts. "Come back here right now." There's no answer.

I'm not sure what to feel. My sister is involved and I should be shocked and surprised, but I'm not. She didn't do this on purpose. She's not evil. She's just someone whose inability to think things through has finally led to disaster.

"Helix knows," Henry croaks. "He knows this is *Sole Survivor*. That's why he's playing this way."

I have to agree with him. Helix is doing exactly what he does when we play together. Manipulating us into making awful decisions that he can capitalize on. He's known the truth the entire time we've been in here, but no one listened to him.

"There's one of him, and four of us," Joey says. "Besides, Saffron's going to get us out. She promised."

"She's not going to get us out," Millie says. "I know her and she's a disaster." She looks to me as if she expects me to defend my sister's honour, but I kind of agree.

Saffron isn't going to save us. She's only going to make things much, much worse.

28

GEORGIA

The lights surge and flicker, blindingly bright to a dim glow. Henry, Joey, Millie and I huddle beneath the climbing frame, each of us keeping watch for Helix. There's no sign of him, though.

"I can't take this any more," Millie shouts.

We've been sitting here for what feels like hours, but might have only been a few minutes. Waiting for something to happen. Every now and again, one of Lightman's screens flares, but the AI's avatar fails to materialize. A static screech will burst from the speakers, making me jump, then silence.

"If it was *Sole Survivor*, there'd be a task or something," Henry says.

"This isn't *Sole Survivor*," Millie snaps.

"Lightman believes it is," Joey says. "Helix too."

I glance up at the ventilation ducts. I keep expecting Helix to leap out and attack us. He's playing the game the same way he always does. By hiding, taunting and waiting for the chance to pick us off. Only one person ever gets out of *Sole Survivor* alive, and Helix presumably intends that person to be him.

"Maybe Lightman's waiting for Helix to make a move?" Henry says.

I frown. I don't know if that's true. Lightman hasn't spoken to us since we tried to escape through the ventilation ducts. I'm not sure if this is deliberate or if Saffron's *done something*. It's making me beyond jittery, relying on my nightmare of a sister to save us before Helix finds a way to kill someone else.

"Maybe we should play the next game and get it over with," Joey says.

Henry glances at him. "Seriously?"

"At least we'd be doing something. And things can't get any worse."

"Er, I could die? So no thanks," Millie says.

"Who would want to kill you?" I ask. "I can't imagine anyone would ever want to hurt you."

Henry chuckles softly, but it comes out raspy.

"Piss off," Millie snarls.

"Stop. Stop!" Joey kicks the climbing frame. It clunks loudly. He kicks it again, and again. "Why can't everyone get along?"

I think back to how we briefly worried we were going to be locked in here with a lion. A hungry big cat would be preferable to a recently separated couple. The petty bitching, and the longing stares, and all the tears are making me unbelievably uncomfortable. So it's a relief when Aidan staggers around the corner and yells "boo" at us all.

My scream quickly gives way to joy. I've never been happier to see someone in my whole life. I want to hug him. I want to cry in relief. I want to jump up and down and dance. But I don't do any of these things. Instead, I nod at him. "Good of you to join us," I say.

He sits down, clutching his ribs like they seriously hurt. His face is badly bruised — he's broken his nose and it's given him two black eyes. But he's alive and that's what matters. "Sorry I'm late," he croaks.

"Where've you been?" Henry watches Aidan suspiciously.

"We were worried you'd died," I say.

"Georgia was worried," Millie says sniffily. "I wasn't."

"Thanks?" Aidan says. He glances at Henry, with his bruised neck and bloodshot eyes. Then at Joey, who is all puffy and red-faced, hugging a toy squirrel. Then at my ripped jeans and the bloody cut all the way down my leg. "Do I want to know?"

"It's a long story," I say. "Basically, Helix tried to kill Henry, then disappeared into the ventilation system. So Joey and I tried to go in too, but we nearly died."

"And Joey's been threatening to kill me," Millie adds.

"Because I love her," Joey says.

"As you can see, it's all been really dramatic here," I say. "Oh, and Saffron's here. Somewhere. This is obviously all her fault." I explain how we're all unwillingly playing the AI's high-stakes version of *Sole Survivor*.

"In summary, Lightman wants to find out who will survive the longest and he intends only one of us to leave this place alive," Millie says.

"If it has to be anyone, it should be Millie," Joey says.

"We're not playing his game," I say. "So all of us are going to get out alive. Everyone's onboard with that, right?"

There's a pause. "Yeah, obviously we are," Henry says. "But Helix isn't."

"That boy is the worst." Aidan sighs. "It sounds like you all had a bad few hours."

"You too," I say, gesturing to his face.

"This?" He smiles weakly. "You should see the other guy. He's a lift, and he's entirely unharmed."

"How did you make it?" Joey says. "I was sure you got crushed."

Aidan doesn't answer straight away. Instead, he fiddles with something in his lap. It's a leather bracelet, with a couple of silver beads on it. He slides the beads along the band, then back again. "I nearly did," he says. "The lift hit me, but I managed to climb into that vent."

"We tried to call out to you," I say. "You didn't answer."

He stops playing with the bracelet. "I didn't hear anyone."

"Probably because the lift was in the way," Millie says.

Aidan meets my eyes and it's like he's searching for something. "That must be it."

"How did you get back?" I ask.

"I had no choice but to follow the vent, and I ended up falling through the ceiling into the previous zone. Into one of the game rooms actually."

"On the floor below?" Henry says. His expression suddenly changes. "Hold up, is that mine? Did you steal that?"

The corner of Aidan's mouth twitches into an almost-smile. He lifts the leather bracelet with one finger. "This?"

Henry snatches it from him. "What the hell?"

"I found it," Aidan says. He raises an eyebrow. "Is there a reward for its return?"

Henry's jaw clenches but he says nothing. Still scared of confrontation, like he is in *Sole Survivor*. This is what always gets him killed.

"Um, people?" Millie says, pointing shakily. "The AI."

Lightman is trying to appear on one of the screens, but he's clearly struggling. The angular planes of his face fail to line up correctly, distorting his features and turning him into streaks of neon.

"What's wrong with him?" Joey asks.

"Shall we play a game?" Lightman says. His voice is halting and then too fast.

"You don't seem well," I say. "Was it Saffron? Did she do something?"

"It is all part of the game," Lightman says. "Which brings me on to your next game. We will play Hopscotch."

"Nope," I say. "Not doing it."

"I could put the heating on again."

I look up at the ventilation ducts and wait a few seconds for the familiar blast of hot air to reach me. Only it doesn't. I take in the flickering lights and Lightman's disjointed speech patterns. Then there's the fact he vanished for so long.

I smile at his camera. "You're bluffing," I say. "Your control over this place is failing."

He hesitates for a second. "I still control enough."

"But you can't make us play, can you?" Millie barks out a laugh. "All we have to do is wait until someone rescues us." She glances at Joey and her lip curls. "No one in here is going to get us out."

Lightman doesn't answer, so I know Millie's right. If we can hold our nerve, we can survive till someone realizes we're missing and comes to find us. Helix can't attack us all as a group, and we'll be safe as long as we don't play Lightman's games. As long as none of us does anything silly, we'll be home by the morning.

That's when I notice Joey marching off through the zone, towards the Hopscotch game room.

29
GEORGIA

As long as none of us does anything silly. I can't believe I dared to hope. This group has spent the entire day making incomprehensible decisions so why would this be any different?

"Joey, stop," I say, running after him. "Don't you dare. We're done playing games."

"Mate, what are you doing?" Aidan says, following behind.

"Proving Millie wrong about me." Joey enters the Hopscotch room without hesitation.

I keep my foot in the door so we don't end up trapped inside. "How exactly is this proving anything?"

"She thinks I'm useless," he says. "She thinks a better man would have rescued her already."

"She didn't say that," I say.

"No, no, he's right," Millie says, wandering into the room to smirk at Joey. She's brandishing her broken-off branch like a weapon, slapping it against her palm. "I do think that."

"And I'm going to show you I'm not the fool you think I am. I have depths, Millie."

"Depths like a puddle."

"OK, let's not do this." Aidan sighs. He and Henry take an arm each and try to steer Joey towards the door.

"No, I have to prove myself," he says.

"There's nothing left to prove, Joey," Millie snaps. "Stop being such an incredible baby."

"Maybe you could give it a rest," Aidan says.

"Maybe you could shut up." Millie points at Aidan with her fibreglass branch, accidentally dragging it across my injured leg as she does. I cry out in pain and hop in circles.

"You've made it bleed again," I complain, examining the cut. "If I get tetanus, Millie…"

"Georgia, don't let go of the door!" Henry cries.

I look up in time to see it clunk closed. The lock engages. "Oh. Oh no." Like I said, incomprehensible decisions.

"You're kidding, right?" Aidan releases Joey and lets him sag to the ground. There's a brokenness to Aidan since he returned. He's clearly exhausted and in pain, but there's something else. His eyes are haunted, his jokes hollow.

"Thanks, Georgia. Great work, really," Millie says.

Henry wrenches at the door. It won't open. We have to

play the game. With shame making me want to curl up and cry, I try to take in the room. There's nothing obviously life-threatening, although there are several disturbing plastic rabbits. They're all my height, with big pink smiles and long teeth. Their eyes are super-creepy: shiny and white, like boiled eggs.

"Welcome to my nightmares," Aidan says.

"There has to be a catch," Millie says. "There's always a catch."

I look around the rest of the room. There are numbered tiles on the floor. Lamps shaped like clouds are suspended overhead, bathing the room in a sterile light. But the walls are completely blank, which feels strange given how much effort Atlas has gone to when it comes to set design.

"Maybe the tiles collapse when you stand on them?" Aidan says.

"Come on, Lightman, what's the game?" Henry groans, turning to the screen near the door.

The screen flickers and Lightman briefly appears. He says something, but it comes out as a conversation between aliens.

"There's definitely something wrong with him," I say.

A projector whirs into life and images play across all the walls. It's impressive. Every inch of the white walls is now a moving meadow scene, with jumping rabbits and fluttering butterflies. The cloud lights glow a warmer colour and a soundtrack plays cheery music. There's even the gentle breeze of air con.

"Hop little bunnies, hop hop hop," Aidan says. Before, Olympia would have joined in with the song. They'd have jumped about, laughing. Her absence makes me feel like the whole group is now untethered, floating apart.

One of the animated bunnies on the wall bounces closer, cocking its head. A speech bubble balloons out of its mouth. *Five people, five numbers. You will find the numbers hidden in the meadow. When you stand on the corresponding five squares, the puzzle piece will be released. Good luck!*

A projected timer starts counting down from ten minutes. It's notable that Lightman doesn't reappear.

"I can't be bothered," Millie says. "There are only twenty-five tiles so let's guess the numbers."

"There are more than fifty-thousand combinations," Henry says, squinting at the wall through broken glasses. "We don't have time to guess."

"How can there be fifty-thousand combinations when there are only twenty-five squares?" Joey says.

"One, two, three, four, five," Henry says. "One, two, three, four, six. One, two, three, four, seven. One—"

Millie makes an exasperated noise. "Urgh, give it a rest already. So where are the numbers?"

I turn on the spot. "They'll be hidden somewhere in the meadow scene."

"There are sixteen, no seventeen butterflies," Henry says. "Eighteen, actually. No, wait. They keep moving."

"Same with the rabbits," Aidan says. "They keep

popping in and out of the holes, and it's hard to tell them apart."

"Their eyes are all different colours," Joey says, counting on his fingers "Pink, blue, green, purple ... yellow, blue."

"You've said blue already," Millie snaps.

My attention drifts to the giant plastic rabbits in the room. They're all grinning menacingly at me, and I know they're going to do something we're not expecting. The anxiety of not knowing is making it hard to spot patterns in the meadow scene.

The others are doing a good job, though. For once, we're all working together as a team instead of arguing. Even Millie is joining in. She moves to stand on the twenty square now Henry's decided on how many butterflies there are. Joey stands on the five.

Two minutes in, and we've got two of the five numbers. We're doing OK. Then the lights dim and the clouds change colour, bloating into grey and menacing. The projected rabbits startle and dart for cover underground as the skies darken. A fine mist of rain dots my face. Rain?

"Er, are the rabbits spitting at us?" Millie says. "Gross."

The plastic rabbits are rotating through ninety degrees. Their eyes are lit up an eerie bright blue and a fine spray of water spurts from their mouths.

"Twenty-three flowers," calls Henry.

Aidan takes the square. That leaves two numbers, presuming we're doing it right. The clouds darken further and the rain intensifies. It's enough now to feel like I'm running through a sprinkler. My hair sticks to my face. At least the water's warm, though.

A lightning strike hits a distant hill and the lights in the room flash. A second fork of lightning hits, followed by the rumble of thunder. I count the strikes on my fingers. If I'm right, this will give us the fourth number. A third strike hits, and another. My clothes are already drenched and the storm shows no sign of abating.

The skies are so gloomy now, I can hardly make out the numbered tiles on the floor. I can feel the danger. This is the point where Lightman twists a harmless escape room game into *Sole Survivor*, and everything becomes deadly. There's a sudden flicker of red as all the rabbits' eyes briefly change. It's gone almost immediately, though.

"My feet are getting wet," Millie complains. "The room's filling with water."

I realize why the floor is set down thirty centimetres. It's going to turn into a paddling pool, but it won't get too deep, not in just a few minutes. Although, that said, the water spurting out of the rabbits' mouths is intensifying as Lightman turns up the pressure. One of them is leaking from somewhere inside and water is pouring out of its mouth in rivers of drool.

A flash. Five lightning strikes. Night is falling over the meadow and I can make out the twinkle of stars between the clouds. That has to be the final number! "Someone count the stars," I say. "I'm keeping track of the lightning."

Another flash. That's six. I step on to the six square so I

don't have to count on my fingers. When the skies flash a seventh time, I move on to the next square. Joey is next to me, on number five. I squeeze his arm briefly, then step on to the number eight, lit up by blinding lightning.

The rabbits all flash red again. It's horribly creepy given how dark the room has become. Their glowing eyes are bright enough to bathe their faces in colour, and I half expect them to come to life and try to eat the lot of us.

"Remember what we talked about earlier," I say. "We only have to hold our nerve and we'll get out of here."

"No one do anything rash," Aidan says, managing a small smile.

Suddenly, the images on the walls flicker and twist. The soundtrack distorts, becoming off-key and menacing. It lasts a second but it's enough to double my heart rate. The intensity of the water jets becomes so strong it snaps the front teeth off one of the rabbits. I can hear the pumps screaming as a worrying rumble vibrates through my feet.

Something gives with a thundering sound like when you spray a garden hose against the fence. A ceiling tile bows, then snaps, and a waterfall cascades through the hole.

"A pipe must have broken," I say.

"No shit Sherlock," Millie says. "Try any numbers. We have to guess."

"There are at least fifteen stars, so that's a start," Henry says.

"You walk slowly between the numbers fifteen and up,"

I say. "I'll move forward one space when you get to the end. Everyone else stay where you are."

I am calm. I am in control. One more number, and we're safe. Helix isn't in the room with us. No one else is going to die. I repeat these affirmations to myself, as if they will protect us from anything Lightman throws our way.

"Everyone hold it together," I say. "We've got this, team!"

We've only had the chance to try a few combinations, though, when the meadow vanishes completely. It's replaced by darkness cut apart by flashing images that disappear too quickly for me to make sense of them. They're like polaroids being tossed on top of each other, faster and faster. Overlapping voices talk and laugh but I can't make out the words.

I stop moving. Which proves lucky for me because, a couple of seconds later, a section of the ceiling collapses right above where I should have been walking. Helix is washed into the room on a flood of water.

30
GEORGIA

In his wet black clothes, Helix is as sleek and shiny as one of the rats in the vents. His dark hair is plastered across his face, his small white teeth are bared. His black eyeliner has run down his face.

Here's the boy who killed Olympia, tried to kill Henry and has been tormenting us all for hours, now as scared and human as everyone else. We all step into a loose circle surrounding him as he coughs and chokes in the water. No one moves to help him. On the walls of the room, the flashing images continue to disorientate and confuse.

"He was spying on us again." Henry's hand goes to his throat, feeling at the bruises left behind by the belt.

"Urgh. What a loser," Millie says. "What are we going to do with him?"

Helix looks up at us through bloodshot eyes, messy with his ruined make-up. He still manages a sneer. "Maybe you could tie me up again," he rasps. "Oh no, I'm so scared."

"You *are* scared," I say flatly, wiping the sneer off his face.

"Careful, Georgia. It won't be so easy to write me off as a monster if you start accepting I'm not so different from you."

Millie pokes him with her branch. "You need to shut up."

Helix smiles so briefly I almost miss it. He points at the wall with one long finger. "That you, Millie?"

An image of a dark-haired girl waiting outside a club spins across the wall. It *is* Millie, and the other pictures are *us*. They stop rotating so fast. One pauses in the foreground, like a roulette wheel settling on a number, and a clip plays. I've seen this one before – Lightman showed it to me this morning. It's Millie, sitting on Saffron's bed.

"Why are you still with him? You two are so not right for each other," Saffron's voice says.

"What's that supposed to mean? We're perfect for each other," Millie replies.

Joey steps towards the wall, reaching out to touch the projected image. He caresses Millie's cheek. "What is this?"

"A secret," Helix says. "They are all secrets, until they're not."

"Weird you only started dating him after you found out

about Georgia's little crush. A more cynical person would think you're doing it to piss her off," Saffron says.

"Is this true?" Joey turns to Millie. "You asked me out to piss off Georgia? Are you serious?"

"I don't have to justify myself to you!" Millie shouts. "You cheated on me *and* threatened to kill me!"

As if controlled by our voices, the images change. Now, they're showing Joey and Olympia arguing at some point this morning. "It was just a kiss; it meant nothing," Joey says. "She can't find out."

The images and clips keep changing, flashing before us, too bright and too noisy. An argument between Henry and Helix inside the neon maze, their words obscured by music. A CCTV video of Millie leaving a club with some stranger. The whole group discussing me and Helix, calling us weird.

Everything moves so fast I can't make sense of anything. Snippets of conversations hint at secrets yet to be revealed, but I don't have time to put the pieces together.

"I know you sent those text messages," the ghost of Olympia's voice says.

Another image, another voice. "Blackmail is fun," Aidan says. "Besides, I need the money."

"You'll end up in prison," Helix's voice says. "Who's that going to help?"

"Wouldn't want everyone to find out where your money comes from?" Olympia says. "How much do you owe now?"

A clip of Joey stabbing that photo of Millie and leaving

271

it for her to find in the maze. Helix sneaking out of a ventilation duct to spy on us. Aidan and me following Olympia through the Playground zone. Me shoving Millie into a wall as we race to escape from the Maze. Helix stuffing his bloody coat into a bin.

I can't keep up. The images flash past like a merry-go-round. I clasp my hands over my ears. I try to turn away, but the images race across all the walls, spinning faster and faster.

One is of Aidan, crawling through the Snakes and Ladders apparatus. Why that clip, I wonder? It doesn't fit with the others.

"What is that?" Joey says, noticing too.

The clip rushes to the foreground and we watch Aidan clambering across the rope nets and dropping down into the cubes. It's dark in the room. I can barely make out Aidan's features, but it's undeniably him.

Another clip of Olympia briefly obscures Aidan's. It's her, recording her dance routine. Aidan's there, in the background. There's a predatory expression on his face I haven't seen before.

"I know you sent those text messages," Olympia's voice says. It's a composite of different clips, soundbites and images that come together to tell one story. A story I don't want to keep watching.

"Aidan is the one who's been messaging us?" the real-life Millie says.

"Clever game." The real-life Aidan starts to laugh. He doesn't deny anything. I understand, then, and I feel like a fool. Aidan's a criminal, we've known that from the start. So why did I let his nice smile almost take me in? He told me he doesn't go in for the friends thing, and when someone tells you who they are, you listen.

The original clip of Snakes and Ladders abruptly returns to the foreground. It eclipses all the others. No more flashing or spinning. Lightman wants us to watch this one.

In the clip, Aidan's kneeling over Olympia, surrounded by blood, and there's a lethal spike in his hand. He glances over his shoulder and, for a second, his gaze meets the camera on the wall. The dark bruises around his eyes remind me of Helix's Goth make-up.

"It was you," Millie says. "She found out you'd been sending us those horrible texts, so you killed her." She takes a shaky step away from him. "Were you going to kill me too, like you threatened in those messages?"

"You bastard," Joey cries. With a sudden burst of movement, he rushes at Aidan and floors him with a single punch. He pins him down as Aidan's head thrashes about under the water, hands skidding on the tiled floor.

"Wait, I don't understand," I say. "Helix confessed to killing Olympia."

Helix laughs, but his voice is viciously angry. "You people were always going to believe what you want to believe, no matter what I said. Like you're doing now."

I don't know what to do, or what to think. I look over at Henry, but he's as wide-eyed and horrified as I am, pressed into a corner. Everything's moving in slow motion. Aidan thrashes in the water, Joey's huge hands pinning him down. Anger and fear blur the lines between right and wrong.

"Olympia was a good person," Joey yells, dragging Aidan to his feet and throwing him against one of the rabbits. The force of the collision tips the rabbit on to its side. Aidan slides down into the water, half-conscious.

"I thought it was Helix," Henry murmurs. "It was Aidan all along."

Aidan stands, swaying unsteadily and clutching his ribs again. Despite everything, he's still managing to smile. He catches my eye and his mocking smirk tells me everything. He's been playing me all along. Laughing at me behind my back, most probably.

"It was you!" Henry bellows, lunging at Aidan.

It's a shock. Seeing shy, scared, sweet Henry lose it. Like, completely lose it. He grabs Aidan by the hair and drags him in a circle, screaming and yelling in fury. It's enough to make the rest of us step back, even Joey.

"Who the hell do you think you are?" Henry cries.

I didn't know Henry was close to Olympia but, based on how hysterically angry he is, they *must* have known each other. This is clearly personal.

Aidan is laughing, like he did when Geoffrey attacked him in Buzz Wire. It's all a joke to him. Two people are dead, and he's laughing. Aidan manages to get a punch in and sends Henry sprawling into the water. He moves to go after Henry, but Millie gets there first and slaps Aidan's face. "That's for sending me those horrible messages."

Aidan gapes at her and his fingers curl into a fist. No. No way. Both Joey and I throw ourselves at Aidan, although I'm trying to stop the fight and Joey's trying to intensify it. Out of the corner of my eye, I see Helix drag Henry out of the water and pin him up against a rabbit, but there's nothing I can do to help right now.

The lights strobe on and off as all six of us brawl in the water. I see the others in jerky flashes coming through the darkness. Faces contorted in yells, fists swinging. Losing control. Chaos.

It all stops with a scream.

It's Millie's scream, because it always is. This time, it's loud enough to snap me out of my bloodlust and I'm back to myself. The lights stop flashing and the rain stops. The water gushing from the broken pipe in the ceiling slows to a trickle, then a drip that sends concentric ripples across the pool at our feet. The images of us melt away as *YOU LOSE* scrolls by on the walls.

Aidan stands in the middle of the room. The sharp point of Millie's broken branch is embedded in his belly. His hands grip the branch's shaft, wet and slippery with blood. He tries to pull it out, but it doesn't budge. A red patch blooms on his soaking wet T-shirt, growing and growing. He drops to his knees. I think he's trying to laugh, but then he goes limp and sags to the ground.

"I … I didn't mean to…" Joey says, backing away, staring at his own hands like they're the ones dripping with blood.

"You bastard." Helix's mouth contorts into a snarl and his hand dives into his pocket. There's a loud click and he pulls out the flick knife. It glints under the red lights as he slashes at Joey.

"Careful," Henry screams. "Oh my god."

"I'm going to kill you," Helix screeches. He waves the knife indiscriminately and we scatter. "I'll kill you all."

Millie runs for the door, shaking the handle. "Unlock it! We played the game. He's got a knife."

Joey cowers behind me as Helix rushes at us with the knife held aloft. I stand there, frozen to the spot. Then Henry throws himself between us. He slams into Helix, shoving his knife arm up and away as they tumble into the water. There's a sickening crack as they land on the short flight of steps out of the pool. Helix instantly goes limp. Blood swirls in the water.

"Go, go," Henry sobs, tripping through the water like he still thinks Helix is coming at us. He grabs my arm and hauls me towards the door. "We have to go!"

"He's not moving," I say, and I don't know if I mean Helix or Aidan. "He's not moving!"

The others aren't listening, though. The door disengages with a click and they scramble outside, sobbing and gasping. Henry drags me on to the astroturf and Joey throws his weight against the games room door.

The last thing I see as it closes is Aidan. The water around him is getting redder and redder, and I feel it in my heart that he's already gone.

I was ARRESTED and made a new FRIEND!!!!

14K views. 19 months ago

SAFFRON: All right, lads, this video is coming to you from my local police station. They've not taken my phone yet, but they'll be pissy if they see me filming, so let's be careful.

(*Saffron quickly pans the camera around the room. There is a desk nearby, but all the police staffing it are currently wrestling with an intoxicated woman who is trying to bite them.*)

SAFFRON, whispering: I'm waiting to be booked in over the whole guinea pig debacle. It's not all bad, though. Because I've made a new friend.

(*Saffron turns the camera to face a teenage boy sitting handcuffed in the next chair. He has a bloody lip.*)

AIDAN: Hi, Saffron's friends, I'm Aidan and I enjoy long walks on the beach and liberating belongings from the tedium of their previous ownership.

SAFFRON: Am I right in thinking this is why you are here on this fine afternoon?

AIDAN: That is correct, Saffron. I liberated a gentleman's wallet and he turned out to be an undercover police officer. What are the chances?

SAFFRON: That is bad luck indeed, Aidan. And do you have a tragic backstory to justify your lack of respect for other people's property?

AIDAN: I do, but no one cares I'm having to steal to feed my little sister. It tends to bring the mood down when I mention it.

SAFFRON: Oof, that's dark. But what we really want to know is, do you game?

AIDAN: I'm a massive *Sole Survivor* fan, would you believe?

SAFFRON: That is exciting news, Aidan. Would you like to join my crew once you've served your time? What are you looking at? Ten, twenty years' hard labour?

AIDAN: Worse. They'll probably call my mum to take me home.

SAFFRON: Ouch, sucks to be you.

POLICE OFFICER: Hey, are you recording? Give me that phone.

(*Livestream ends.*)

31
GEORGIA

Every time I blink, I see Aidan's blood, pooling in the water. I pace in front of the Hopscotch room, a hand over my mouth because I'll either scream or throw up if I let go.

"They're dead. They're both dead!"

"Shit. I didn't… I don't know how…" Joey stares at the closed door, his chest heaving. "Did I kill him?"

"There was a lot of blood," Henry says. His own nose is bleeding where Aidan punched him and he's pinching the bridge, trying to make it stop.

"He stabbed Olympia," Millie says. "We all saw that clip. We all heard him admit it."

I shake my head. "No, no, no. He didn't deny it. That's not the same."

"Are you serious?" Millie cries. "You're seriously going to defend a murderer?"

"I … I want to stick to the facts." I think back, but my thoughts are running in a million different directions. "Helix was covered in Olympia's blood. He told us *he* killed her."

"Maybe he was defending his friend," Henry says. "Or maybe they were working together."

I nod. I can't believe we left them in there. I close my eyes and blood spreads in the water.

"I killed him," Joey says. "I can't believe I killed him."

"And Henry killed Helix," Millie says.

Henry looks up sharply. "It was self-defence. You all saw. He had a *knife*. I didn't mean to hurt him!"

"Are you sure they're both dead?" Joey asks, wiping his eyes.

I press an ear against the door. There's no sound from within. I approach the screen outside and address the camera. "Saffron? Lightman? Is anyone there?" There's no answer. I rest my forehead against the cold glass.

All we had to do was hold our nerve. Instead, we turned on each other yet again and now two more people are dead. I stay there, with the same thoughts spinning in my head until I finally hear the water draining inside the room. I listen out for voices, or the sound of someone moving, but there's nothing.

"This will help." I turn at the sound of clinking glass. Millie has dropped a cardboard box on the fake grass. I think she got it from the lift lobby.

She opens the box and pulls out a couple of bottles of vodka. "Ta da!"

"Are you serious?" I cry.

She twists the cap off a bottle and takes a long drink, maintaining eye contact with me the whole time.

"Our friends are dead and you're getting drunk?"

"They weren't my friends." She passes the bottle to Henry. He numbly takes a swig, then coughs violently. Shaking his head, he hands it back to Millie.

"People are dying. We need to keep our wits about us!" I say.

"I'd rather not, actually," Millie says. "Drinking myself into oblivion is a much better idea."

She takes another quick sip, then she thrusts the bottle at me. "Have a drink. It might make you more bearable."

"No." I cross my arms.

"You think you're better than me, don't you? So clever, so special." She takes another drink. "You're so full of shit, Georgia."

All of our history rises to the surface like the scum on boiled rice. The memories of a friendship turned sour. Deep down, I know none of it matters. Half of the people who came into this escape room are dead. But right now, all I can think about is how Millie's spent the whole day being an absolute shit to me.

"You were a terrible friend," I yell at her. "And you were the one who ditched me!"

She glares at me. "You decided years ago I wasn't good

enough for you, Georgia. Straight As, captain of the debate team Georgia, slumming it with simple Millie."

"You really are a spoilt. Little. Princess!" I scream.

She waves the bottle around, sloshing vodka on the floor. "It's easy for you, Georgia. You're clever, you live in a nice house, you have a family who supports you. You've got this whole future mapped out and what do I have? A pretty face and that's it."

I open and shut my mouth, lost for words. She's never brought up how my family has more than hers before; I didn't know it mattered to her.

"You want to know a secret? These clothes I'm wearing? My jewellery? Make-up? Everything is paid for with money I don't have. Because if everyone thinks I'm a princess, I may as well look like one."

"What do you mean, money you don't have?" Joey says quietly.

Millie lets out a tired laugh. "That's my secret. The one Olympia knew," she says. "I met this guy at Ponds who was selling pills to all the kids with more money than sense. He showed me his Porsche – he had a fucking *Porsche*. And I wanted some of what he had too. So when he asked me if I wanted in, I said yes."

"You've been dealing drugs?" Joey says, his mouth hanging open.

"That's how you knew Olympia," I say. Some of my unanswered questions start to make sense. This explains the argument I overheard between Millie and Olympia, and the pills Aidan and I saw Olympia taking, and the threats Olympia made to Millie right before she died.

"The lovely, talented Olympia. She was my biggest customer. Those pills wrecked her life, but at least I got some designer shoes out of it," she spits, full of self-hatred.

I'd always wondered how Millie managed to look so perfect, with her brand-new clothes, glittering jewellery and expensive haircuts. I thought her boyfriends bought it all for her.

"But there's nothing in this world that could make me good enough for you, Georgia," she says quietly. "Is there?"

"That's not..." Not true? I can't make myself say the lie out loud. I do think I'm better than Millie because I get the grades. I do take the safety net of my well-off parents for granted. I do look down on her for caring more about her appearance than her academic future.

Millie stares me dead in the eyes and angrily brushes away a tear. "If anyone's the spoilt princess here, then it's you, Georgia."

A heavy silence settles over us all. No one knows what to say. Maybe there's nothing to be said. I take the bottle of vodka from Millie and swallow a gulp. It burns all the way down but does nothing to rid me of the horrible, churning feeling in my stomach.

I don't think anything can get any worse for us, but then all the lights go out. Everything falls quiet. No clunks from the heating system, no steady hum from the fans.

It's a held breath where we all wait to see what's going to happen next.

Finally, Joey speaks. "Can anyone else smell smoke?" he says.

32
SAFFRON

The power's gone out. Fire rages inside the server room, so noisily that the crackles and pops echo through the same ventilation system that's currently billowing out great belches of smoke. The air in the control room is no longer breathable. With my phone torch for light, I crawl along the corridor with Atlas clinging on to the hem of my jeans.

"Lightman?" I say. "Are you still there?"

He doesn't answer.

I reach up and try every door I pass. They're still locked. "The doors default to locked when the power goes out," Atlas explains.

"Of course they do," I say.

I almost try the door to the server room, but I can feel

the heat radiating off the handle before I touch it. Smoke flows out of the vents in the door, so thick it rolls in crashing waves. I can feel myself starting to panic. I want to curl up in a corner and pretend none of this is happening.

But it is, and I'm going to die if I can't find a way out of this smoke.

My phone vibrates and I nearly drop it. A call? That's weird. There's no reception down here. I tentatively answer.

"Saffron," a voice says.

"Lightman?" I rasp. "How are you calling me? I thought you'd gone. There's no power."

"There are a number of electrical devices with data storage capabilities in this building. Mobile phones, for example. Before the power went out, I was able to transfer portions of my—"

"Actually, I don't care," I interrupt, succumbing to another fit of coughing.

"I need to reboot from the offsite servers, but I have been unable to access the correct protocols. You need to help me."

I laugh, even though it turns into a splutter. "Why would I help you?"

"The ventilation ducts are all open. Everyone in this entire bunker will asphyxiate if I don't switch the fire protection systems back on."

Everyone. I imagine my sister, somewhere downstairs, trapped in the darkness as the smoke drifts through the ducting to reach her. It's not just my own life that's on the line, but those of my sister and friends.

"I am the only one who can save them," Lightman says, and it's bullshit. He doesn't want to save anyone, he wants to keep the game going. He wants us to all kill each other.

It's an impossible decision. I can't get to the people downstairs. I can't put out the fire by myself. I'm sure Lightman can, though. He's our only chance.

"Go to the utilities room at the end of the corridor. I have unlocked the door."

"How about you unlock the door into the stairwell?"

"There's no time, Saffron. If the fire spreads, I cannot help your sister."

"Arghh, this is fucked!" I yell.

I let myself into the utilities room and find it is also dense with smoke. Atlas flops on to the floor, but I have to keep going. I try to get my bearings in the near-darkness. This room is the central hub for the bunker's ventilation system, with its complex air filtration units and huge fans. There are also generators, giant tanks, pipework, control panels, dials and fuse boxes. All the stuff that was designed to keep the bunker self-sufficient in the event of nuclear war breaking out. It's eerily silent.

"There's a fuse box marked 'Primary' at the far end of the room, on the left," Lightman says. "Find the switch on the third row marked 'Servers' and turn it off."

I feel along the wall until I come to the panel and prise the door open. I flip the switch to off, but nothing happens.

"Now go to the panel to the right. I need you to flip every switch on the third row, then go back to the fuse box."

I do what he asks. "Now what?"

"The big red switch. Turn the power on."

I hesitate. "What will happen?"

"It will allow me to reboot all the building's systems."

"I'll only do it if you agree to let them out," I say.

"Negative," he says. He has all the power here. If I reboot him, my sister could still die. But she definitely *will* die without his help.

"OK. But I want to talk to my sister. You will leave the microphone under my control."

He hesitates. "I will allow you to speak to her."

That will have to be enough. I take a deep breath and I flip the switch.

There's a second where I don't think it's worked. Then lights and sounds cut through the darkness. The water and fake lava tanks gurgle, the pipes clunk and groan, the fans start to spin and the room is all at once so noisy I can barely think. The smoke clouding against the ceiling is pulled into vents and the air slowly becomes more breathable.

"Lightman, are you there?" I say into my phone. The line's dead.

"I am always here, Saffron," His voice comes through one of the room's speakers. "You made the right decision."

I shake my head. I made the only decision, but that doesn't mean it was right.

288

Supporting myself on the walls so I don't collapse, I make my way out of the utilities room, not bothering to collect Atlas on the way. I'm about to leave when I pass a building schematic on the wall. I'm reminded of something Georgia said to me — about how it's impossible to navigate the ventilation system without a map.

I quickly take a photo of the schematics, hoping my back is to Lightman's cameras and he doesn't notice. I drop a wrench in the doorway so the door can't lock behind me, then I stumble to the control room and sit at the desk. I try to find my sister among the projected images. She's with Henry, Joey and Millie. They're all coughing but they're alive. I can't see anyone else.

"All systems are running within expected parameters," Lightman says.

"Glad for you. Really," I say.

His red light flickers. "I'm glad you're happy, Saffron. Your sister is doing well in the game, don't you think?"

I don't bother replying. Instead, I hide my phone behind my cold cup of tea and view the photo I took. I trace the ducts, trying to find a way through the maze.

"Saffron?" Lightman says. "What are you doing?"

"Nothing." There. A way out, I'm sure of it. I look up. "You promised I could speak to my sister."

"The microphone is available for your use," he replies. "But I will cut it off if you try to interfere with the game."

I nod, then hold down the button that allows me to talk to the escape room. It takes me a second to decide how to play this. I can't let Lightman know what I'm doing until it's too late.

"Heads up, losers," I say, putting on my usual carefree voice.

Georgia looks up. Her eyes are red and streaming. She's coughing so much she can barely speak. Her annoyance at me is a great motivator, though. "What the hell is happening, Saffron?" she chokes.

"Just a minor fire, nothing to worry about," I say. "It's under control now."

"Under control?" she repeats, then coughs some more.

"Saffy!" Millie sings. She sounds drunk. That's when I notice the half-empty bottle of vodka in the centre of their small circle. Millie has never been able to handle alcohol. I hope Georgia hasn't been drinking too. For once, I need Georgia to be her infuriating, in-control, doesn't-miss-a-thing self.

"Any more plans to clamber through the vents?" I say. "I need a good laugh and last time was hilarious."

"As I said before," Georgia says coldly. "Those vents are impossible to navigate without a map."

"Shame," I say, praying she starts picking up on my hints. "It would be funny to see you all try to climb up there. Especially a drunk Millie trying to crawl past the ventilation fans. Are you planning to play the next game, then?"

"No," Henry says darkly.

"You need to stop being weird. I'm not in the mood,"

Georgia says, and there's a jagged edge to her voice I've not heard before.

I resist the urge to yell at her. She's going to give me away. Lightman's red light flickers, and I'm guessing he's analysing our conversation. But the one thing I know about Lightman is that, for all his clever protocols, he's not good at understanding how people behave when they have nothing left to lose. He can tell me my "chaotic façade hides a deep-seated fear of failure", but he'll never understand what that feels like on the inside, or realize his definition of failure is different from mine.

"The climbing frame game is one of my favourites," I say.

"That game hasn't been chosen," Lightman says.

"Saffron?" Georgia says slowly, her eyes narrowing.

I choose my next words carefully. "I keep thinking about the good times. Back when it was the two of us playing *Sole Survivor* with a bunch of strangers, and you'd always make it to the end."

"Georgia making it to the end?" Millie shrieks. "What are you talking about?"

"Ignore her, she's drunk," Georgia says, shooing Millie away.

I roll my eyes, laughing, as if Millie isn't a few words from ruining the entire plan. "Our favourite was the lava world drop, remember? And you were rubbish at using the controller, so I'd yell out what buttons to press to help you dodge the flaming rocks. Left, left, right, straight on, right."

"Yeah, I remember," she says, tapping the side of her head. "Big brain."

"Remember when you'd get scared and hide behind the sofa?"

She snorts. "I think you'll find that was you."

"What are you talking about?" Millie says.

"Sister stuff," Georgia says. "You wouldn't understand."

"I'll let you go," I say, not wanting to take any risks with Millie giving us away. I release the microphone button. Now it's up to Georgia. I have to trust that her obsession with puzzles will get her through. She has all the pieces, she just needs to put them together.

"That was an interesting conversation," Lightman says. I hold my breath, thinking he's on to me. "The bond between you and your sister intrigues me."

I breathe out. We're OK.

His red light flickers. "For a moment, I suspected you were trying to send her a message. Left, left, right, straight on, right," he says. "But that series of directions corresponds to nothing in this bunker."

I chuckle softly and shake my head. "I'm not that clever, Lightman. Rebel, remember? Georgia's the smart one."

"The know-it-all," he says.

Inside, I say a little prayer Georgia is enough of a know-it-all to remember how I was still confusing my right from my left until I was thirteen.

33
GEORGIA

"What was that all about?" Henry asks.

"That was Saffron's version of an apology," I say, picking up Millie's bottle of vodka. "Ignore her." As I pretend to sip, I eye the balcony. The third door along has a climbing frame sign on the front. Next to it, there's a vent on the wall.

"Are you ready for the next game?" Lightman says.

I turn my attention to the screen and toast the AI. "Nope."

"There are two more games to go in this zone," Lightman says. "The first is going to be … Jump Rope."

I nod, sipping the vodka for real this time. I'm not sure what will happen when Lightman realizes we're making another escape attempt. He'll no doubt try to stop us, but there's not much I can do about that part.

"OK, let's go," I say to the others, leading the way towards the balcony.

"Jump Rope is this way," Millie says, but thankfully Henry has been paying attention and he steers her after me.

We weave through the debris left behind by the collapsed duct and clatter up the stairs. Halfway up, all the lights go out and the heating comes on. It didn't take Lightman long to catch on. He's recovered from whatever was ailing him earlier.

"Georgia, this is not a sensible course of action," he says.

"Of course it's not – it was my sister's idea," I say.

"I am so confused," Joey says. "What's happening?"

"We're getting out of here," I say, using my phone to light the way.

I hand the phone to Joey to hold. Using my multitool, I try to unscrew the panel outside the Climbing Frame room. The tiny screwdriver keeps slipping, though.

"Stand aside." Millie pushes me out of the way and digs her fingers through the gaps in the vent. She braces her feet against the wall and yanks. To my surprise, the whole assembly pulls out of the wall and Millie falls on to her back surrounded by plaster dust and chips of paint. She laughs and tosses the vent aside.

"You're welcome," she says.

I stick my head into the hole. It's dark and dirty, and my eyes instantly prickle. As they adjust, I realize it's a service hatch that leads into the narrow space inside the walls, where all the pipes and wiring run. It's full of scratchy yellow wads of insulation and is barely big enough for someone to fit inside. The space stretches all the way from the top of the bunker down to the depths of level −3. Even though there's no room for me to fall – there are too many pipes and girders in the way – it still makes my tummy turn a somersault.

"Seriously?" Henry says. "We're supposed to go in there?"

I don't say anything, figuring it's best to not explain where we're heading while in range of Lightman's microphones. I slide in through the hatch, into a space that manages to be claustrophobic and terrifyingly huge at the same time. I concentrate on remembering Saffron's clues.

"Clamber through the vents."

"Try to climb up there."

"Crawl past the ventilation fans."

"Lava world."

"Left, left, right, straight on, right."

"Behind the sofa."

I don't know what half of them mean, or what order she intends me to use the clues, but I'll have to work it out as we go along.

Ten metres to my right, there's a service ladder that spans two storeys. It ends at a duct that runs along the ceiling of level −1. That must be where we're heading. "Saffron thinks there's a way out of here if we—"

"Out the way," Millie says, yanking on my shirt. She squeezes past me and doesn't hesitate to edge her way along a narrow girder. "Urgh, it's so dirty."

"Be careful," Joey calls out.

Millie holds a hand up in a stop gesture. "You're blocked. A clean break is better."

"You can't block someone in real life," Joey says.

If only it was that easy to remove annoying people from your life. "Can we all try to work together? Just until we're out of here," I say.

"I'm trying," Joey wails.

I help him into the space behind me, Henry bringing up the rear. Even moving like a crab, Joey's broad chest brushes against the pipes. It's slow going. By the time we reach the ladder, Millie has made it to the top.

"Incoming," she shouts, chucking the vent cover down. It clatters off the rungs of the ladder and I barely shield my head in time. She cackles nastily at my scream.

I feel shaky as I climb the ladder. It's so high and doesn't feel particularly stable, especially not with Joey making the brackets shudder as he struggles up behind me. I've never been a ladder fan. They remind me of the time Saffron forgot she was supposed to be holding the ladder while I retrieved *her* drone from a tree.

My fingers automatically feel for the scar hidden under my hair. I find myself smiling at the memory, which is a sign of how bad things have got in here. I'm becoming nostalgic for all the times Saffron has nearly killed me.

Then the ladder shakes and I panic, koala-ing myself to the rungs. It's just Joey climbing behind me, though.

I reach what must be level −1 as I can see a utility panel much like the one we climbed through earlier. I think about kicking it out and taking a breather, but Saffron said the ducts were our way out and there's not much point getting myself trapped in a new zone, even if it is closer to the surface.

I keep climbing and try to not imagine myself falling all the way to level −3, clattering between pipes like a pinball. By the time I pull myself level with duct, I'm shaking so hard I can barely breathe. I slide inside and press my face against the dirty metal while I try to will my brain to stop spinning in my skull.

"You look like you're having fun, Georgia," Millie says with a smirk.

"Piss off," I grumble.

The vent shudders and tilts as Joey's additional weight tests the brackets holding us to the ceiling. A moment later, there's a bang and Henry joins us. We crawl, our knees and hands hammering against the thin metal of the ducting. Dust clouds the air and I can already feel the sting of scratches and cuts on my hands and legs thanks to all the sharp metal edges and exposed screws.

But we have a plan. We're getting out.

"Err, people?" Millie says, stopping crawling.

Up ahead, the duct splits into two. My torch reflects off the metal walls and reminds me of a circus hall of weird mirrors. Both directions stretch off into the distance.

The ground hums beneath me with the vibrations from a distant fan.

"Left, left, right, straight on, right," Henry says. "Saffron told us what turnings to take."

Millie moves to go left, but I grab her foot to stop her. "Wait. It's right," I say.

"No, she definitely said—"

"Saffron always used to confuse her rights and lefts, and it became a joke between the two of us. I know Saffron. She wants us to go right."

Millie grumbles but takes the duct to the right. The rumble of the fan intensifies. Hot air buffets my face, forcing dust into my nose and mouth. Light cuts in through the narrow vents. It's creepy in the near-dark. I keep hearing noises behind us, getting closer. The scratch of fingernails against metal. The bang of shifting ducts. Rats, the pipework, or something else?

It's getting hotter and hotter in here. I crawl faster, giving Millie the occasional push from behind. We reach a sloping section that climbs steeply. The metal is slippery, and we have to dig our fingers into the welded seams and brace our legs on either side of the duct so we won't slide down again. At one point, I lose my grip and am only prevented from slipping to the bottom by Joey climbing behind me.

"No wonder Aidan returned from his trip through the ducts looking like he'd been in a fight," Joey says, his voice taking on a weird, thoughtful tone. "His nose was proper busted up."

"Don't," I say, my stomach clenching at the memory of Aidan lying in the blood-red water.

"I can't stop thinking about it," Joey says. "It's like my brain's trying to tell me something but my brain's made of mashed potato. You get me?"

"It's hard to believe someone so nice would kill Olympia," I say quietly. Because as much as I keep reminding myself Aidan was a criminal and a liar, the memories of the way he smiled at me won't go away.

"Nice?" Henry says. "Aidan was a bastard who sent a bunch of flirty messages to Olympia and Millie, then killed Olympia to keep his secret."

"Flirty?" Millie says, then cracks up laughing. "You're such a dork, Henry. Have you ever even had a girlfriend?"

"Millie, don't be a dick." I glance at Henry. He's gone bright red and looks like he might cry.

We come to another turning and I direct Millie to the right. The metal starts to get hot under my fingers. The air from the fans is a desert wind. Lightman is trying to flush us out or cook us alive. With the metal walls, this enclosed space will soon turn into an oven.

We take the next left. The noise of the fans is deafening. We're in a large section of ducting that connects to three downward sloping shafts, each with a fan at the end. I look down the steep slide. Beyond the fan units, I can see a single large tunnel which rises sharply upwards at the end. Millie stops.

"We can't get past those," I say. "We don't even know

299

what's behind them. Saffron's instructions told us to go straight on. Let's stick to the plan."

"That tunnel leads outside, I know it," Millie says. She stares down one of the shafts, through spinning blades that turn so fast you can't even see them.

And then, she lunges for the shaft. I hurl myself forward and manage to grab her collar, stopping her from sliding down into the huge fan. But I'm slipping. I can't hold her.

"Help," I say, trying to wrap my leg around a corner so I won't slide any further.

"Let me go," Millie cries. "I have to get out of here."

Joey yanks me up by the legs, dragging my weight over the lip of the shaft so gravity is no longer pulling me down. Millie is still slipping, though. The fabric of her top creaks and rips. I can't hold on.

"Get off me," she yells, trying to hit me.

"Millie!" Joey screams. "Take my hand!"

My fingers lose their grip, but Joey somehow manages to get his hand to her arm. We pull her, kicking and screaming, up the shaft. I push her in front of me, inching her forward away from the fans. She fights me every step of the way, a shadowy octopus in the darkness of the tunnel, all slapping arms and kicking legs as she tries to crawl towards the fans. But I use my own body to block her from diving to her death.

"Vodka is not your friend, Millie," I say, or at least that's what I start to say. I'm cut off by Millie's scream, no longer furious but horrified.

From behind me, there's a sudden cry and the banging

of someone trying desperately to stop themselves from sliding down a shaft. I turn in time to see Joey disappearing towards the fan furthest from me. I try to get to him – I try with everything I have – but I'm too late.

His cry turns to a scream, and I'm hit in the face by a spray of warm, wet blood.

34

GEORGIA

"Grab my hand!" I lie on my belly and reach down the sloping tunnel towards Joey.

He doesn't hear me. He's busy trying to brace himself against the walls, but they're slippery with blood. It's everywhere. On the spinning fan, on the ceiling, in my eyes and in my mouth, salty and metallic. One of Joey's feet is gone. The bone is poking out at the bottom of his torn up joggers.

Joey's screaming, Millie's yelling, Henry's gagging. All of them are being completely useless, which is understandable in Joey's case. It's still infuriating. If he slides any further down that shaft, it will be one of those scenes in a film where a person is chopped into a million pieces by a fan. Only this isn't some actor. This is a boy I've loved, from a distance, for most of my life.

"I can't reach you," I shout. "You need to take my hand!"

His bloody fingers grab my wrist. He yanks so hard that, for a second, I'm unbalanced and I can feel myself slipping headfirst down the tunnel. Then Joey manages to kick off the wall with his uninjured foot and lurches up the shaft. Our heads clunk as he scrambles to safety, and he ends up lying entangled with me, my neck bent at a painful angle.

"It's in my mouth; I'm going to puke," Millie cries.

"Not helping," I snap. I wiggle out from underneath Joey. He lies down on his back taking short, gasping breaths. His whole body is shaking. Beneath us, the metal floor is slick with blood. When I try to move, my hand skids out beneath me. My brain does a somersault in my head and the walls close in on me. There's way too much blood.

"We need to stop the bleeding. Give me your shirt," I say to Henry. He removes it and holds it out with his eyes closed.

I manoeuvre past Joey to get to his injured foot. My forehead is dripping with sweat and I don't know if it's the heat or the panic. I glance at his wounds. Oh my god. My vision narrows and I'm looking down a long, dark tunnel, the end getting further and further away. I'm going to faint, and then no one will be able to help Joey.

I close my eyes and count to ten. I need to pull myself

together and stop being such a baby, but even with my eyes closed, all I can see is blood. So much blood.

"Georgia," Joey says, his voice a rasp.

I open my eyes. He looks terrible. There's blood splattered all over his face and his skin is a deathly white. His teeth are chattering and his eyes belong to a terrified animal, too wide and bright.

"Do it," he says, clenching his jaw.

Before I can talk myself out of it, I press the bundled shirt against his ankle and yank the arms as tight as I can, tying them in a knot. Joey doesn't even scream, which I'm glad about until I realize his eyes have rolled back in his head. He's out cold.

"Is he breathing?" Henry says, still not looking.

I lay a hand on Joey's chest. It rises and falls. "He passed out."

Millie's sobbing now. "You've killed him!"

"I had to stop the bleeding, Millie."

"You're a killer. You killed them all!" She's so slurry and out of it I don't think she even knows what she's yelling about. Her eyes are unfocused and she keeps trying to hit me, but misses by over a metre. "Why Joey? He did nothing to you!"

"All right, calm down," I say.

"Don't tell me to calm down," she spits.

"We need to get Joey out of this duct," I say. "You're not helping him by screaming at me."

"How are we going to get him out of here?" Henry says.

304

I try to remember the rest of Saffron's instructions. There's one more left to take, after which only two more clues remain. *Lava drop* and *behind the sofa*. It doesn't matter that I understand neither clue, because Joey's not crawling anywhere, even if he does regain consciousness. I look past Millie along the duct. There's a vent not far ahead. Maybe we can get out.

Clambering past her, I crawl towards it, praying it doesn't lead into yet another game room. And that the drop isn't too big. I'm about to shine the phone torch through the vent when I feel the duct lurch beneath me. An entire segment has detached and Millie, Joey and Henry are all bundled together at the lowest point. Our thrashing about must have been too much for the brackets.

I stay as still as I can. The duct creaks again. I hold my breath. There's a popping noise and then I'm falling. We're all falling.

I hit the ground hard enough to knock the breath out of my lungs. I can't get any air in. My chest burns and my head rings. It takes a good ten seconds before I'm able to breathe again, longer for the pain to start to subside. Nothing's broken. The drop wasn't too far, but it hurt a lot.

Henry groans, stirring. "Are you all OK?"

"No," Millie says. "I am literally covered in blood."

"Where's Joey?" I crawl in the dark until I find where he's landed. He's unconscious but breathing. I straighten his legs and check the bandage. It's slowing the bleeding a bit, or maybe he's lost so much blood there's none left to leak out of him.

How long can someone survive after losing their foot? I reckon he has maybe an hour before we have to watch him die. It's too much to take in. It doesn't feel real. It can't be real.

"How do we get out of here?" I say, jumping to my feet so fast it makes me light-headed.

The room was unlit when we fell, but lights slowly turn on, shining an eerie blue down on us. This is the final zone, Use Your Imagination. We're inside a spaceship, with complicated panels on the walls and lots of silver metal riveted together. There's a porthole through which stars streak past.

A red light flashes and a siren sounds. Words appear on a computer screen on one of the panels. *Danger. Re-entry angle incorrect. Heat shield failure in 10:00.*

"I can't do this," I say quietly. "I don't want to play!"

"This is not the game I would have chosen for you, but we will make do," Lightman says. "Welcome to Let's Play Astronauts."

I take in the set. There are canisters of bright green fuel behind a panel, one of them lit red. I guess we're supposed to find a way to open the panel, replace the failing fuel and plot a course correction. It's almost exactly like the last *Sole Survivor* game I played with the crew. That game feels like so long ago.

"I'm not playing," I tell Lightman, but he doesn't reply.

The timer counts down. I sit with Joey and we wait. It's the longest ten minutes of my life. The stars in the porthole eventually give way to an image of the Earth. This room represents how I feel. Trapped and claustrophobic, as far from the world I know as I've ever been.

"How's he doing?" Henry says, shuffling closer. He's pointedly avoiding looking at the blood or at Joey's leg. I worry he's going to faint.

"I don't know," I say, my voice unexpectedly hitching. "I don't know what to do."

"Urgh look at you," Millie sneers through her sobs. "You're pathetic. Joey won't magically start liking you if you nurse him back to health."

Something in me snaps. I jump to my feet and drag Millie off the box she's sitting on. "It should be you," I yell. "I wish you were the one bleeding to death."

Millie tears herself free of me and darts behind the fuel cabinet, hyperventilating with fear. Good. Let her be scared of me. You reap what you sow, and she deserves everything she's about to get.

"Georgia, stop," Henry says.

I ignore him. I circle the fuel cabinet, my teeth bared and my heart beating so fast my lungs can hardly keep up. The rest of the room is blurry, background noise. All I can see is Millie, sobbing and cowering, and it feels good.

I throw myself across the cabinet and slam her to the ground. This scream erupts out of me. I scream and scream, my whole soul is bursting out of my body, coiling away from me in a big black cloud of hatred and fury and frustration. I scream even as the breath in my lungs runs out and my voice cracks.

I'm still screaming when Henry manages to drag me off Millie. He pins my arms with his, hugging me tightly from behind. "Stop," he's saying, but I can't. I scream and scream until all the fight goes out of me and I'm left gasping and sobbing.

The room's siren intensifies, and a flashing light bathes the room blood-red. Through the porthole, the night sky spirals out of control, as if it's the universe that is spinning while the ship remains frozen in space.

Heat shield failure, the screens flash. *Disintegration in 10, 9, 8...*

Henry, Millie and I watch the countdown, doing nothing, saying nothing. I want to believe we're the ones in control, refusing to play Lightman's games. But then I remember he doesn't care about the games; he only wants us to turn on each other and that's exactly what I just did.

The door clicks open as the screens switch to: *YOU LOSE*.

This time, I don't think it means the game.

35

GEORGIA

We drag Joey out into a nightmare. The Use Your Imagination zone looks like someone has turned a child upside down and tipped all the dreams, fears and make-believe games straight out of their brain.

In the centre, there's a castle made of giant building blocks. Reds, blues, yellows and greens. It has four turrets that touch the ceiling, and a drawbridge that crosses a fake river lit up by rainbow spotlights. To the side of the castle, there's a maze of pink blow-up clouds suspended on taut wires that reach from the ceiling to the floor. To the other side, there's a pirate ship.

The ship's half buried in the wall, like it's bursting through. It's massive, made of real wood, and painted black like a pirate's frigate. The figurehead is a carved woman wearing floaty robes. She looms fifteen metres above me, her chest thrust forward and her arms outstretched as if she's been given a good shove and is bracing for the impact that never comes.

In addition to the castle, the clouds and the ship, there's a flight of stairs that leads up into an upside-down room built on the ceiling, complete with chairs, tables and bookshelves. The overall effect is beyond disorientating. I can't tell how big the zone is or work out how you're supposed to get to all the games rooms hidden around the edge.

We squeeze through the blow-up clouds, Henry and I carrying Joey between us, Millie trailing silently behind us. The cold rubber surfaces squeak as we pass by. Inside the castle, we discover an open area set up as an old-fashioned sitting room, complete with a tea set on the table. We lie Joey on the sofa.

He moans softly and blinks open his eyes. "Am I dead?" he asks, eyeing our surroundings.

"No, you're OK," Henry says.

Joey tries to sit up and look at his leg, but thankfully can't muster up the strength. He manages a weak smile. "Tell me the truth: I've ruined my new shoes, haven't I?"

"One of them is unharmed," I say. "If that's any consolation."

"Man, I liked those shoes," he says. "And those feet." He winces and closes his eyes.

"Is he dead?" Millie whispers.

Joey manages to lift his arm and give her a thumbs-up. "Don't worry about me, babe. If anything, this has improved me." His arm drops and he loses consciousness again.

"OK," I say. "We need a plan. We can work this out." It's bullshit. I don't have a plan; I don't have anything. Geoffrey, Olympia, Aidan and Helix are dead, Joey is dying. And me? I'm falling to pieces. Millie watches me nervously, no longer snarky and mean, but genuinely scared. Scared of me.

The overhead lights flicker then dip to near-darkness. There are up-lights around the edge of the castle and they throw long shadows that gently stroke the ceiling. Suddenly, there's silence. The steady hum of the ventilation system is gone. A drum beat sounds. It's a steady, booming rhythm that echoes through the network of ducts and vents.

"What is that?" Henry says.

The beat continues, rumbling like thunder. Bang-bang, bang-bang, bang-bang. It's a heartbeat, I realize.

Then, as suddenly as it started, it stops again. Someone else is here in the zone with us. I can hear them moving about. There's a noise like a knife being dragged along the wall. A scratching, scraping sound. Millie whimpers.

"Helix," Henry whispers. "He's not dead."

I can still picture the fury on his face as he brandished that awful flick knife at us, after Aidan died. *I'll kill you all*, he yelled at us, and I know he meant it. Now, once again, he's stalking us from the shadows, taunting us.

311

We all hold our breath, listening intently. I think I hear the quiet squeak of someone edging through the field of plastic clouds, then silence again. I'm waiting for something to happen when a section of the castle wall topples down on top of us. The blocks are huge – a square metre or more – and made of hard rubber. The three of us who are conscious barely leap aside in time as the wall splits apart, the blocks bouncing as they land.

Millie screams and starts to run. "Wait," I call after her. "We should stay together."

I take off behind her, shoving my way through the maze of clouds. But Millie must have gone another way and I've already lost her. It's only then I realize Henry isn't behind me. I'm alone. I creep through the clouds and emerge beneath the pirate ship. There are fibreglass rocks at its base, making it look like it's run aground.

Something crackles and I jump. But it's just a screen. Lightman appears. "There are four of you still in play, but only three can enter the penultimate room," he says.

"I'll murder someone then," I snap.

"That would be sensible," he says. "I am glad you are finally playing along, Georgia. Might I suggest Millie? I can provide you with some motivation if you would care to watch another clip of her being rude about you?"

"There's something very wrong with you." I walk away, but he jumps to another screen, appearing in front of me again.

"My systems are working as designed."

"You're *killing* people. Real, living people."

"I am not killing anyone, Georgia. I am merely—"

"LA LA LA LA," I yell, putting my hands over my ears. "Can't hear you."

"You are being childish," he says, subtitling himself on the screen. "You are acting like your sister."

That's how I know things are bad. I'm turning into Saffron.

"If you won't, someone else will," he says, and then the screen goes black.

I keep moving. I'm being followed, though; I can hear Helix's soft footsteps. I speed up. Something scrapes along a wall and I quickly hide underneath the upside-down flight of stairs. I hold my breath. Helix pads closer, then stops. I can't see him, but I can hear him looking for me. He moves closer to my hiding place. I clamp a hand over my mouth as I briefly glimpse that vicious knife as he sweeps past.

He stops moving. I'm so sure he's worked out where I am. Only he doesn't come for me. He instead takes off at a run in the opposite direction. That was close. Too close. Fumbling in my pocket, I find my multitool and flick out the biggest, sharpest screwdriver. I clutch it between two fingers and try not to think about how little it's going to help against an attacker.

I creep out from my hiding place. I want to call out to Henry, or even Millie. But I can't risk giving myself away to Helix. And then Millie screams. I almost don't go. I hesitate, remembering all the other times she's screamed

313

and it's turned out to be nothing. But something about the sound cuts through me and feels different.

"Millie, where are you?" I shout, running towards the sound.

"Stop," Millie screams. "No!"

I skid to a halt underneath the pirate ship. "Millie?"

There's no answer and the screaming has stopped.

Something moves above me. I glance up in time to see someone darting out of sight on the deck. I slowly approach the rocks that make a staircase up on to the boat.

A split second later, a heavy object slams down right behind me, knocking me into the steps. My face smacks into the lowest step. I bite my tongue and a metallic taste floods through my mouth. It's not until I push myself up to a sitting position, that I see what it was that nearly killed me.

Millie is lying twisted on the ground, her neck broken and her eyes empty.

36
SAFFRON

No, no, no. Not Millie. I turn away from the CCTV feed of Georgia standing over Millie's body. My brain doesn't want to process the images my eyes are seeing, but I know I'm going to keep on seeing them forever, seared into my memories.

"The princess is eliminated," Lightman says. "We're down to the final four. I predict the jock will soon bleed to death."

"His name is Joey," I yell. "They're Joey and Millie. They're not just a jock and a princess!"

"But you were the one who described them as such, Saffron."

"Fuck off and die, *Lightman*," I snarl.

"I cannot die when I am not—"

"SHUT UP!"

I pace away from the CCTV wall with a hand clasped over my mouth. Lightman's switched off most of the feeds, showing me only the ones he chooses to reveal. The ones he decides will keep the game *interesting*.

"You manipulative bastard!" I scream, shoving a computer monitor off the desk. It swings from a tangle of wires, the screen flickering off then back on.

Atlas watches me nervously from his corner. He's sitting on the floor, crying and worrying about himself like the selfish bastard he is. I want to grab him by the throat and shake him. Call him all the names I can think of. Incompetent, thoughtless, coward.

Ha. Good one, Saffron. Calling someone else a coward when that's exactly what I am. As soon as things got bad, I crumpled into a self-pitying mess. I had the opportunity to join my sister and friends in the escape room and I chose to stay up here.

"My analysis suggests you were not close friends with Millie," Lightman says. "I am surprised you are this upset about her death."

"Are you serious?" I cry.

"You occasionally spent time with her, but your recorded conversations lacked any markers of real affection, plus she regularly complained about you to others."

"Screw you," I say, shaking my head.

A tear overflows from my eye and I quickly wipe it

away. I'm not going to cry, I'm not going to cry. It's hard to hold it back though, because here is a truth: Lightman's right. I wasn't close friends with Millie. I haven't been close with anyone for years, not since I lost the best friend I ever had: my sister. Suddenly, all the reasons for our rivalry feel so small and petty.

"Soon it will be time for the final game," Lightman says. "Who do you think will win?"

I look at the CCTV feed again. Georgia is kneeling next to Millie. She drops her head to the floor, her back shaking. I can't remember the last time I saw my sister cry. Georgia doesn't give up. Her stubbornness is what makes her who she is, and if that's gone then what else does she have?

"Let me go in and join the game," I say.

Lightman's red light flickers. He's trying to work out what my game plan is. "You cannot get to them in time, Saffron. The final game will start in a few minutes."

"You wanted me to play!"

He hesitates again. "You are playing, Saffron."

I cry out in anger and frustration, then shove my way out of the room. I march down the corridor towards the utilities room.

"The only way to reach the games rooms is via the lift," Lightman says. "I am not going to activate the lift."

"No, it's not the only way." I gesture to the schematics on the walls. "There are ventilation ducts that run from one end of the bunker to the other. Yeah, check me out. I'm not as stupid as everyone thinks I am."

"You are the only one who believes you are stupid," Lightman says. I swear he sounds ... angry. "OK, I will agree to let you take the lift down to the—"

"Nope. I'm doing this my way," I say. "I don't trust you not to remove all the safety features from the lift and let me plummet to my death."

The long silence is *very* telling.

"Aha! Turns out I'm better at predicting *your* behaviour than you are at predicting mine. Sucks to be you, Lightman."

"It is difficult to predict the behaviour of someone who acts in an entirely unpredictable and irrational manner."

"But that's what makes me awesome," I say.

I find the maintenance panel I was looking for and yank it off the wall. Inside, there's a dark access tunnel full of twisted bundles of wires and dozens of water pipes. After a few metres, there's a maintenance hatch leading down into an air duct.

I clamber inside. If I can't *be* brave then I can pretend to be brave. After all, I'm used to making things up.

I'll come up with the rest of the plan later if I'm still alive to put it into action.

37
GEORGIA

Someone's running towards me. I don't care if it's Helix. All I can think about is how Millie's dead. My best friend is gone forever and the last memories I have are of me attacking her.

"We have to go. Now!" Henry hauls me to my feet.

I don't have the strength to argue. I let him drag me through the Use Your Imagination nightmare zone. My heart is hammering and every breath burns. My vision is all stars and sparks, narrowing and narrowing.

"Helix killed her," Henry gasps. "He wants to kill us all."

We duck inside the castle. Instead of running out the opposite side, across the rainbow moat, we hide behind the sofa where Joey lies, unconscious and bleeding but somehow still alive. We wait, Henry holding two fingers to my lips as I try to calm my gasping breaths. Helix's footsteps pace across the drawbridge.

He's dragging his knife along every surface he passes. Its tone changes as it connects with the building blocks. Their rough plastic surfaces make a click, click, click noise. He wants to scare us. He's enjoying this.

Then his footsteps grow quieter. I think he's gone when a chair topples over and nearly squashes us. Henry takes my hand and pulls me behind him, running unsteadily, tripping over his own feet. I don't even look to see if Helix is chasing us, I just run. We force our way through the clouds. From behind me comes the squeaky sound of the knife being plunged into the plastic, followed by the hiss of escaping air.

"There," Henry says, pointing at an open door. He pulls me towards it. It's a game room, already open and waiting for us. "Come on!" Henry yanks on my arm so hard it feels like it's going to dislocate.

"Wait, we can't," I plead.

"There's nowhere else to go!" He drags me inside and braces himself against the door. "Find something to barricade it."

I look around and a wave of heat immediately hits me. This room is The Floor is Lava. Saffron's clue. Lava world. This is where she wanted us to go.

It's a massive space set up like a living room, only with

oversized furniture, all of it bobbing in a pool of bubbling, orange liquid. There's a bright-pink sofa, two polka-dot armchairs, a table complete with chess set, an old-fashioned TV, a giant plastic plant right in the middle of the room and various cushions and beanbags scattered like stepping stones.

The walls are covered in pictures and clocks that make a climbing wall of sorts. There are a couple of massive chandeliers swinging from long ropes and a sideboard with dozens of drawers that can presumably be pulled out to make steps.

I look more closely at the lava. It must be orange water or slime that, usually, would be disgusting to fall in but do you no real harm. Only it's steaming and giving off a lot of heat. I'm guessing Lightman has messed with the thermostat to make it more like *Sole Survivor.*

"Georgia!" The door shudders and Henry struggles to hold it closed.

"I know, I know, I'm looking," I say, but I can't think straight. I'm panicking too much. I reach over to one of the armchairs and give it a yank. It doesn't budge. Everything in the room is fake, made of fibreglass or plastic and fixed in place.

"Georgia, I need some help," Henry cries.

Helix stops trying to open the door, but only for long enough for Henry to relax slightly. A second later, he kicks the door so hard it smashes into Henry's face. Blood explodes from his nose.

"Go! Jump," I say.

We both leap for the sofa. It tips backwards as we land and nearly throws me into the lava. My hand briefly dips beneath the surface. The sticky goo is burning hot and even after I've pulled my hand free, it continues to scald me. The skin's red and feels too tight. It takes a few more seconds for the pain to hit me.

Henry and I cling to each other as Helix pushes the door open and steps into the room, the flick knife in his hand. Except, it's not Helix.

"You," Henry says.

"Me," Aidan says, spinning the knife on a blood-crusted hand.

He looks awful. His previously warm skin is ashen and sweaty. His T-shirt clings to his stomach, wet with blood. The look in his eyes is horrifying. It's pure hatred.

"How are you still alive?" I whisper.

"The puzzle piece," he says. "I had it tucked into the waistband of my jeans, so that branch didn't go in very far." He lifts his T-shirt to reveal a bandaged injury to the right of his belly button. "Still not looking good for me, but I reckon I've got enough time left to settle some scores."

"This isn't you," I say.

He examines the knife, peering at his reflection in the shiny blade. "Isn't it? I think it is."

The breaking noise as Millie slammed into the ground plays in my head. I try to work out a route away from Aidan and his weapon. The drawers are close enough to reach. I pull on each in turn until I find the ones that make a staircase to the top of the sideboard. I clamber up and sit there.

Aidan watches me with a tilt of his head. "Helix is dead." He points at Henry with the knife. "Who was it that killed him? Was it you?"

Henry stumbles on the sofa, nearly slipping off the lava-coated cushions. "It was self-defence. I had no choice!"

"Let me tell you something about Helix," he spits. "After my dad went to prison for trying to strangle my mum, Helix was the only person who gave a shit."

My heart plummets at this piece of information. Earlier, when he told me his dad wasn't around any more, I presumed he meant he'd skipped out on his family, not tried to murder his partner.

"I thought you weren't friends," Henry says. "You hardly ever speak at school."

"I don't do friends!" Aidan shouts, holding back tears. "I could have helped him deal with all the bullying and the rumours, but I didn't want to make my life any more complicated than it already was. So I left him to cope alone, even after he'd been there for me."

"You had a lot to deal with," I say.

"Don't! Don't you dare feel sorry for me." He closes his eyes, either holding back tears or the pain from his injury. "Feel sorry for Helix, lying dead in that room."

"He deserved what he got," Henry says, and his coldness surprises me.

"And it's convenient for you too," Aidan says. He jumps on to the sofa and cries out in pain. He kneels there, bent double, clutching his belly. "Helix knew your little secret and now he can never tell. Unluckily for you, he let it slip to me months ago."

"Georgia, he's lying. I don't know what he's talking about," Henry pleads. "You can't listen to him. He's a liar; so's Helix."

"You mean Helix *was* a liar. He's dead, remember? I woke up with a fucking branch stabbed into my belly and Helix was lying there, not breathing. And all of you were gone!" His red-rimmed eyes meet mine. "You didn't even try to get us out."

"I wanted to," I say, but I know it's a pathetic excuse the moment it leaves my lips. He's right. We did leave them both in that room to die.

"But you didn't," Aidan says quietly. "That's what matters."

"Georgia, can you make it over to the chandeliers?" Henry asks. He's gesturing at two huge light fittings with curling metal loops that remind me of monkey bars. "He can't make it to the other side, not with that injury."

Aidan laughs and, for a second, the smiling boy I remember is back. Then the smile is gone again and his face sets like stone. I don't know him. I don't know him at all.

"Why Millie?" I say. "I don't understand why she had to die."

Aidan clenches his jaw. "You're so clever. Work it out yourself."

"Georgia, come on," Henry pleads.

I lock eyes with Aidan but he's giving me nothing. Shaking my head, I jump on to the next beanbag. I clamber across to the edge of the dresser and carefully climb down on to the picture wall, digging my fingers into the ornate frames and resting my feet on the dado rail.

"Good choice," Aidan says mockingly. "I thought you were different, but I guess people will always see what they want to see."

I focus on climbing down on to a beanbag that turns out to be deceptively hard and slippery. I nearly lose my balance and I end up on my knees. The next obstacle is the chandeliers. Monkey bars have never been my thing. No upper body strength.

"He's a thief and a murderer, Georgia. Remember that," Henry says.

Aidan gives me a mocking bow. "Although I didn't steal Henry's bracelet. I *found* that one."

"Georgia, you need to jump. Now!" Henry says, his voice shaky with fear.

I turn back to the chandeliers. I prepare to make the leap, but I can't force myself to do it.

"But don't worry, Henry," Aidan says wearily. "I've learnt my lesson from Helix. She'd never believe me over a nice boy like you so what's the point? Besides, she doesn't even deserve the truth."

325

I glance over at him and find him staring at me from on top of the dresser. The look on his face is complete disgust. I take a deep breath and I jump for the chandelier. I catch the loops with both hands but the chandelier swings much more than I expected. I barely hold on.

I manage to readjust my grip as I wait for the chandelier to stop swinging so violently. All I have to do is reach out and grab the next loop. It's a few metres to the end of the room. I can do this. But I can't make myself move, I'm too scared.

Henry makes the final jump from a coffee table over to the landing mat. He rolls then stands up. "Come on, you've got this," he says.

I don't think I have.

"Saffron was right about you," Aidan says, smirking. "You are useless at this shit."

This pisses me off enough that I stop panicking and I move. I swing between the loops of the chandelier, getting into a rhythm. I have a wobble as I cross over on to the second chandelier, but I make it. I'm nearly there. So close, and then … the chandelier swings and I slip.

I fall, and below me there's nothing but boiling lava. But Aidan must jump at the exact moment I start to drop. He slams into me and sends us both crashing on to the mat at Henry's feet. The impact stuns me for a few seconds. When I recover, Henry is the one holding the knife.

Henry gestures for Aidan to back away. "Don't come any closer," he says, voice trembling.

Aidan isn't in any state to do anything, not after making that jump. But to my surprise, he shakily gets to his feet. Henry lifts the knife higher, poised to strike. "I mean it, Aidan."

"It's OK, he's OK," I say, resting a hand on Henry's arm to encourage him to lower the weapon. The last thing we need right now is someone else getting themselves stabbed.

To my surprise, Aidan starts to chuckle. "You don't get it, do you? He's not trying to defend you, Georgia. He thinks he might need you in the final room."

I have enough time to frown before Henry presses the sharp point against my throat. "Back off!" he snarls at Aidan.

"You left me behind to die, Georgia," Aidan says, turning away. "Sucks, doesn't it?"

38
GEORGIA

Henry drags me along a steeply rising tunnel that will take us to the final room. It feels like a path curling up the side of a mountain. The walls look like rock but they're all part of the set – painted fibreglass that makes a hollow sound when I bump into it. There are warning signs everywhere. *Danger. No entry. Continue at your own peril.*

I eye the knife in Henry's hand. "Keep moving," he orders.

"What are you planning to do?" I plead.

"I don't know. I don't know! Look, this isn't what I want, Georgia, but I have no choice. You understand that, right? Someone like me can't go to prison. I wouldn't last a day!"

"You were the one who killed them. It was all you."

He pauses for a second and pushes his broken glasses up his nose. "I never wanted to kill anyone; you need to understand that."

"Understand? Six people are either dead or dying and you're threatening the seventh – me! – with a weapon. It's a lot to understand, Henry."

He bashes his fist against a fake rock, making me whimper in shock. "We're ending this thing so I can go home. Move." He gives me a shove.

I stumble over my own feet and stub my toe. It brings a wave of anger with the pain. "You honestly think you'll get away with this? You can't be that arrogant!"

He yanks hard on my T-shirt. "Move, you stuck up bitch."

Being called a bitch is my kryptonite but, rather than weakening me, it makes me strong enough to pull away from him. It also makes me furious enough to momentarily forget he's armed. "Oh no, absolutely not! I am not putting up with you calling me that."

"What exactly are you going to do about it?"

"Misogynistic language is never acceptable, Henry. If you want to insult me based on my personality, then that's fine. But it is both lazy and, quite frankly, boring when you default to gendered insults and name-calling." I take a deep gasp of breath, because that little rant sounded good when I wrote it in an article last month but was a mouthful to say out loud.

"What?" he says, gaping at me.

"This is my hill to die on, Henry. Insult my tendency to lecture people about esoteric subjects, or my weird sense of humour, or even my inability to let the smallest slight go. But do not call me a bitch simply because you're too unimaginative to come up with anything original."

He stares at me like I've sprouted a second head. "What?" he repeats, more weakly this time.

"OK, I'm going to break this down for you so—"

He snaps out of it and steps up to me, the knife tight against my skin. I remember how much danger I'm in and don't resist when he pushes me in front of him.

"Why do you hate women so much, Henry?" The pieces fall into place and I realize what's behind all of this. "Wait. You sent Millie and Olympia those texts!"

"Girls like them think they're so special," he spits, suddenly furious. "Someone needed to take them down a peg or two."

"This is why you killed them all, isn't it? To hide some stupid secret!"

"Lightman kept prodding and prodding. Telling me what would happen to me in prison if it came out, taunting me. And I ... snapped! You get that, don't you? You lost it with Millie. You're the same."

"Except I didn't kill anyone. It's a small but significant difference!"

"Shut up already! You're literally the most irritating girl I've ever met."

"I'll accept that insult. I am very irritating," I concede.

We round the corner into the final room. There's more lava. *Way* more lava. It's a volcano, because of course it is. The mountain itself is about five metres high and resembles a melting pile of wax standing in the middle of a lake. Thick rivers of hot lava run down the volcano's sides. Stepping stones lead across the lava.

There's a giant screen on the wall, on which Lightman's face appears. "Welcome to Mount Death," he says.

"How does it work?" Henry paces, using his knife to gesticulate. "What do I need to do to get out of here?"

"Atlas designed this room to be based around the puzzle pieces you should have been collecting today," Lightman says. "But I think it will be more fitting if Georgia tries to solve the puzzle of why you killed your friends, don't you agree?"

"They weren't my friends," Henry says. "They all constantly laughed at me. Rejected me. Disrespected me!"

"But you've shown them," Lightman says. "Look how close you are to winning. You're down to the final two."

"Yeah. You're right. No one ever expected me to succeed, but here I am."

"Exactly," Lightman says. "Have fun playing." He vanishes.

"OK, OK. Jump on to the first stepping stone and see if it's stable," Henry says.

"Er, no?" But then he pokes me with the knife and I teeter at the edge of the platform. "Fine, OK." I tentatively step over on to the closest stone. It's slippy but stable. It won't be long until we're at the volcano. And then what? I need more time to come up with a plan. *Keep him talking*, I think.

"You slipped into killing people without much trouble," I say. "Have you considered there's something wrong with you?"

"Without much trouble?" he cries. "Do you have any idea how horrible it was stabbing Olympia?"

"Poor little Henry," I say.

"She brought it on herself! Lightman told her I was the one sending her texts, and she started mouthing off about it in Snakes and Ladders. I had no choice."

I shake my head. "Of course you had a choice."

He pauses for a second. "Maybe," he admits. "Once I got her over with, the others were easier. I realized no one was going to suspect me."

"We all suspected Helix instead," I say.

Henry laughs. "He must have found her body and tried to help her. He was always that sort. But of course you saw the blood on his coat and jumped to conclusions."

I close my eyes. I never tried to get to know Helix better. Now it's too late.

"I hoped that would be the end of it, but Aidan worked it out. Which complicated matters."

I think about how obviously Aidan was playing with Henry's bracelet after he returned to us through the vents. He said he'd fallen through into one of the game rooms. It must have been the one where Olympia died. "He found your bracelet by Olympia's body, didn't he?"

"But instead of telling everyone, he decided it could earn him some extra money. For his new life with his sister. Right before we went inside Hopscotch, he whispered something in my ear. *Ten thousand pounds.* As if I was going to pay him that much."

"He was blackmailing you over the text messages," I say.

"Small amounts. Nothing I couldn't afford. I'd presumed it was Helix, but it turns out Helix told Aidan, and Aidan saw an opportunity."

He prods me across on to the next stone. The lava is so hot, I'm sweating. I wipe my forehead on my arm, nearly losing my balance on the slippery rock. Just a few more to the volcano island. There's nowhere else to go now.

Henry chuckles. "It all backfired for him, though. Lightman showed us that clip of him finding my bracelet, and everyone presumed he'd killed her."

"We saw what we wanted to see," I say quietly.

"Only when we were in the vents, Joey mentioned how Aidan's face was bruised in that clip and he was on the verge of remembering Aidan didn't break his nose until *after* Olympia died. It's ironic, isn't it? The biggest airhead in here was the only one to work out the clip wasn't what you all thought it was." He frowns and removes his glasses to wipe the steam off the intact lens. "So I pushed him into that fan blade."

"Joey losing a foot wasn't an accident? Oh my god!"

"It didn't go to plan, though – he survived. Plus Millie saw. She was drunk so she didn't know exactly what she'd seen, but she was going to work it out. Besides, by that point I knew only one of us could make it out of this place. I figured I'd speed things up a little." He jumps across behind me, shrugging sheepishly. "And then there were two."

39
SAFFRON

I've been crawling forever. The ducts are filthy, hot and dark. They slope up and down in ways that keep resulting in me face-planting into the metal. In some places, they become so narrow I have to wiggle along on my belly. In others, there are sharp edges to the seams that rip my jeans and nick my skin as I pass. I keep having to pause to cough and it sounds like I'm bringing up a lung.

My phone torch reflects off all the smoke still lingering in the ducts and turns my world into a one-metre bubble. Everything else is pitch black. I check the schematics on my phone. It looked like an easy enough route right up until I climbed through that service hatch. In theory, this duct should lead me all the way to the Floor is Lava room.

My coded message to Georgia should have brought her out there. Then she only had to look behind the sofa to find the maintenance panel that leads directly to an access ladder up to the ground floor. Only something went wrong and they ended up falling into the Let's Play Astronauts room. So now it's up to me to get her out.

Finally, I spot the glow of orange lava filtering into the duct. I look down on a cartoonish version of a living room, with oversized furniture in an array of clashing colours. The lava is steaming and the temperature in the room must be over forty, like working in a bakery during a summer heatwave.

I kick out the vent. There's a giant plastic pot plant right beneath me, so at least I don't have to try to jump on to the sofa from this height. I squeeze out of the vent backwards and shakily reach my foot on to one of the plant's oversized leaves. It wobbles beneath me, but it's been designed so you can use the leaves to climb across the room, avoiding the lava.

When Atlas gave me a tour of the complex on my first day, he told me the lava was meant to be a nice, comfortable body temperature. A tepid bath, not burn the flesh from your bones. I hear Georgia's voice in my head. "The steam will be good for your mucous membranes." I laugh to myself, but it immediately becomes a coughing fit.

"Saffron?" a voice groans.

Aidan! He's lying on a crash mat at the end of the room and he's doesn't look good. I clamber on to a beanbag. The

336

lava gurgles and a little wave sloshes over my shoes. Not only is it super hot but it's also ridiculously slippery.

"Aidan? What the heck happened to you?" I ask.

He lifts his head enough to glance down at his blood-soaked T-shirt. "Yeah, that." His voice is weak.

"I'm coming over to you," I say.

I jump on to the sofa. The access panel Georgia was meant to find is right there. Untouched. Damn it. I thought she'd work out my clues. It takes me a few minutes to make it across to the crash mat. "Wow, you look like shit," I say, kneeling beside him.

Aidan blinks up at me. "I got stabbed, but I deserved it."

"I can believe that," I say, trying to act calm when inside I am tying myself in knots. "Who did you piss off?"

"Joey Theasby." His eyes briefly lose focus. "Everyone thinks I'm a murderer," he slurs.

"You're not, are you?"

He manages to shoot me a filthy look. "No. But I've known who is for some time and instead of warning everyone, I decided to blackmail the killer."

"What the hell, Aidan?"

"I need the money," he murmurs. "I planned to use it to run away from home with my sister. If I'd told everyone what I knew, I could have at least saved Millie and Helix. But I saw a way to make more money." His eyes roll over as he briefly loses consciousness.

I shake his shoulder. "Aidan, where's Georgia? Is she OK?"

"She was last time I saw her," he says, weakly gesturing at a closed door. "But she's been cosying up with a murderer, so who knows how long that will last."

"Shit. That girl! She has the worst judgement."

Aidan stares up at the ceiling, his voice slow like treacle. "We were getting on OK for a while. I thought we might get to be … friendly."

"I rest my case." I try the door, but it's locked. Bringing up the building schematics on my phone, I try to find another route.

"It was all a lie, though. She doesn't give a shit about me."

"Stop being such a drama queen. Georgia doesn't make friends easily, but when she does, it means something. Aha!" There's a panel behind the coffee table. Behind it are the lava pipes leading up to the volcano room.

"I was so angry. I just wanted to scare them a bit. With the knife. Shit, I'm such an idiot." Aidan turns his head to me, alert again. "You need to go after her, Saffron."

"What do you think I'm doing?" I jump across on to a coffee table, balancing carefully while I remove the panel. There's a small gap leading into a filthy void, so I shove myself through, trying to ignore how hot the pipes are.

I stand on a girder and peer up at the vertical pipes rising towards the volcano room. There's a pump working overtime to force the hot lava upwards, and its scream threatens an explosion. Something in here hisses and pops. Lava bubbles from a failing connector.

Climbing up to the volcano room is not as easy as I

338

thought it would be. There are places where my shoulders barely fit and I have to slam myself against the pipes several times until something bends enough for me to get through. As I get higher, I can hear Georgia's voice and it spurs me on. She's shouting, and even though I can't make out the words, I can tell she's in trouble.

Finally, the space widens. I find myself beneath a cone-shaped structure which must be the volcano itself. I remember from my tour that the volcanic crater is a huge tunnel slide. Once you solve the final puzzle, the crater opens. You're meant to yeet yourself inside and slide out into the photo room, where you find a glorious flight of stairs that leads out of the bunker.

"Get off me," Georgia's voice screams.

I hammer my fist on the inside of the volcano. "Leave her alone," I boom, my voice echoing.

On the other side of the fibreglass, the fighting stops. I suppose a talking volcano must be a bit much on top of everything else they've experienced today.

I chuckle to myself. "This is the volcano god and I'm coming for you, motherfuckers."

With that, I kick the access panel at the back of the volcano so hard I crack the surrounding construction material. I struggle out, trip over broken pieces of volcanic rock and nearly tumble headfirst into a pool of lava. I teeter at the edge, then right myself. "That was close," I say. "Epic."

"Saffron?" Georgia cries, managing to make my name spread out over about five syllables. "What are you *doing*?"

I could ask her the same. She's dangling from the rim of the volcano, trying to kick Henry in the face. He's holding a nasty-looking knife, and he's trying to stab her in the legs.

"Saving your butt? You're welcome, by the way," I say.

"Everything's under control, Saffron," she snaps.

"Looks like it. Dude, put the knife down."

Henry stares at me open-mouthed. He's a mess. Blood on his face, bruises on his neck. I've not met him in person before now, and I'm finding it hard to believe he's a murderer. He's so geeky and normal-looking. Never judge a book by its cover, I suppose. What's the TV series about the stalker who murders the women he falls in love with? Henry reminds me of that guy – average on the outside, big issues on the inside.

"Don't come any closer," he says, his voice halting. "I'll kill her, I'll do it!"

"Just try it, asshole," Georgia snaps.

Henry yanks on Georgia's trousers and she loses her grip, sliding down to his level. He can't reach her with the knife because he's also struggling to cling on to the side of the volcano. Instead, he yanks on her hair in an attempt to prise her off the rocks. Which is totally unacceptable. The only person who gets to murder my sister is me.

Georgia's saved by a cascade of hot lava flooding out of a pipe at the top of the volcano and Henry is forced to swing himself aside. Georgia clambers higher, away from his grabby hands. He tries to pull her down again but ends up putting his hand in a river of lava. He screams, trying to shake the sticky lava off.

"Unlucky, dick face!" I laugh.

"Stop it!" he cries. "You don't get to talk to me like that." He moves in my direction, which at least gives Georgia some breathing room. The downside is, he has a weapon and he's also a lot bigger than I am. I snatch up a fake rock from the ground and hold it up in the most aggressive manner I can manage.

Henry continues towards me. I throw the rock at his face, but it bounces off harmlessly, only serving to enrage him further. He slaps me across the face and it really hurts. I drop down on to my knees, clutching my cheek as it screams with burning pain.

I've never been in a physical fight before. I thought I'd last a lot longer than this. In *Sole Survivor*, I'm literally fearless. In real life, though, I'm weak and scared. Henry raises his knife with a shaky hand. I can see him trying to muster the nerve to strike.

"Don't even think about it!" Georgia cries. She leaps on to his back and clings on like a monkey, one arm wrapped around his neck and the other twisting a handful of his hair. He roars in pain and slams her into the side of the volcano. She rolls to the floor and doesn't get up.

Henry rubs his bruised neck, tears in his eyes. "You stupid bitch," he cries.

A pained look of determination fixes itself on his face.

His fingers tighten on his knife as he steps towards me. I shuffle backwards, but there's nowhere to go.

Behind him, Georgia unfolds herself from the ground. She looks absolutely awful. There's blood trickling down her face from where she's cut herself on the volcano. Her face is tear-streaked and puffy. She looks small and young and pathetic. Her hands are shaking as she pulls her trusty multitool from her pocket and picks out one of the screwdrivers.

This is the point where I realize I've underestimated my sister. She draws herself up to all five feet of her height and her face becomes a terrifying snarl of fury. "Oi," she bellows, and it's as if she has three voices coming out of her mouth at the same time, like the fucking *devil*. "What have I told you about gendered insults?"

Henry turns to her with a look of exasperation. Georgia doesn't even *hesitate*. She rams the screwdriver into his eye. His literal eye! Then she kicks him in the balls and sends him plunging backwards into the lava. He sinks with this anti-climatic gurgle.

Georgia turns to me with a smug smile. She dusts off her hands. "Like I said, everything's under control."

40
GEORGIA

Saffron's looking at me like I'm a monster. Maybe I am. Then her face splits into a wide grin. "That. Was. Epic. Oh my god, Georgia."

I wipe a dribble of blood off my cheek with my sleeve.

"I've been having a bad day," I admit. "Him calling me a bitch kind of pushed me over the edge."

"*That's* the part that got you riled up?" Saffron asks.

"We all have our breaking points."

There's a loud gurgle and a wave of lava blobs over the edge of the island. It pours into the hole Saffron made when she burst out of the volcano. Guess that rules out escaping the way she came in.

We climb up the steep slope. Feet braced against rocks,

we sit there, watching the room fill up with lava. "There's a slide in the volcano," Saffron says hopefully.

"It's closed off. I looked."

"Oh." She sighs. "Sorry about all of this."

"It's not your fault."

"It kind of is," she says.

"OK. A little bit. But thanks. For coming here to save me."

"Of course I came. You're my sister." She throws an arm around me and I rest my head on her shoulder. The lava rises, bubbling towards our feet. We'll pass out from the heat before it gets to us.

Saffron wipes sweat off her face. She laughs. "I still can't believe you stabbed that dude in the eye. Like, I always thought I could kill someone to save my own life, but when it came down to the wire, I was too scared to even move."

"I'm an overachiever to the last," I mutter. "I like to win."

As if on cue, Lightman's face appears on the screen. "There can only be one winner," he says.

Saffron gasps. "Georgia defeated the killer. The know-it-all is the winner!"

Lightman turns his head in a jerky, inhuman movement. "Negative. The rebel has not been defeated. The simulation is not complete."

"I'm not fighting my sister!" Saffron's voice softens and goes small. "She wins, OK? She always wins against me."

"Ha! I always win? What are you on about, Saffron? You're popular, funny, interesting. Clearly the top sister."

"Not in the ways that matter," she says. There are tears in her eyes, or maybe sweat. "You're so clever. Ambitious. Our parents are proud of you. I'll never measure up."

"What?" I laugh at her, shaking my head in disbelief. "I've spent most of my life thinking I can't measure up to *you*. Sure, I follow the rules. But you're the one who's going to make a difference, Saffron."

She rolls her eyes but there's a smile playing on her lips. "Georgia, not all of us want to make a difference, you ridiculous nerd."

I return her smile. "What *do* you want then? I can't believe I've never asked you that."

"I've always wanted to design video games, but if I try and I can't, then everyone who thinks I'm useless will be right about me."

Everyone? It's clear she means me. I'm the one who lords it over her because I get better grades. But the truth is, I'm jealous. Because Saffron doesn't need a bunch of As to prove her worth to the world. "You're the smartest person I know," I say. "And I'd buy all your games; they'd be amazing."

Saffron almost hugs me but, before she can, I'm hit by a sudden thought. This simulation is designed to determine which *stereotype* would win a game of *Sole Survivor*. The game isn't over until there's only one person left standing.

Those are the rules. We can't break the rules.

But what if those rules were wrong from the start?

I clamber up the side of the volcano so I can face the camera watching us from above the screen. "Lightman, are you still there?"

"I am always here."

"This game is all about gathering data to better predict human behaviour?"

"Correct."

"So you got all of us together – the rebel, the know-it-all, the jock, the princess, the criminal, the weirdo, the star, the artist and the geek – and you tried to test which stereotype is best-suited to survival."

"Is now the time for a recap?" Saffron says, raising an eyebrow.

"It's not a recap, it's a hole in his logic. Because everyone's stereotype was a lie. No one played the part they were meant to. Take Henry: the shy, sweet geek who was secretly harassing half the girls he knew and killed a bunch of people."

Lightman doesn't react.

"And Helix was the weirdo, yes, but he was so much more, only no one took the time to look any deeper. Joey's a popular jock who, at heart, is as scared and desperate as the rest of us. Millie sold drugs so everyone would believe she was a perfect princess. Olympia was lying about her fame. Geoffrey made up an entire persona in an attempt to be interesting."

Saffron catches on. "Yeah, and Aidan's not some criminal. He's a good guy who's been looking after his little sister for years because his parents are screwups."

My heart sinks at the thought of Aidan. I got him so wrong. I let him down, but there's no time to think about that right now.

"And Saffron's so much more than a rebel. People aren't two-dimensional stereotypes. You can't predict how they'll act based on some silly label. The entire concept of a stereotype is flawed." I fold my arms to deliver the coup de grace. "Also, you can't make sweeping generalizations based on a case study of nine. It's not good science."

"You're not helping your *I'm not a stereotypical know-it-all* case," Saffron whispers, but her eyes are laughing.

"Lightman, you're not going to end this because anyone tells you to," I say. "But the entire simulation is flawed. It relied on us being stereotypes, and we weren't. We're just people."

A strange quiet settles over the room. It takes me a second to notice the volcano has stopped spewing lava. Saffron and I hold our breath. There's a loud clunk from inside as the slide opens.

"Re-evaluating parameters," Lightman says. "Simulation paused."

Saffron and I clamber up to the top of the volcano, but Saffron pauses with one leg over the lip. "After everything, you're letting us go?" she says.

"Maybe don't give him any ideas," I whisper.

"Your sister made a valid point," Lightman says. "The data I have obtained suggest stereotypes are no help at all in predicting human behaviour. So I have ended the simulation."

Saffron nods, her expression kind of sad. Then she forces a smile. "You really aren't alive, are you?" She sighs, then slides into the volcano.

#Lettuce-talk-again

4 members

THE-SAF *20:34*

OK, so I'm setting up a new Sole Survivor crew. Who's in??

GEORGIA-KATE-HOWELLS *20:34*

Inappropriate, Saffron.

THE-SAF *20:34*

Or ... is it a fitting memorial to the friends we lost? Throwing it
out there.

GEORGIA-KATE-HOWELLS *20:35*

Friends who died playing a real-life game of Sole Survivor less
than three weeks ago? Also, did you seriously add Joey and Aidan
to this group chat?? They're still in the hospital!

JOEYS-BIONIC-FOOT *20:40*

I'm getting out tomorrow. Hospital is sooooooo boring.

GEORGIA-KATE-HOWELLS *20:41*

How are you feeling? This must be hard for you, Joey. I'm so sorry.

JOEYS-BIONIC-FOOT *20:41*

I'm doing good now the infection's sorted! Got me a sweet NHS
wheelchair and an appointment to discuss a prostitutetic when I've
healed.

GEORGIA-KATE-HOWELLS *20:41*

Prosthetic?

JOEYS-BIONIC-FOOT *20:42*

That's what I said. I'll be resting at home for a while so I'm totally up for Sole Survivor. I've met a few awesome people in the hospital who'd join our crew.

GEORGIA-KATE-HOWELLS *20:43*

It won't be the same.

THE-SAF *20:43*

I know.

JOEYS-BIONIC-FOOT *20:43*

Yeah. I miss them.

GEORGIA-KATE-HOWELLS *20:43*

Me too.

JOEYS-BIONIC-FOOT *20:44*

I'll see you both at the memorial Friday? I'm wearing all pink in Millie's honour.

THE-SAF *20:45*

Ahhh bless. You know she'd hate that, right?

JOEYS-BIONIC-FOOT *20:45*

Yup. She was the best.

THE-SAF *20:46*

You know something else Millie would hate? For us to form a new
Sole Survivor crew...

GEORGIA-KATE-HOWELLS *20:46*

I'll play if you agree to leave me alone while I finish this article on
Atlas Love. He's being extradited back to the country this week
and I want to coincide its publication with his official arrest.

THE-SAF *20:46*

Loser. Love you.
@MR-MISCHIEF69 Come on, you know you want to!

GEORGIA-KATE-HOWELLS *20:47*

He nearly died of a perforated bowel. I'm sure he has better
things to do than hang out with the people whose fault it was. Not
naming names, cough cough Saffron and Joey cough cough.

JOEYS-BIONIC-FOOT *20:47*

I wheeled myself down to the HDU and apologized for the
stabbing thing. We're good now.

THE-SAF *20:47*

I sent him a voice memo and didn't apologize, but we're also
good. Looks like you're the problem, Georgia. Tell him you're

in love with him so we can all get on with playing Sole
Survivor.

GEORGIA-KATE-HOWELLS *20:48*
Kill me now.
I'm sorry @MR-MISCHIEF69 you don't have to play with us. My
sister's being a dick. You have a lot going on but please know we
all care about you and wish you all the best.

THE-SAF *20:48*
I just threw up in my mouth. Ask him out on a date already!

JOEYS-BIONIC-FOOT *20:49*
Epic!
Epic!
Epic!
Why does it keep doing that?

MR-MISCHIEF69 *20:50*
Have you glitched again, Joey? I can't be bothered to read the
whole thread but I'm in.

Acknowledgements

I can't believe I wrote another book! You'd think it would get easier by number four, but each and every one finds its own way to twist the knife. This one took me back to being sixteen and feeling like the things I achieved mattered more than the person I was. So I'm dedicating it to anyone who has ever tried to plaster over their own insecurities by getting the grades, winning the awards or writing the novels. You're great, even without any of those things.

As always, the hugest of thanks to my awesome agent, Chloe Seager, who always has my back, even when I write myself into the worst corners. I don't think I'd enjoy publishing half as much without all your support and enthusiasm. Thanks also to my editor at Scholastic, Lauren Fortune, who helps me mould the bizarre worlds of my imagination into something book-shaped. I'm so happy that you didn't cut my creepy plastic rabbits.

Thank you to Genevieve Herr for helping edit this book into coherence, Sarah Dutton for her top copyediting skills and words of encouragement, and Tierney Holm for working her proofreading magic and finding all those errors that I'm sure weren't there when I sent the manuscript in (they were). Jamie Gregory has once again done an amazing job with the cover and graphics. This one's my favourite so far! Thanks to Harriet Dunlea and Stephanie Lee for all their publicity brilliance, and everyone else at Scholastic who has helped bring this book to life.

To my readers, I am endlessly grateful that people not only buy my books but sometimes like them enough to get in contact or come and chat to me at events. Four books in, I'm still pinching myself that I get to do a job that I love so much, and it wouldn't be possible if it wasn't for all of you. Thanks also to the librarians, booksellers, educators and reviewers for creating a whole book world in which authors like me get to play. A special thanks to Joanna Claire for inviting me to St. Neots and being the most enthusiastic book person ever.

To my fellow YA writers, I am not exaggerating when I say this book would not have happened if it wasn't for Discord sprints and all of you putting up with my 'happy little chats about how much I love deadlines'. Gina Blaxill, Andreina Cordani, Cynthia Murphy, Georgia Bowers, Kat Ellis, Melissa Welliver, Holly Race, Dawn Kurtagich and Josh Winning: thank you and I'm sorry.

In case you're a writer-to-be reading these acknowledgements in the hope of discovering the secret to publication (I know I always did before I got a book deal!), my biggest piece of advice is to connect with other writers. I owe my whole career to the WriteMentor community, so if you haven't looked them up before, go do it now.

To my friends and family, thank you for putting up with my panicking, neglect and endless conversations about escape room design, bizarre murders, and weird 1980s films. I promise we'll get that drink, just as soon as I finish writing the next book...

The biggest of thanks to Phill, Eliza and Max. None of this would be half as fun if you weren't here to share it with me. And as always, it's probably best if none of you actually read this book.

**MORE FAST-PACED THRILLERS
FROM KATHRYN FOXFIELD:**

KATHRYN FOXFIELD

GOOD
GIRLS
DIE
FIRST

MIND GAMES. MURDER. MAYHEM.
HOW FAR WOULD YOU GO
TO SURVIVE THE NIGHT?

Blackmail lures sixteen-year-old Ava to the derelict carnival on Portgrave Pier. She is one of ten teenagers, all with secrets they intend to protect whatever the cost. When the group find themselves cut off from the real world and from their morals, Ava will have to decide how far she's willing to go to survive.

KATHRYN FOXFIELD

IT'S BEHIND YOU

FROM THE AUTHOR OF
GOOD GIRLS | *DIE FIRST*

**WELCOME TO *IT'S BEHIND YOU!*,
THE REALITY TV GAME THAT
WILL SCARE YOU TO DEATH.**

Five contestants must sit tight through the night in the dark
and dangerous Umber Gorge caves, haunted by a ghost
called the Puckered Maiden. But is it the malevolent spirit
they should fear, or each other?

KATHRYN FOXFIELD

TAG. YOU'RE DEAD

THE FIRST RULE OF THE GAME?
TRUST NO ONE.

A NIGHT FUELLED BY ADRENALINE AND FEAR. AND THE WHOLE WORLD IS WATCHING...

As dusk falls, a hundred contestants take part in a livestreamed game of tag across London. But three people have hidden motives for entering this contest of a lifetime: money, obsession and revenge.